S0-BDP-459

ALSO BY LIZZIE SHANE

The Twelve Dogs of Christmas
Once Upon a Puppy
To All the Dogs I've Loved Before

Pride
&
Puppies

LIZZIE SHANE

FOREVER

New York   Boston

Forever
Hachette Book Group
1290 Avenue of the Americas, New York, NY 10104
read-forever.com
twitter.com/readforeverpub

First Edition: November 2022

Forever is an imprint of Grand Central Publishing. The Forever name and logo are trademarks of Hachette Book Group, Inc.

The publisher is not responsible for websites (or their content) that are not owned by the publisher.

The Hachette Speakers Bureau provides a wide range of authors for speaking events. To find out more, go to www.hachettespeakersbureau.com or call (866) 376-6591.

Library of Congress Cataloging-in-Publication Data

Names: Shane, Lizzie, author.
Title: Pride & puppies / Lizzie Shane.
Other titles: Pride and puppies
Description: First Edition. | New York : Forever, 2022. | Series: Pine Hollow series | Summary: "Dr. Charlotte Rodriguez has a history of dating jerks-and she blames Jane Austen. She made the brooding Darcy types sound so appealing, but when Charlotte is dumped by the latest in a long line of not Darcy-caliber boyfriends she decides to swear off men and convinces her best friends to join her in a Puppy Pact, lavishing all their affection on sweet little puppies who actually deserve it instead of the man-children who most definitely do not. The absolute last person she expects to tempt her back into the dating pool is the new physical therapist in town, George Leneghan. George is a total teddy bear-and not at all Charlotte's type-but he's kind, he's patient, and he's determined to get out of the Friend Zone. Now all he has to do is convince Charlotte that the best heroes wear their hearts on their sleeves"—Provided by publisher.
Identifiers: LCCN 2022026044 | ISBN 9781538710319 (trade paperback) | ISBN 9781538710333 (ebook)
Subjects: LCGFT: Novels. | Romance fiction.
Classification: LCC PS3619.H35457 P75 2022 | DDC 813/.6—dc23
LC record available at https://lccn.loc.gov/2022026044

ISBNs: 978-1-5387-1031-9 (trade paperback), 978-1-5387-1033-3 (ebook)

Printed in the United States of America

LSC-C

Printing 1, 2022

For Jane. And Colin Firth.

Chapter One

The more I know of the world, the more I am convinced that I shall never see a man whom I can really love. I require so much!

—*Sense and Sensibility*, Jane Austen

I blame Colin Firth."

Charlotte Jane Rodriguez, MD, PhD, and self-proclaimed total badass, stood in the center of her living room, weaving only slightly from the four shots of tequila she'd downed in the last hour—one for each month she'd dated Jerkface Jeff—and glowered at the stern, brooding face currently occupying her television screen.

It was all Colin Firth's fault.

At the tender—and romantically precocious—age of nine, Charlotte had seen the BBC version of *Pride and Prejudice* for the first time. Colin Firth had smoldered onto the screen, and Charlotte had fallen hopelessly, irrevocably in love.

Other little girls could keep their Prince Charmings. She was devoted to Mr. Darcy.

Charlotte had always seen herself as the heroine of every story. Her father was very easily imagined as Mr. Bennet, calm and intelligent and kind—and while she only had two sisters rather than four, she still felt a definite kinship with Lizzy. She, too, was from a small town filled with gossip. She, too, was far too clever to be wasted on a Mr. Collins— even if her mother had made the unconscionable blunder of naming her after Charlotte Lucas. And she, too, had a mother who frequently took to her bed—though it was chemo and not the vapors sending her there.

One might argue that Charlotte's feelings for Mr. Darcy bordered on pathological. When examining her fixation, her therapist might point to the fact that the BBC miniseries was the last thing she ever watched with her mother—who was herself a Jane Austen aficionado—and say Charlotte was using her obsession in an attempt to avoid processing the trauma of her mother's death when she was a girl. She might say that Charlotte's lifelong quest to date a Darcy was unrealistic and problematic.

She might be right.

"Don't blame an innocent actor," argued Magda, one of Charlotte's two very-best-friends-in-the-whole-wide-world. She slumped with her legs crossed on the floor, having sunk there after taking four sympathy shots. Magda, sadly, lacked Charlotte's ability to turn alcohol into manic energy. "Blame Darcy," Mags advised. "Or better yet, blame Jane Austen. She created him."

"I'm sorry." Kendall, Charlotte's other very-best-friend-in-the-whole-wide-world, raised a single index finger in dissent. "Jane Austen didn't make you date a series of assholes. You did that all on your own."

Charlotte swung her glare to Kendall, who had an unfortunate tendency to call her out on her bullshit right when she wanted to have a good wallow. "She gave me unrealistic expectations of men."

"You just keep picking the wrong men," Kendall insisted. "Smug assholes aren't all Mr. Darcy under the surface. Sometimes a brooding, self-important dick is just a brooding, self-important dick. You gotta listen when people tell you who they are."

Charlotte narrowed her eyes even more. "So I was supposed to know that Jeff was going to cheat on me *on Valentine's Day?*"

She hadn't even found out about it until today, over three weeks later, when the idiot had posted about it on Instagram.

It had been quite a day.

Surprise! Your boyfriend of four months has a secret second girlfriend! Surprise! Your boyfriend has a separate Instagram account he's been using to post photos with that other girlfriend for six months!

Which technically made *Charlotte* the other woman. Which was squicky for all sorts of reasons. She didn't want to think about how long she would have continued dating Jeff if he hadn't forgotten to log out of the account she followed before posting gushy I-love-my-girl stuff with Valentine's photos of the wrong girlfriend.

Who posted Valentine's pictures in March anyway? It was practically St. Patrick's Day.

Kendall had the grace to wince. "Well, no, not that specifically. But you already knew he wasn't worth your time." She met Charlotte's eyes with her usual brand of tough love.

"You didn't really *like* him, did you? Or else you wouldn't be pissed off and blaming Colin Firth. You'd be heartbroken and sobbing." She waved a finger in a circle to encompass Charlotte's righteous irritation. "This is no Warren."

She might have a point. There had definitely been sobbing with Warren. But Charlotte refused to be derailed by Kendall's logic. She tilted her chin up indignantly. "I am perfectly capable of being heartbroken and pissed off at the same time. I contain multitudes."

"Has anyone else noticed the room spinning?" Magda asked from the floor. The four shots had undeniably been a bad idea, since Mags almost never drank, but she'd insisted on throwing them all back in solidarity.

Charlotte might need to change her break-up ritual—or start having shorter relationships—just for Magda's sake. During the Viking funeral for her relationship with Warren, they'd watered down Magda's sympathy shots, but tonight Charlotte hadn't had time to prepare, and they'd all been drinking the hard stuff.

She headed to the open-concept kitchen to grab Mags a glass of water without interrupting her discussion with Kendall. "I'm processing my grief over the death of my relationship. This is how I process."

"Yes, I know. By doing shots, torching everything he ever gave you, and watching *Pride and Prejudice*. By the way, are you keeping those ruby earrings as your memento mori? Because if not, I want to claim them before they go into the charity pile."

Charlotte paused with Magda's water in her hand, frowning as Kendall's words penetrated, carrying with them a galling realization.

Kendall was right.

This wasn't a ritual to deal with her pain anymore. It was a routine. A habit.

She didn't feel heartbroken.

She didn't feel... *anything*. Except irritation. And maybe, if she was being completely honest with herself, a tiny little bit of relief.

She'd dated Jerkface Jeff—so dubbed by her sister, Elinor, who had the annoying tendency to be right about Charlotte's boyfriends—for four months. She'd poured all her energy—and Charlotte had a *lot* of energy—into making the relationship work. She'd accommodated. She'd bent over backward. She'd made excuses and allowances. She'd done what she always did.

But she wasn't sure she'd actually cared.

After Warren, it had been hard to get her hopes up again. Hard to believe the fairy tale she worked so hard to spin for everyone else. She'd thrown herself into the relationship as much as she could, but she had disappointment fatigue when it came to men.

It wasn't Mr. Darcy's fault. It was Warren and Hunter and Landon and Bridger and freaking Jerkface Jeff. It was all the men who weren't worth her time, but whom she kept giving it to, over and over again. Kendall had dubbed them the Darcys, but not one had turned out to be hero material.

"Are you going to give Mags that water?" Kendall asked. "Or just stand there like one of those living statue people until we tip you?"

Charlotte jolted back into action, shoving the water into Magda's hand. Then she took a step back, facing her best friends—and Jennifer Ehle, who was now on-screen—and squaring her shoulders to declare "I'm doing it. I'm swearing off men."

Magda's brows pulled together in a puzzled frown.

Kendall cocked her head. "Is that a yes on the ruby earrings?"

The reminder of the earrings catapulted her into motion, and Charlotte charged down the short hall in her cozy little two-bedroom condo.

She hadn't had time to gather all the things Jerkface Jeff had given her. The Instagram incident had escalated quickly, and they'd been officially broken up less than an hour after his accidental post. She'd texted Magda and Kendall while still angrily messaging with Jeff and her friends had come over right away—which, since Kendall lived a short walk and Magda lived a short drive away, meant Charlotte hadn't had time to do more than change her relationship status online.

She snatched the ruby earrings off the dresser, along with an Hermès scarf and the ugliest heart pendant in the history of heart pendants, which he'd given her as an apology for being busy on Valentine's Day—apparently busy with his *real girlfriend*.

Charlotte started out of the bedroom—and paused, her gaze catching on the open door to her walk-in closet.

On impulse, she darted into the massive walk-in, which had made her fall in love with the condo in the first place, and snatched a small decorative box off the top shelf. The box was light, just cardboard, but in the shape of an old-fashioned hardback edition of *Pride and Prejudice*.

She carried it out to the front room, where Kendall and Mags waited.

The memento mori, as Kendall called them, were the solitary items from each of Charlotte's past relationships that she kept tucked away after she'd evicted every other trace of her exes from her life.

Charlotte set the box, along with the remnants of her relationship with Jeff, on the coffee table and stared down at them, coming to a long overdue decision.

"I'm getting rid of all of it."

"Really?" Kendall asked, her voice rife with skepticism.

"Even the box," she declared.

"It isn't the box's fault," Magda protested.

"It's tainted by the bad memories," Charlotte insisted. And the good ones.

The good ones were always harder to let go.

Charlotte flipped open the lid, and there they were. Remembrances of boyfriends past.

The silk scarf Bridger had gotten her. Landon's locket. The pearl earrings Hunter had bought her because all the women in his family had them and his future bride needed her own pair—though he'd never proposed, and he'd broken up with her as soon as he realized she wasn't going to quit med school to be his trophy wife. And then there was the diamond tennis bracelet. The one she'd woken up one morning to find fastened to her wrist, with Warren smiling down at her, his stupid Colin Firth–esque brown eyes glinting.

And now Jeff's contributions.

All gifts that had more to do with her exes and who they wanted her to be than they ever did with her. Because none of those men had ever bothered to know her.

She'd tried so hard to make things work, but she was the only one trying. For years she'd worried that she was too needy, too demanding, that she wanted things too much. That she wanted *love* too much. She'd only ever wanted to be someone's whole world, to be the person that mattered most to them, but she needed to reset those wants.

She tossed Jeff's gifts into the box and snapped it shut, then shoved it across the coffee table toward Kendall.

"Give it all away. I don't want any of it."

Kendall eyed the box. "You don't want me to pawn them? I'm pretty sure the tennis bracelet alone is a mortgage payment. Maybe several. You suffered through dating Warren. You should at least get something out of it."

"Pawn it, give it away, whatever. I need to stop holding on to things. I'm swearing off men."

Charlotte ran through her memories of her relationship and felt foolish for all the times she'd believed Jeff. She should have known. Even Elinor's dog, Dory, who loved everyone, had hated Jerkface Jeff. Dogs always knew.

"I need to get a dog."

As soon as she said the words out loud, the sheer genius of them seeped into her. The absolute *rightness*.

"A dog?" Magda echoed.

"In lieu of a man?" Kendall drawled sarcastically—but Charlotte wasn't joking.

"Exactly." She bounced a little on the balls of her feet. She *loved* dogs. She'd always wanted one, but while completing med school hadn't felt like the right time, and then she'd been dating Warren, who never wanted to share her attention with anyone. But now...

"It's time I directed my affection at someone who actually deserves it, someone who will love me back, unconditionally." God, it was *brilliant*. "I'm getting a puppy."

Her best friends stared at her.

"You know, that isn't a terrible idea," Kendall said after a pause.

"It's *genius*," Charlotte insisted, her enthusiasm expanding to fill the room. "We should all do it. Swear off men and adopt puppies."

"I don't have any dating prospects to swear off, and okay, yes, I'd love to get a dog, but I'm pretty sure a puppy in my kitchen would be a health code violation," Magda, Pine Hollow's star baker, protested.

Charlotte waved away her concerns. "So you keep him away from the ovens and don't let him lick any of the baked goods."

"Magda doesn't need to swear off men," Kendall argued. "She needs to go wild." Magda glared at Kendall, who shrugged. "Well, you do."

"I can't go wild without the entire town knowing about it. The first time I open the bakery late because I don't make it home in time from my walk of shame, I'll be the star of the *Pine Hollow Newsletter* for *months*. My whole family, from my grandmother on down, will hear about it. And, shockingly, not many men want to go wild with me on a schedule that lets me be home in bed by nine so I can start baking at five a.m."

"But dogs *like* it if you wake up early." Charlotte spread her hands to indicate the perfection of the plan. "Elinor's always complaining about what an early riser Dory is."

"You're really hooked on this dog thing, aren't you?" Kendall eyed her suspiciously, as if trying to see through to the hidden reason behind her determination.

Charlotte made exaggerated pleading eyes at Kendall.

"It'll be more fun if we all do it. You said you wanted to get another dog after Darby, and you're always saying dating in a small town is an exercise in futility. Why waste our energy worrying about that nonsense? Come on. *Puppies.* Everything is better when we do it together," Charlotte coaxed.

"And you hate doing things alone, I know. But I don't have time for a puppy right now any more than I have time for a relationship," Kendall reminded her. "My job never lets up."

"That's precisely why you need a dog!" Charlotte waved her hands in a gesture to say *obviously.* "Something to distract you from all that. And the ski season's almost over. You'll have a break."

Kendall shook her head. "My dad wants to expand the summer business—he's trying to get a bunch of conferences and events to book the resort during the off-season, which means all the staffing headaches of the ski season, only year-round." Kendall had been working at her family's ski resort ever since her athletic career suddenly ended—and her voice always had that pinch of stress when she talked about her job. She needed something in her life that just made her happy, and Kendall had always loved dogs.

She needed this.

They all did.

"We're making a pact," Charlotte declared. "Right now. A Puppy Pact. No more wasting time on men who don't deserve it. No more throwing our feelings at guys who take them and give nothing back." She met Magda's eyes first, knowing exactly who Mags would be picturing when she said those words.

A grim determination settled on Magda's face as she nodded. "Okay."

Charlotte turned her gaze to Kendall. "No more putting ourselves last. No more killing ourselves for thankless jobs. We only give our love to adorable puppies who are pure and perfect and deserve our devotion. And one another," she amended, then added, "and our families."

"Forever?" Kendall asked dubiously. "That sounds very... celibate."

"Fine. For..." Charlotte waved a hand, pulling a number out of the air. "Six months. A man detox. No more dating jerks."

Kendall arched an eyebrow. "Does it count as dating if it's just a convenient booty call?"

"I don't even have that," Magda muttered.

"No more feeding the jerks," Charlotte insisted. She thrust out her hand, and Magda dropped her hand on top of it. "We are too good for them, and we respect ourselves too much to waste another second on them."

"Do we though?" Kendall asked.

Charlotte narrowed her eyes—and Kendall caved, slapping her hand onto the pile.

"Fine, yes. No more jerks."

"Only puppies," Charlotte declared triumphantly. "Trust me. This is exactly what we need."

Chapter Two

Where the heart is really attached, I know very well how little one can be pleased with the attention of any body else.
—*Northanger Abbey*, Jane Austen

Well? How did it go?"

George juggled his phone as he unlocked his front door, marveling at his sister's eerily perfect timing. "How did you know I was home? Your psychic powers are uncanny."

The lock released and he bent to greet Duke, who was waiting, as always, two inches inside the door, wriggling with euphoria at his return. "Hey, buddy." He stroked the Bernese mountain dog's silky head until Duke went to fetch his current favorite oinking pig toy for George to admire.

"I still have your Ring password from that time you went camping and wanted me to be able to keep an eye on things from afar," Beks answered blithely—as if that wasn't deeply stalkerish. His closest sister—both in age and affection—went on cheerfully, "Though I'm not sure what you wanted me to do if you got robbed. I'm three thousand miles away."

"Twenty-one hundred," George corrected absently. He didn't need it to sound any farther than it was. He already felt like he was in a bubble on the other side of the world.

Moving to Pine Hollow, Vermont, had seemed like such a good idea eighteen months ago. A fresh start. Full of possibilities. But now...

"So how was the date?"

"The same way they all are," George muttered, the phone held away from his face as he stripped off his jacket and hung it up.

"What was that?" Beks demanded.

George sighed, putting the phone back to his ear. "It was fine."

They were always fine. And never anything more.

"Well, crud," Beks said, understanding perfectly. "No sparks?"

"Oh, there were sparks." He toed off his shoes. "I'm pretty sure that after she told me she hoped we could be friends she went back to get the bartender's phone number."

Beks groaned. "Okay, that's not ideal."

"It's just frustrating," he said. "I thought things would be different here. Small town. Get to know people face-to-face. Build connections organically over time. No more apps where everyone is looking for insta-love in five profile pics or less. But now I'm still on the apps, only with a smaller population base." He opened the patio door to let Duke out to pee, since the Berner had been cooped up for hours while George drove halfway across the state for his date. "I'm literally running out of options."

"Literally?" Beks challenged. She had strong feelings about people misusing that word.

"I got a message the other day that my app didn't have anyone left to show me. I didn't know it was possible to get that message until I moved to Vermont."

He propped a shoulder against the doorjamb, keeping an eye on the white patch of Duke's fur in the darkness as he sniffed for the perfect spot. Usually George took him to the greenspace behind the complex, but it was thirty-eight degrees and raining—Duke would have to make do with the swath of grass in front of the patio tonight.

"You could always move back to Denver," Beks reminded him, a singsong lilt to the familiar refrain. "I never understood why you ran away to Vermont when I'm here and I'm awesome."

"I didn't run away. I just needed a change."

He'd been treading water in Denver, stuck in a series of relationships that never seemed to go anywhere. Then, two summers ago, his girlfriend had dumped him, and he'd decided to take the romantic hiking vacation through New Hampshire and Vermont they'd planned on his own. He'd tripped across the Pine Hollow Fourth of July celebration and fallen in love with the charming little town.

It had seemed like the kind of place where people took time for one another, where there was more of an emphasis on community than convenience. Long after he left, he'd found himself daydreaming about the kind of life he could build there.

When he'd gotten home, he'd looked up job listings in Pine Hollow on a whim. The ad he'd found for a physical therapist seemed like a sign. A chance to change one crucial variable in the ongoing experiment that was his love life.

"That's the definition of insanity, right?" he said. "Doing the same thing over and over again and expecting different results?"

"You'll get different results," Beks assured him. "You just haven't found the right person yet."

George made a noncommittal noise. As he waited for Duke, his gaze drifted across the courtyard of the complex to a certain third-floor balcony in the building opposite his. Lights shone through the curtains.

Charlotte was awake.

"This isn't about the hot doctor, is it?" Beks asked, reading his mind as she had the awkward tendency to do.

He should have known his sisters would never let it go once they realized he had a crush on Charlotte.

He'd been fascinated by his neighbor and coworker since the day they met, when she'd read him the riot act after he mistakenly assumed the physician RODRIGUEZ, CHARL on a chart was a Charles. Her rant about internalized misogyny had reminded him so much of his sisters he hadn't been able to stop smiling, which had only made her rant more.

He'd been calling her Charles ever since. Which now made her roll her eyes and smile.

But they were just friends.

"She's unavailable," he reminded his sister, putting in his earbud to free his hands to dry off the wet dog as Duke came back to the door.

"I didn't ask if she was suddenly single," Beks said dryly. "I asked if she was the reason you were feeling so frustrated about your dating prospects. I don't want you wasting your time pining for her."

"Not pining," George assured his sister as he crossed to the kitchen to fill a glass of wine from the box on the counter.

Even if she hadn't been dating someone else, Charlotte had made it clear that she wasn't interested in anything romantic. She'd even tried to set him up with her sister. And her best friend.

"I just worry that you're giving off friend-zone vibes to everyone else because you're fixated on this unattainable woman in some kind of romantic defense mechanism," Beks said.

"Are you reading relationship psychology books again?" George settled onto the couch, and Duke immediately flopped on his feet, pinning him in place.

"Fine, don't listen to me. This wasn't why I called anyway. Have you talked to Dave lately?"

"Not since last week." His best friend Dave, who was married to one of Beks's best friends, had moved to Western Australia a few years ago, and it had made keeping in touch more of a challenge. Spurred by the mention of Dave, George eyed the bass guitar he never remembered to practice.

"I just got off the phone with Sophie," Beks said. "They're thinking of moving back."

George froze in the act of reaching for the bass. "Back to the States?"

"She's applying for a job in Denver, and if she gets it, they'll come home. I just thought, you know, you could too. Move home."

Home.

The word resonated surprisingly sharply.

Beks jokingly badgered him to move back all the time, but this wasn't the usual teasing—and George found himself actually considering it. His lease was up in six months. The two-year contract he'd originally signed at the Summerland Estates retirement community also expired at the beginning of September. He didn't have any long-term commitments. There was nothing really keeping him here.

When he'd moved to Vermont, he'd thought he'd be settled by now. He liked his job—but he hadn't magically found the sense of community he'd imagined, and he was starting to miss the things he'd left behind. His family. That feeling of home. Being able to be there for them. Three of his four sisters were still in the Denver area.

It was funny, but one of the things he was realizing he missed most was being needed by someone.

He'd loved Pine Hollow from the day he arrived—but he still felt like an outsider half of the time. He wasn't really a part of things here. After a year and a half, he was still the new guy.

He'd actually gotten an email this afternoon asking him if he could help out at the parade tomorrow, and he'd been excited at first, thinking it was finally an overture from the town. A sign that he was being accepted as one of them.

Until he scrolled down and saw the rest of the email chain, where the organizer had begged for help from half a dozen people before someone finally suggested she try the "new guy."

He wasn't *needed* here. And he hadn't found true love and domestic bliss. The marriage and 2.2 kids he'd been hoping for.

"Maybe I *should* come back."

He didn't even realize he'd said the words aloud until Beks yelped, "Really?"

George chuckled at the happiness in her voice. "I don't know, maybe." Then self-preservation prompted him to add, "Don't say anything to the family, okay? I want to think this through without Maggie and Lori going berserk on the group text."

"My lips are sealed," Beks promised, barely suppressed excitement beneath the words. "And I know I always tell you what to do, but I'm not *really* telling you what to do. You know that, right? I support your decision whatever it is and all that crap. But selfishly, I would love it if you—" Her giddy voice broke off. "Oh, crud. I just heard a crash. I need to make sure the kids are still alive. Talk later?"

"Yeah. Go."

"Love you, Punk Face."

"Love you, too."

Beks was already shouting, *"You better not have broken any—"* as she disconnected the call, and George grinned, feeling that tug of home again.

He picked up the neglected bass and sat with Duke at his feet, absently thumbing a bass line and letting the idea of going back to Colorado roll around in his mind.

Home.

Part of him still wanted to stay, but that might just be stubbornness. A refusal to admit defeat.

If nothing was going to change, maybe it was time to move on.

Chapter Three

The very first moment I beheld him—my
heart was irrecoverably gone.
   —*Northanger Abbey*, Jane Austen

I t was love at first sight.

Charlotte hadn't been entirely sure she believed in the concept—that it was possible to completely lose your heart in an instant—and then she looked into those liquid black eyes and everything changed.

He was perfect. And tiny.

"He won't be ready to leave his mother for at least another month," Ally said. The proprietor of Furry Friends Animal Rescue was playing with the rest of the litter inside a sort of modified playpen while Charlotte acquainted herself with the love of her life.

Charlotte had woken up this morning brimming with enthusiasm. She'd bounced out of bed, thankful for the metabolism that meant she was never hung over, even after multiple celebratory toasts of their pact. Her body processed alcohol as energy, and she had a *lot* of it, so she threw on her running gear and laced up her sneakers.

Kendall lay passed out facedown on her couch, so Charlotte paused long enough to set a glass of water and a pair of Advil on the coffee table beside her.

Last night, they'd poured Magda into a Lyft since she had to be up ungodly early to open the bakery. Charlotte had decided on impulse to return Magda's car and then jog the half dozen miles back to her place—it was too beautiful a morning not to, even if there was a layer of frost on the car door handle and her breath fogged in the air.

But then, as soon as she'd parked the car behind the bakery and used her spare key to drop Magda's car keys inside—sneaking back out because Mags hated being interrupted when she was baking in the morning—Charlotte had started thinking about the Puppy Pact again.

She'd trotted through town, her muscles loosening pleasantly. Pine Hollow was perfectly still around her, before even the early birds were stirring, and she queued up her Girl Power mix, lengthening her strides as the music took hold.

Sometimes her genius ideas—particularly those midwifed by alcohol—didn't turn out to be quite as genius in the light of day, but last night's revelation seemed even more inspired the more she ran.

The Puppy Pact was *brilliant*. So brilliant, in fact, that Charlotte veered away from her favorite forest path, the most direct—and hilly—route back to her condo, and headed instead along the road toward Furry Friends.

She'd known they probably wouldn't be open—most people didn't wake up at dawn on foggy Saturday mornings—but fate had been on her side. Right as she'd been bounding up the driveway, she'd seen Ally emerge from the farmhouse, where she lived with her family, and start across the gravel driveway toward the barn that housed the animal shelter.

Five minutes later, Charlotte had met the love of her life.

"He'll have to be neutered," Ally went on now. "He's purebred and from an AKC champion line, but the stitches around his eyes are from a birth defect—his eyes didn't open on their own, something about an extra ligament."

Charlotte gazed into the most perfect eyes on the planet, set in a little golden face with the black stitches making him look like he was wearing mascara.

"He had to have surgery, and one of his littermates was born with a benign cyst. Apparently this is the second 'imperfect' litter this mom has produced, so the breeder wanted to rehome both her and the puppies as quietly as possible. He could have sold them as family pets—golden retrievers will always sell—but he was worried if it got out he had a history of birth defects in his litters it would hurt his reputation, and his prices. So here they are."

A golden retriever.

Charlotte felt like sunshine had burst through the clouds inside her chest and was pouring out of her skin, the sheer *rightness* of the moment enveloping her. She couldn't have picked a better breed if she'd been picking out of a puppy catalog. Sweet, smart, cuddly—Kendall's parents had a golden retriever when she was a kid, and it was *exactly* what Charlotte had pictured when she'd envisioned the ideal puppy to receive all the devotion she wouldn't be giving undeserving men.

The puppy leapt onto a ragged rope with what was probably supposed to be a fearsome growl—and came out more like a squeak. Charlotte was grinning like a fool, but she just couldn't stop. "He's perfect."

"They'll go fast," Ally warned. "Goldens always do. We haven't even advertised we have them yet and already all but the two with birth defects and the mom have been claimed. If you want him, I'd recommend getting in your adoption application and deposit this morning. I have a feeling they'll all be spoken for by this time tomorrow."

Charlotte gazed down at her puppy—he was definitely hers—and marveled at the rightness of it all. "It's fate. I am meant to have this dog."

If Jeff had idiotically posted the wrong photos to his Instagram account even *one day* later, her puppy would have been claimed already. He would be the love of someone else's life. It was almost too perfect, how everything was falling into place. Like the universe was rewarding her for finally seeing the writing on the wall and swearing off men.

Even the fact that her baby wouldn't be ready to come home with her for another month was perfect. It gave her time to puppy-proof her condo and read up on the responsibilities of pet ownership. She wanted to do this *right*.

Her puppy tripped over his own feet, tumbling onto his side, and Charlotte took the opportunity to tickle his little belly. He twisted his head around to look at her upside down—and her heart flipped.

Ally grinned. "You know, I think you're right. Sometimes the universe knows what we need before we do."

Charlotte met Ally's smiling eyes. "Where do I sign?"

The application only took ten minutes to fill out, and Ally promised to process it right away. Charlotte wanted to stay and play with her puppy all day, but he'd fallen asleep, and she knew Ally had her own day to get to. Instead she volunteered to come back later and help with the Furry Friends float in the Fire and Rescue Appreciation Day parade.

Ally had said the application was practically a formality in this case—it probably helped that Charlotte's sister Elinor was one of Ally's best friends—but nervous energy still pulsed through Charlotte's veins as she jogged down the long driveway away from Furry Friends.

She queued up the Girl Power mix, but even the feeling of the miles disappearing beneath her feet couldn't entirely dispel her agitation. She wanted her sweet golden puppy *so badly*. And when she wanted things this badly, they had a tendency to blow up in her face.

Impatient to tell someone, as if that would make it real and less likely to be snatched away from her, she paused the Girl Power mix and called Elinor.

Surely her oldest sister, who adored her own dog and had made no secret of her dislike for Jeff, would want to hear the good news.

"Hello?"

Charlotte had forgotten that it was still early, even after her dawn visit to Furry Friends. Her oldest sister's groggy voice reminded her that most people didn't wake up with the sun on Saturday mornings, but Charlotte had too much energy to be deterred.

She started with the news Elinor would probably like the most. "Jeff and I broke up. Actually, *I* broke up with *him*."

The words resonated with power. It was the first time she'd ever been the break-upper, rather than the break-uppee. The fact that it had taken catching him in the act of two-timing her with another girlfriend to get her to break up with him probably said unfortunate things about her tendency to cling, but she was focusing on the positive. Look at her! Powerful! Independent! Adopting a dog!

"Charlotte?"

Charlotte knew Elinor generally took a while to process things when she was first waking up, so she repeated the headline. "I broke up with Jeff. I'm swearing off men and getting a dog."

"Swearing off and getting..." Elinor muttered sleepily. "Are those things related?"

"Yes," Charlotte declared definitively, her sneakers thumping a satisfying rhythm as she ran. "They are."

"Okay..." Elinor mumbled—and Charlotte had to shove down a flicker of childish disappointment. She'd expected a little more fanfare from the woman who had been quietly campaigning against Jeff for months.

Then the deep voice of Elinor's fiancé rumbled something in the background, reminding Charlotte that she might have called a tiny bit too early for a Saturday morning. *Other* people still had love lives.

"I'll let you go," Charlotte chirped, since Elinor clearly wasn't listening anymore. "Give my love to Levi. See you at the parade!"

Elinor muttered something unintelligible and disconnected the call as Charlotte's running shoes thudded onto the packed dirt of the mountain path. Tree roots snaked across the trail, but Charlotte knew them like the back of her hand and placed her feet with expert precision, falling into the automatic, unthinking rhythm of the run.

She'd always been terrible at yoga and meditation. Sitting still with her thoughts invariably felt like someone had poured a bucket of ants all over her body, but running...running was heaven. Especially in nature, when everything in her seemed to expand to fill the vast open spaces of the outdoors. When the breeze through the trees felt like her breath and the birds singing their morning songs like the music of her thoughts. *This* was her Zen. Her happy place.

The fact that she was *this* happy the morning after breaking up with Jeff doubtless said something unfortunate about her supposedly blissful relationship and how deeply deluded she'd been, but that was a reality to be faced on another day.

Today was about who she was becoming, not who she'd been.

She was still bursting with energy and the desire to tell everyone about her bright new plan for a bright new life when she emerged from the forest path. Packed dirt gave way to paved sidewalks, and the towering trees ceded to the landscaped lawns and gardens of the recently developed area near the ski resort.

The NetZero Village condo complex was reasonably large—four multistory buildings with rustic stone accents and architecture that would have looked right at home in the Alps, surrounding a pond which became a skating rink in the winter and contained a small fountain in the summer.

With the proximity to the ski resort, most of the condos

were empty vacation homes owned by weekenders from New York and Massachusetts who were looking for someplace to park their extra money. Which meant the fitness center, parking lots, and geothermal-powered hot tubs got crowded on the weekends during the high season, but the rest of the time the complex was nearly abandoned, with only a quiet little cluster of full-time residents.

As she jogged into the complex, she spotted one of those residents playing with a big black-and-white-and-brown dog beside the pond. At the sight, Charlotte's heart lifted, and she immediately bounded in that direction, an automatic smile spreading across her face.

She knew that figure. The mussed-up sandy hair. The Clark Kent glasses. The crooked smile with that one lopsided dimple.

Exactly the person she wanted to share her news with.

"George!"

Chapter Four

I may have lost my heart, but not my self-control.

—*Emma*, Jane Austen

George was unprepared for the sight of Charlotte Rodriguez bouncing toward him in head-to-toe skintight spandex on a Saturday morning.

He hadn't been expecting to see anyone near the pond where he'd brought Duke to play, but the sight of *Charlotte*, looking like she'd stepped right out of one of the fantasies he absolutely was *not* supposed to have about her, nearly had him swallowing his tongue.

He'd seen her in work clothes. He'd seen her dressed up for New Year's Eve, or for some night out with whatever guy she was currently dating, and he'd occasionally seen her from a distance in jogging gear—but none of that had prepared him for the full impact of the swinging ponytail, sunshine smile, and skintight everything as she bounded over to him.

"You're up early," he managed in a reasonably normal tone.

Duke intercepted her while she was still six feet away from George, the Bernese mountain dog nearly bowling her over with his delight. Charlotte laughed, bending at the waist and cooing, "Hello, baby! Who's a good boy? Who is?"

George silently reminded himself of his favorite slightly revised commandment. *Thou shalt not get turned on by thy in-a-relationship, only-interested-in-you-as-a-friend coworker.*

He knew Charlotte liked to look good. She made jokes at her own expense about her vanity all the time and had a seemingly endless supply of cute little dresses, but he most frequently saw her at work, where she tended to wear tailored slacks, glasses she didn't need, and a white lab coat. She'd once explained to him that some of the older residents at the Summerland Estates retirement community would only listen to a doctor in a lab coat and glasses. He knew she was nearly thirty, but she looked more like a perky college student than a practicing orthopedist. Especially when she was dressed like Track Star Barbie in pink-and-black Lycra with her thick brown hair in a high ponytail.

She continued to coo baby talk at Duke, who shamelessly lapped up the attention, until George cleared the blockage in his throat and asked, "How is it someone who loves dogs as much as you do has never gotten one?"

Charlotte looked up at that, her big brown eyes wide with the manic enthusiasm she got when she was on a mission— like when she'd set him up with her sister.

"I am getting one!" She gave Duke's ears one last ruffle and then closed the distance to George, beaming at him. "I broke up with Jeff."

The words were a mule-kick to the chest.

She sounded so proud of herself that he didn't think

condolences were in order, and he somehow doubted his un-filtered reaction of *Thank you, Jesus* would go over well. Still, George couldn't help the little surge of hope at her words.

She was single. Maybe it was time to finally do something about this crush. Not that he would ask her out right away—he didn't want to be the rebound guy—but eventually...

He kept his expression mild as he searched for a neutral response. "Jeff didn't like dogs?"

"For all I know Jeff has a dozen dogs with his other secret girlfriend, but that is no longer any of my concern."

"Ouch." George winced sympathetically, pointedly ignoring the way his heart rate was accelerating eagerly. *Not a good time. Wait a decent mourning period...*

Duke whined at the loss of Charlotte's full attention, and George bent down to grab the ball the dog had abandoned. He flung it across the courtyard, sending Duke leaping after it.

"He never deserved my time," Charlotte declared.

George kept his wholehearted agreement silent. He'd made it a policy never to comment on Charlotte's love life. Duke returned with the ball, and George received the slobbery offering, winding up to throw it again.

"But none of that matters now. I'm in love."

"Oh..." *Shit.*

The ball flew out of his grip, somehow hurtling in the right direction. Duke took off after it.

It was bound to happen, wasn't it? Charlotte never stayed single for long. He hadn't even found out she'd split up from Warren until she was already dating Jeff.

"Wholly, completely, ridiculously in love. He's perfect," Charlotte gushed. "I just met him this morning—"

Seriously? It wasn't even nine o'clock yet and already she'd managed to fall in love?

Duke raced back with the ball.

"You should see him, George. He's so cute. And smart. I just know it's the best decision I've ever made. I should have gotten a puppy months ago. Years!"

"A puppy?" This time the ball slipped from his fingers, barely going three feet, though Duke didn't seem to mind, pouncing on it with his tail waving.

"A puppy! A golden retriever! Ally still has to okay the paperwork, and he can't come home with me for a month, but you should see him, George. He's *everything*."

A puppy. She was getting a puppy.

She's single.

"That's awesome." His heart was racing without his permission, but it wasn't like he could ask her out *right this second*. Duke bumped his foot—reminding him that the ball had been retrieved and placed against his shoe to be thrown again. He bent to pick up the gooey mess. "Congratulations, Charles."

"Thank you! Elinor didn't seem nearly excited enough when I told her I was swearing off men and getting a dog, but I think I woke her up."

He paused in the act of winding up for a throw. "You're... what?" He couldn't have heard that right.

"My gravestone will read: *Charlotte Rodriguez: Terrible taste in men, excellent taste in dogs*," she declared, making a banner with her hands and radiating pleasure at her decision.

"So you're..."

"Giving up dating and lavishing all my affection on the

four-legged love of my life. No more men. Ever. Or at least six months. Total detox."

"Oh..." *Shit.* "Wow."

Duke whined at the delayed throw, but George could only stare at Charlotte.

She was gorgeous. She was funny. She was bossy and mercurial and impatient, but also gentle and endlessly kind. She would do anything for her friends, her family, and her patients. When she loved people, her love was a huge, all-consuming thing, which was why he'd never understood why she insisted on dating men who didn't seem to appreciate how incredible she was.

She drank her coffee black but never seemed to need it to fuel her endless reserves of energy. She was always out and about early, even when she stayed out late. Her mind was terrifyingly quick, and she would boast about her genius so exaggeratedly that he was never sure if it was ego or insecurity talking—though she was, undeniably, brilliant.

She loved hiking and dogs...

And he'd had a crush on her ever since she'd taken him mini-golfing.

He'd still been new to the Estates then, new to working with seniors who ranged in age from their sixties to nineties. One of his favorite clients had been put on hospice care, and it had hit him hard. Charlotte had seen that and declared she was taking him out to cheer him up. He'd been expecting a commiserating drink at the local pub, but instead she'd driven nearly an hour to take him to the closest mini-golf place with a roof because it had been pouring rain.

She'd invented ridiculous rules, declaring whoever won

each hole got to dictate how they played the next one—eyes closed, legs crossed, hopping on one foot. When she got a hole-in-one—with her eyes closed, no less—she'd run a victory lap around the course, pumping her arms over her head like Rocky. On one hole, she'd promised him a "creemee" if he won, and then nearly fell over laughing at the look on his face when he'd mistakenly thought that must be something much dirtier than Vermont soft-serve ice cream.

She'd made it fun. Light. Making him laugh on a night when he'd been sure he wouldn't.

He'd walked off the course grinning, while Charlotte accused him of bribing the mini-golf gods to make the trick hole at the end repeatedly spit out her ball and secure him the win.

On the drive home, they'd talked about anything and everything. First, the helplessness of losing patients to brain cancer—which he as a physical therapist and she as an orthopedist could do nothing to stop. Then why they did the work they did. And how rewarding it was to be able to help someone get back some mobility or independence they thought they'd lost.

When they'd gotten back to Pine Hollow, he'd felt a kind of peaceful acceptance—and *she'd* thanked *him* for listening, since her boyfriend at the time didn't like it when she talked about her work.

George, though not a violent person, had wanted to smack that boyfriend with a mini-golf club.

And he'd had feelings for her ever since.

What did you do when the woman you were secretly half in love with declared she was swearing off romance?

If you were George, you smiled and supported her.

So that's what he did.

"I think that's a great idea."

Charlotte beamed at George, irrationally delighted by his stamp of approval. "Right?" She bounced a little, her enthusiasm pushing through the soles of her sneakers. "It's all about the puppies."

"So you're getting a golden retriever?" He'd paused in his throw, but he released it now, his shoulder muscles flexing beneath his coat. The ball flew all the way across the courtyard to the far path, bouncing high in the air, with Duke racing after it.

"You have to see him. He's an angel. Ally said he would have been taken if I'd waited even one more day. It's destiny."

"You can't fight destiny."

Charlotte grinned. "I always enjoy it when the universe decides to validate my choices. Don't I, Duke?" The last was directed at the dog who had returned, triumphant, with the ball. Charlotte knelt to admire his ball-retrieval efforts. "I feel like the universe has been trying to tell me to do this for a long time, and I was just slow to spot the signs. Sometimes you've gotta listen when life keeps shoving your nose in your fate."

She glanced up to find George was watching her with a slight frown on his face. The expression was so foreign on him that she nearly frowned too—but she was in too bright and shiny a mood for anything to bring her down. "Everything all right?" she asked.

For a moment something seemed to pass in his dark eyes behind his Clark Kent glasses, but before she could decipher it, it was gone. "Yeah." He collected himself. "I was just thinking about the parade. Are you going?"

"As of this morning, I'm volunteering with Furry Friends. You?"

"I'm helping with the Estates float. Last-minute request. That's why I was trying to get Duke's energy out before I have to leave." Duke had flopped down on his belly, panting, and George pointed over his shoulder toward his building. "In fact, I should probably get going. I need to get Duke settled before I head to the Estates to pick up the residents who want to be in the parade. You know how they are. On time is late."

George reached down, clipping on Duke's leash.

"Right. Of course," Charlotte agreed, hating the bereft note in her voice. She didn't *need* his company. She just liked it. George was always so easy to be around. "I'll see you there," she confirmed.

George lifted one hand in a wave, already turning back toward his apartment. Something in his posture snagged at her instincts, and Charlotte watched man and dog walk away—until an alarm went off on her Apple Watch and she remembered she needed to get going herself if she was going to shower and change and get back to Furry Friends before the parade.

Today was all about her puppy.

Chapter Five

We can all begin freely—a slight prefer-
ence is natural enough; but there are very
few of us who have heart enough to be
really in love without encouragement.
—*Pride and Prejudice*, Jane Austen

"Careful there."

George gently helped Mr. and Mrs. Johnson up
onto the Estates float, a flatbed truck which got redecorated
every time Pine Hollow decided to have a parade. Mr. Johnson helped his wife of sixty-plus years settle onto one of the
benches on the float, and George tried not to be jealous of
the way the older couple still held hands everywhere they
went.

Was it so wrong to want that?

Old Mr. Blake frowned at George as he climbed onto the
float with his little dog, Hemingway. "What's this all about
today?" he demanded.

Mr. Blake had been getting confused more and more
often lately—though in his defense, it *was* hard to keep all

the Pine Hollow events straight. The residents loved any excuse for a parade.

"Fire and Rescue Appreciation Day," George explained.

Mr. Blake nodded, his confusion clearing. "Ah, right."

"You there! New guy!"

George looked up at the shout—and then silently groaned to himself that he was responding to *new guy* now.

Judith Larson, the parade organizer with a clipboard and a helmet of silver hair, beckoned him imperiously. "New guy! Over here!"

George was generally an even-tempered guy. Most irritations rolled right off him, but today the little frustrations caught at his skin like nettles he couldn't shake off. He found himself tensing as he excused himself from the Estates residents who were settling themselves on the float and approached the impatient Judith.

"It's George, actually," he reminded her.

"Of course it is, dear. And I'm Judith Larson," she said, as if they hadn't been introduced half a dozen times. "I run the inn."

There were half a dozen inns within the town limits, and all of them seemed to be called "the inn" by the locals, who somehow always knew which one was meant.

When he didn't immediately react, she clarified. "The *historic* Pine Hollow Inn?"

He'd been trying to learn them all and he was pretty sure he'd heard something about the oldest inn in town being the one out by the covered bridge. "That's the one with the barn, right?"

"Oh, heavens, no!" Judith released a high, trilling laugh. "That's the Inn at Pine Hollow! Don't mix those up in front of Zella Newton! We're the lovely brick Colonial, right off the square."

"Right. Of course." He glanced back toward the Estates float, still trying to figure out why she'd flagged him over.

She peered at him over the clipboard. "I just wanted to make sure you were clear on your responsibilities. We just need someone to ride with the seniors and help them out if anyone needs anything. You're a nurse?"

"Physical therapist."

She frowned. "I could have sworn you were a nurse."

Not last I checked. "I've helped on the Estates float before." *On a parade you organized.* Though he'd been pulled out of the crowd at the start that time. "We'll be fine."

"Excellent." She patted his arm. "I'm sure you'll be lovely, dear." Her attention veered to the side. "Andrew! Andrew, the marching band is in the front. The *front*!"

Judith Larson bustled off to deal with the pre-teen, who was struggling with a tuba, and George turned back to the Estates float, catching sight of Charlotte across the muster area. She was wearing a Furry Friends T-shirt and cuddling a little golden pup.

She caught him watching her and beamed, waving one little paw at him. His heart spasmed at the cuteness overload.

Charlotte said something to Ally over her shoulder and jogged in his direction, her puppy tucked close against her chest.

"I thought you might want to meet the love of my life," she announced as she came into range. The fluffy golden retriever puppy lay trustingly in her arms, blinking sleepy black eyes as if he'd just woken up from a nap. "Behold, my soul mate."

"He's a cutie," George said, extending his fingertips for the tiny little nose to sniff. The golden snuffled at him and then leaned into his chin scratch adoringly.

Charlotte smiled, her eyes soft. "I think he likes you."

"I am irresistible. To puppies."

"I wanted a girl—because the last thing I need is male energy in my life right now—but as soon as I saw this little guy it was love at first sight."

"He's pretty irresistible too," George acknowledged, as the little furball practically fell out of Charlotte's arms in his quest for more chin scritches.

"Did I already tell you I can't take him home with me for at least a month? Which feels like forever, but that gives me time to get my place ready and do some research. I'm going to be the best pet owner in the history of pet owners."

"I bet you will be." Charlotte never did anything by half measures.

He focused on the puppy, trying to ignore the twinge in the region of his heart. It sounded like everything was falling into place for Charlotte, while he felt like he was treading water, the life he wanted always stubbornly out of reach.

Charlotte studied his face and cocked her head. "What's wrong?"

He arched his eyebrows with exaggerated confusion. "How could something be wrong when I'm petting the cutest puppy on earth?"

"You're making the face."

"What face?"

"The I'm-secretly-annoyed-and-trying-not-to-show-it-because-I'm-too-nice-to-ever-admit-I'm-annoyed face."

George suppressed a frown. He'd had no idea he had a

face—or that Charlotte paid enough attention to his moods to realize he had a face. They were friends, but things between them had always been light and playful. Easy. She'd never called him out on faces he might or might not have.

"So?" Charlotte pressed, because she was categorically incapable of letting anything go. "What's wrong?"

He opened his mouth to say it was nothing—because George was always more comfortable as the helper than the helpee—but something about the frustrations of the day got to him and he found himself admitting the truth. "I'm just tired of always being the outsider. How long do I have to live in this town before I become something other than 'the new guy'?"

Charlotte wrinkled her nose. "Forever?"

George waved behind her toward the Furry Friends truck, which had been decked out for the parade. "Ally isn't considered a newcomer anymore, and she hasn't been here that much longer than me."

"Well, yeah," Charlotte acknowledged. The puppy squirmed in her arms, and she adjusted him to a better position. "But she married the mayor. And she used to come visit her grandparents here all the time as a kid, so the old guard remember her when she was still falling off her bicycle."

"So your answer is I'll never be local."

"I didn't mean that. I just think it takes people a while to accept that you're really going to stick around. Give it time. They'll figure out you aren't going anywhere."

The possibility of moving back to Colorado whispered in the back of his thoughts.

A horn honked and Charlotte spun around. "Looks

like we're starting. See you after!" She wagged the little puppy's paw at him again and jogged back to the Furry Friends float.

George watched her go until someone called his name. He jerked to attention and jumped up onto the float to do his part.

⁓

Charlotte walked along the parade route beside the Furry Friends truck, waving and beaming at everyone with the pride of future pet ownership, but even though her sunny smile never wavered, something kept niggling at the back of her brain.

George didn't seem happy.

That was twice now she'd finished a conversation with him today and it had felt like there was something weighing him down. And Charlotte couldn't stand it when the people she cared about were unhappy. The desire to fix, to meddle, wasn't even a desire really—it was a compulsion. She needed George to be okay. To be wonderful.

He felt like an outsider—which seemed ridiculous because she'd gotten so used to having him here it was like he'd always belonged in Pine Hollow—but she could also see why he felt that way, now that she was focused on it. The town was incredibly warm and friendly to tourists, but it could also treat new residents like they were just spectators, only passing through.

All he needed was something to suck him right into the heart of the town and make everyone realize he was here to stay. Something like...

Her attention snagged on Lois Dwyer, standing in front of the covered bridge along the side of the parade route.

Lois ran the town talent show every August, benefiting the historical society. She took her duties *incredibly* seriously, and the various talent show feuds that had developed over the years meant she was always short of volunteers. Especially those who were willing to coordinate the acts from the residents at the Estates.

Charlotte smiled as an idea began to take shape.

George wanted to be part of the town...and you didn't get much more local than doing your time on the talent show roster.

As soon as the parade was over, Charlotte needed to have a word with Lois Dwyer. Meddlers gotta meddle, after all.

Chapter Six

I declare after all there is no enjoyment
like reading! How much sooner one tires
of any thing than of a book!
—*Pride and Prejudice*, Jane Austen

W hat's going on with your face?"
George frowned through the webcam at Beks and
her question as they waited for the rest of their siblings to
join the chat. The family Zoom book club had been a
monthly ritual since before George moved to Pine Hollow,
starting back when his second-oldest sister, Evie, had first
moved to California with her husband.

"What are you talking about? There's nothing going on
with my face."

"You're making that face." Beks pointed a finger at the
screen. "The one where you're trying to pretend you aren't
irritated. What happened?"

"Nothing happened," he insisted, unsure how he felt
about the fact that the sister who knew him best had used
nearly the exact words Charlotte had used this afternoon. "I
don't have a face."

His oldest sister, Maggie, chose that moment to connect to the group chat—the video appearing first as she struggled to unmute herself. "You don't have a face?" she asked as soon as technology cooperated.

"He's making the face," Beks explained. "Something happened, but he doesn't want to talk about it."

"Ooh." Maggie lifted her goblet-sized wineglass and leaned closer to the camera, her face looming larger until another video window popped in. "Is this about a girl? You had a date last night, right?"

"Wait! What did I miss?" Evie frantically checked her phone for the time, the California sun setting behind her. "Am I late? I thought we were starting at seven-thirty my time."

"We are," Maggie assured her. "George is having drama but doesn't want to discuss it."

"I'm not having drama," he calmly reminded his battalion of sisters. "Is John joining tonight?" His brother-in-law sometimes came to book club, and George had a feeling he was going to need male reinforcements tonight. Or a human shield.

"He'll be along later. He got sucked into another bedtime story," Maggie explained. "That man has no willpower where the twins are concerned." Her eye roll was so fond George felt a little kick of jealousy.

"At least he does bedtime. Scott is still giving me the 'oh, but they never settle down when I do it, you're so much *better* at it than I am' bullshit." Beks sounded more exhausted than usual and George studied her, his worry sharpening.

"Don't you hate that?" Evie commiserated. "Like they think if they compliment us, we won't notice that we're doing all the work. Darian actually tried to convince me the reason he never loads the dishwasher is because he isn't *good* at it. Like I freaking care how prettily arranged everything is in there as long as the dishes get clean and I'm not the one who had to clean them."

"Uh-huh. So you're saying you've never criticized his dishwasher loading technique?" Maggie asked archly.

"*One* time! And he had it jammed so full one of the saucers broke—the ones that match those little china cups Grandma gave us, which weren't supposed to go in the dishwasher anyway—"

The final space filled in as Lori appeared, wearing a bathrobe and with her hair still wet. "Sorry I'm late. Baby food disaster. I made Mark take the poltergeist so I could shower. Book club is my one adult hour all week and I refused to do it with mashed peas in my hair." She raised her own glass of wine—white to Maggie's red. "Did I miss anything?"

Maggie lifted her glass for a virtual toast. "Evie scared Darian away from the dishwasher and now regrets it. John is being emotionally manipulated by our children into another five stories, so he'll join late tonight. And George is upset about something, but he's trying not to talk about it—as if he doesn't know that his sisters will always get the truth out of him and *resistance is futile.*"

"Exactly," Beks confirmed. "So, what's up with the face, Georgie?"

"Oooh." Lori leaned toward her camera. "Didn't you have a date last night?"

"Aren't we supposed to be talking about, oh, I don't know, a *book*?" He grabbed the paperback off his desk and waved the cover in front of his camera.

"We'll get to that," Maggie assured him. "I want to know

all the hot Vermont gossip. Beks picked up on a face, and Beks is never wrong."

"Thank you." Beks toasted them with a juice box.

"Is that grape juice?" Lori asked.

"We ran out of wine. Closest thing."

"Don't get distracted," Evie coached. "All eyes on George."

George groaned. Sometimes his sisters were so distracted by their own lives that they didn't seem to notice his. He could come to book club and soak up the familiar noise and nonstop chatter of them and feel more connected to home without ever letting on that he was lonely or envious of what they had.

And then there were times like now.

Four pairs of eyes—three brown, one blue—stared back at him through the computer screen.

He briefly considered feigning technical difficulties. How long could he hold it if he froze in place? Duke wasn't in the shot, asleep on his dog bed out of frame, so he wouldn't give up the game by moving.

But that would only make his sisters hungrier for the truth. He wanted to distract them, not send them into a feeding frenzy.

"The date wasn't worth talking about," he started, trying to defuse their interest. "She had more of a love connection with the bartender than she did with me."

His sisters groaned sympathetically in unison.

"I'm fine," he insisted. "There is no face."

"What about the hot doctor?" Beks asked—with her uncanny instinct for cutting through his bullshit.

"That's never going to happen. She broke up with the guy she was seeing—"

He was trying to gloss right over that part, make it matter-of-fact, but he should have known better. He couldn't get another word out that wouldn't have been completely lost in the squealing.

"Did you ask her out?" Maggie demanded.

He frowned. "They broke up *last night*, Margaret."

"But you're going to, right?"

George shook his head. "She's decided she doesn't want to date for a while."

Beks's brows pulled together. "And she told you this?"

Lori flapped a hand. "Everyone decides that after a breakup."

Beks was studying him with a little frown. She was the only one who seemed more concerned than excited. "Is there something else?"

"She says she's swearing off men and getting a puppy. She's already picked out the puppy."

"Swearing off men..." Maggie repeated.

Evie shook her head. "That's the breakup talking."

"Probably," he agreed, "but it's not like I can say, 'Oh, you're swearing off men? How about dating me?'"

"So you give it some time—"

He interrupted before Lori could get going. "She doesn't think of me that way."

"So you change how she thinks of you—"

"No means no, right?" he countered. "If a woman doesn't want you, she'll let you know—isn't that what you've all been hammering into my head since I was six years old?"

Maggie winced. "We might have been a little too effective in teaching you to be sensitive to what women want."

He frowned at the guilty expression on her face. "What's that supposed to mean?"

It was Evie who answered. "Just that you always accommodate what the other person wants, sometimes at the expense of what you want."

"And you always wait for the girl to make the first move, because you never want to presume she's flirting with you when she might just be friendly," Lori added.

"Which is another excuse for never taking a risk with your heart or letting people know how you feel," Beks finished.

"I don't need to tell her how I feel to know she doesn't feel the same," George insisted. "She set me up with her sister *and* her best friend. Who does that if they're remotely interested in you?"

"She *was* dating someone else at the time," Maggie reminded him.

"Yeah, and when they broke up she didn't even tell me about it until she was already dating someone new. Another arrogant asshole who treated her like crap." He'd been so far off her dating radar that she didn't even think to tell him she was free before she was with someone else.

"Don't do that," Beks scolded. "Don't go the whole nice-guys-finish-last route."

"Ugh, yes, those guys are the worst!" Evie agreed. "The wallowing in self-pity!"

"The bitterness," Beks piled on.

"'Nice guys finish last' is the kind of bullshit dicks say to give themselves permission to act like dicks," Maggie said.

"Exactly." Lori gestured with her wine. "Everyone has good luck and bad luck. It's not like the so-called nice guys are being singled out for crap just because they were so magnanimously good that one time."

Evie lifted a glass of something sludgy and green. "Have you guys ever noticed how in like every rom-com that's centered on a male lead, the girl is in love with the wrong guy? *Made of Honor, Playing It Cool, Wedding Crashers, Four Weddings and a Funeral, IQ, Runaway Bride, Sleepless in Seattle...*"

"They're always getting married too," Maggie added. "It always starts when she's engaged."

Lori wagged her wineglass. "It's the fantasy of the unattainable."

Beks snorted. "It's the misogynistic double standard of Hollywood—in which a man who is single is a stud, and a woman who is single has something wrong with her, therefore she is conferred value and desirability by the fact that someone else wants her. But obviously she's too stupid to recognize that her *soul mate* isn't the guy she's apparently settled for—because she's so desperate for love and babies that of course she would settle for the first guy who asks her—until a brilliant man *shows* her that he's the one she's meant to be with."

"Gee, Beks, tell us how you really feel."

"Is no one going to ask what the hell Evie is drinking?" George asked, still hung up on the green concoction.

"Darian made me one of his health smoothies." Evie eyed the green goo skeptically. "If you add enough rum, it's almost drinkable."

Beks pointed a finger at him, undeterred by his attempt to divert the conversation. "You always liked the unattainable. That's your problem."

Maggie shook her head. "His problem is the friend zone. He's practically built a house there."

"Lack of initiative." Lori tapped her glass for emphasis. "You're too passive."

"Or maybe I just haven't met the right person yet," he said, giving up on diversionary tactics.

His sisters wanted to help. They were all happily married. They all had kids. They had what he wanted—and they knew it—and they'd never been able to stop themselves from meddling in his life. At least he never had to doubt that they loved him, even when they drove him crazy.

"Honestly," he said, "if rom-coms have taught me anything, it's that guys like me are the ones who get dumped when the heroine finds her soul mate. Look at *Sleepless in Seattle*."

"What?" Evie yelped, indignant. "You're such a Tom Hanks!"

"Tom Hanks is the brooding single father widower. I'm the dude who makes awkward jokes at the dinner table."

"I like your awkward jokes," Lori said, staunchly supportive.

"Bill Pullman gets the girl in *While You Were Sleeping*," Evie reminded him.

"Yeah," George agreed. "Because he steals his brother's fiancée while he's in a coma. Can you see me doing that?"

"Well, you don't have a brother," Lori pointed out. "That slows you down."

"I don't know why we're talking about rom-coms," Beks grumbled. "It's not like they're romantic instruction manuals for a happy life."

"Amen," Evie agreed. "In real life a woman just wants

someone who will do the damn dishes without being asked."

"Once you're married, maybe," George argued. "But when you're dating, they all want excitement. They want sparks, and I'm too boring to be the soul mate. I'm no Mr. Darcy."

"So find a Jane!" Lori suggested. "She goes nuts for the Bingley type. You're *very* Bingley."

Find a Jane. It would have been great advice, if he wasn't already stupidly hung up on an Elizabeth. Or, more to the point, a Charlotte.

"It's your own fault we're so invested in this thing with the hot doctor," Maggie reminded him. "You're the one who made us read every single Austen novel for book club when you found out she was into them."

Lori raised two fingers. "And two spinoffs!"

George rolled his eyes. "They weren't spinoffs."

Lori flapped a hand. "Adaptations. Modernizations. Whatever. They were Austen-adjacent. They count."

"At least every book I pick for book club doesn't involve a wife finding out her husband is secretly a killer—*Maggie*." He waved the current selection in front of the camera again. "I'm starting to wonder if you're trying to tell us something about John."

Maggie snorted. "My husband can't even kill a spider. I read about women discovering deep dark secrets about their husbands to remind myself how lucky I am that John's biggest secret is the Oreo stash he thinks I don't know about in the garage."

Right on cue, the chat windows adjusted as a sixth person joined. Even though they were in the same house, John and

Maggie always used separate computers during book club—and proceeded to flirt with each other through the screen for the entire hour.

George couldn't knock it. They had the healthiest marriage he'd ever seen.

"Hi, honey!" Maggie cooed when John's head appeared, round and bald and smiling as always.

John pumped his fists. "Victory! The rugrats are finally out."

"Excellent," George said. "Can we talk about the book now?"

~

"Well?"

"Well, what?" George asked, standing up from his computer desk. As soon as book club ended—with no further discussion of Charlotte, thank God—his phone had rung with an incoming call from Beks.

"When are you asking her out?"

He should have known he wasn't going to get off so easily.

"She *just* broke up with him. I don't want to be the rebound guy." Duke stirred from his dog bed, taking a long, slow stretch before padding after George toward the kitchen.

"Wasn't she with the last rebound guy for like five months?"

"Four."

"I'm just saying. This girl doesn't sound like she's ever stayed single for long."

"But she *wants* to be single now. I'm gonna give it a few weeks." He opened the sliding door to the patio to let

Duke out to pee one last time before bed. "Patience is a virtue, right?"

Beks groaned. "I just don't want you staying in Vermont forever, waiting for the perfect moment to ask her out."

"Is that what you're worried about? I'm still considering coming back. Especially now. She'd rather be alone than with me."

"You don't know that for sure. And the not knowing is the worst. You should just ask her. Rip the Band-Aid off. At least then you'll know." There was a strange edge to her voice.

George frowned, his Spidey sense twinging. "Is everything okay with you? Is there something you're waiting to hear about?"

"This isn't about me. This is about you being so *patient* that you let opportunities pass you by."

Across the courtyard he could see light in Charlotte's windows—it was nearly midnight, and she was still awake. Those lights tried to snag his attention, but he pulled his gaze away. "Maybe the opportunity wasn't there to begin with."

"I honestly don't understand how you're still single," Beks grumbled, as if it was a personal affront. "Emotionally mature, financially responsible, not hideous to look at."

Duke trotted back to the door, and George opened it again to let him in. "We can't all meet the One in college."

"I guess." There was something strange in her voice again. "Did you know you're statistically more likely to get divorced if you get married before the age of twenty-five? So it's actually good you've waited until you're a fully grown adult."

Beks had gotten married at twenty-three. His worry reflex spiked. "Beks. Are you and Scott okay?"

"Yeah. Of course. We're fine."

George frowned, but with Bekah, pushing wouldn't do any good. He was the patient one. He would wait her out. "You know I'm here if you want to talk. Any time. Day or night."

"I know. Thanks. Just tell the hot doctor how you feel. Let it play out—and if it crashes and burns, *fine*. If you never try, you'll never know. " Her voice tightened. "I don't want you to live with regrets."

Her tone sent another jab of worry into his gut. "Beks..."

"And don't be bitter. Bitterness turns people into assholes."

He paused, debating pushing it, but if Bekah didn't want to talk about something, there was nothing he could do to push her over the phone. After a moment, he let it go. "I'll try."

"And?"

He rolled his eyes even though she couldn't see him. "And I'll ask her out, okay? I'll give her a week to process the breakup, and then I'll ask her."

Beks groaned. "I guess that's the best I'm going to get out of you. Just don't wait too long. You deserve to be stupidly happy."

"Thanks, sis. So do you."

Beks made a strange sound he couldn't interpret—and said goodbye quickly before he could press her again.

For a long moment, George didn't move, staring out at the darkened courtyard. Something was wrong with Bekah, and he didn't have the first idea what it was.

Maggie had no verbal filters—she would tell absolutely

anyone absolutely anything, and her troubles were public knowledge—but Beks had always been more secretive. She kept her worries close to the vest—but she usually didn't keep them from George. Maggie, Evie, and Lori were seven, five, and four years older than he was, but he and Beks were less than a year apart. They'd always been close.

If he was there, he'd know what was going on. If he saw her in her house, with her family, he'd immediately be able to spot the source of her worry—whether it was work or kids or Scott. He'd be able to coax it out of her. He'd be able to help.

But he was in Vermont, and she could hang up on him and hide from his concern, always trying to do everything herself.

Everyone had been doing so well when he moved here eighteen months ago. It was part of why he'd come. No one had needed him. His sisters and his parents, they all had their own lives—and he'd been living out the Wrong Guy part in the rom-com script. Not that he'd been engaged. But he'd been considering it. Not because he was so madly in love with Willa. But because he'd wanted what his sisters had. He'd wanted to be the husband who read too many bedtime stories. And Willa had seemed perfectly happy in their perfectly nice relationship—until she met someone who made her heart race. Something he apparently had never done.

He'd wanted to build something in Pine Hollow—but now eighteen months had passed, and he was no closer to being part of the town, no closer to the wife and kids and arguments over how to load the dishwasher.

Lois Dwyer had found him after the parade and asked

him to be on the talent show committee, which felt like a positive step, but would it change anything?

If he was home right now, he'd know what was going on with Beks. He could babysit for Lori. He could be there for his family. And find someone to argue with about the dishwasher with a larger population base to draw from.

But Beks was right. He would always wonder *what if* if he never asked Charlotte out.

His gaze went back to those windows across the courtyard, now dark.

He had the summer to decide. And to make sure he left with no regrets. No lingering might-have-beens.

Which meant telling Charlotte how he felt. When the moment was right.

Chapter Seven

She was stronger alone; and her own good sense so well supported her, that her firmness was as unshaken, her appearance of cheerfulness as invariable, as, with regrets so poignant and so fresh, it was possible for them to be.

—*Sense and Sensibility*, Jane Austen

Charlotte bounced through the entrance to the Estates first thing in the morning with an extra spring in her step. She was officially thirteen days into being single by choice, and she was *loving* it.

She'd always considered herself a happy person, generally cheerful and energetic, but she'd never considered how much of her mental energy was going toward relationship stress until it was gone. No more worrying about finding her Mr. Darcy, or keeping him happy, or not being good enough to keep him when she had found him. She was free of all the emotional baggage she'd been heaping on herself for the last decade—and she felt twenty pounds lighter.

She should have done this *years* ago.

Yes, she'd get a little lonely in odd moments—Charlotte had never done well on her own, and she was probably driving her friends and family nuts wanting to be around them all the time—but that would change as soon as she could bring her sweet little golden baby home. In the meantime, she visited him at Furry Friends every chance she got and spent all her free time puppy-proofing the condo and researching puppy-parenting techniques.

The Puppy Pact may only be half in effect without the puppy part, but even the first half made her feel like a new woman. Charlotte 2.0.

She waved to Suzie at the front desk with a bright smile and headed toward the small medical suite next to the assisted living wing.

She shared her office here, since she split her time about sixty-forty between the Estates and the sports medicine practice near the ski resort. She'd written her thesis on geriatric orthopedics, but even a big, fancy retirement community like the Summerland Estates didn't need a full-time ortho on staff. Most of the time she was here, she was either paying house calls or seeing patients in the exam rooms, so the shared office was just a place to drop her stuff and send emails.

Charlotte punched in the number code on the door and let herself in, reaching automatically for the light switch before she realized the lights were already on. "Oh! George! Hi!"

George looked up from one of the computers, surprise in his eyes. "Charles. You're in early."

"I'm sneaking in an off-the-books appointment with Vivian Weisman. What's your excuse?"

As a physical therapist, he worked primarily at the Estates, though they sometimes loaned him out to the sports medicine practice, but Charlotte hadn't seen him in days. Their schedules hadn't lined up the last couple weeks, and when they had seen one another, it had been rushed and surrounded by their colleagues.

"I'm trying to knock out all my paperwork so I can take an hour off this afternoon—it's the preliminary meeting of the talent show committee. I'm going to be coordinating the Estates acts this year."

Charlotte felt her face light up. "She asked you!"

It wasn't until George's eyebrows flew up and he laughed that she remembered she'd planned to be stealthy and not let on that she'd had a hand in arranging his involvement with Lois Dwyer.

"You meddled," he accused, smiling softly.

She wrinkled her nose. "I might have."

"You know, sometimes you remind me a terrifying amount of my sisters."

"Well, they sound fabulous. And you were the one who said you wanted to be more a part of Pine Hollow," she reminded him. "Though this may be a be-careful-what-you-wish-for situation. Lois takes the talent show *very* seriously."

"So I've gathered. She's sent me an email almost every day since I volunteered, and the show isn't even until August."

"Yeah, but the auditions are in July, and people rehearse their acts for *months*. The spots are very competitive."

He shook his head. "Doesn't everyone get a slot? It's a community talent show."

"Oh no, not since the six-hour marathon back when I

was a kid—apparently the town has a lot of talent. Lois Dwyer took over the following year, and it's been cutthroat competition to get a slot ever since."

"I'm getting that sense," he said dryly, making no move to go back to the computer.

She'd always liked that about George. When he talked to you, he gave you his full attention. None of that absent, I'm-really-in-communion-with-my-phone nonsense.

Behind his glasses, his eyes seemed to be studying her, as if he was looking for some kind of sign. "How's the puppy prep going?" he asked casually.

Charlotte beamed. "So great." She gave a little bounce. "I ordered a dog bed, and training pads, and signed up for a toy subscription service—did you know there were dog toy subscription services?"

"I didn't, but I can't say I'm surprised. Duke goes through a lot of toys. He's very hard on things that squeak." There was something she couldn't quite identify in his voice. A sort of tightness.

"I didn't know what kind my little guy would like the most, so I figured the subscription would let us try out a bunch of them—and the ones he doesn't like I can donate to the shelter."

"Sounds like you've got it all figured out." Definite tightness.

Did he disapprove? Charlotte felt that familiar compulsion to get him on her side, to win his support.

"Seriously, swearing off men and getting a puppy is the best thing I've ever done. Elinor thinks I'm moving too fast," Charlotte said, studying George for signs that he agreed with her older sister. "She keeps saying she's all for the Puppy Pact, but then turns around and says stuff like, 'Are you sure you want to be making major life decisions after a breakup?'" She made a face. "But when else do we make decisions except when we see that something needs to change? And when do you ever see that more clearly than when something blows up in your face?"

"She just worries about you."

"I know." Charlotte spun her office chair slightly back and forth. "I know she means well—and she's not *entirely* wrong. I did sort of jump into dating Jeff five seconds after Warren broke up with me. I was just so sure Warren was my Mr. Darcy, you know? And then Elinor saw what a pathetic mess I was when we broke up."

Bawling that she was going to be forced to marry a Mr. Collins hadn't exactly been her finest moment. But Charlotte wasn't that person anymore.

"Elinor wants me to take time for myself and think things through—but she doesn't see that this *is* me taking time for myself. I'm completely single, not looking for anyone to be my brooding romantic hero—for maybe the first time in my entire life—and I'm *loving* it. I feel *powerful.*"

"That's great." George's face looked strange again. Tight. His smile seemed off, somehow. "So I guess you wouldn't be interested in going out with a guy who's about as far from Mr. Darcy as you can get."

"God, no." She laughed. "I don't want to date anyone. But now I'm curious—who do you know who's the anti-Darcy?"

He spread his arms, his smile self-deprecating. It took her an embarrassingly long moment to realize he meant *him.* George.

"Oh! Oh God, George. Of course. Right. I'm an idiot. I…"

Did George have a crush on her? She'd never gotten that vibe from him. He was obviously crushable himself—sweet and friendly, and that dimple was downright lethal when he flashed it. But she was so *comfortable* with him. They were *friends*. And she'd only mess that up if they dated. She'd already proven she was a relationship time bomb. She needed to figure out how to be by herself before jumping back to dating anyone. Besides, he couldn't really—

"Relax, Charlotte. I was kidding."

"Oh…"

People always said they were joking when they wanted to take it back, pretend it had never happened. Then again, he had compared her to his sisters…Charlotte bit her lip, suddenly feeling tangled up inside instead of powerful and independent.

The office door opened, and Julia, their occupational therapist, walked in before Charlotte could find the right words to explain that it wasn't that she didn't want *him*.

"Oh!" Julia released a startled laugh. "Here I thought I was early, and you two beat me to the punch again. I guess we all have busy schedules today."

Charlotte lunged at the excuse. "Oh my gosh, yes, so busy. In fact, I should—I need to—"

"Say hello to Ms. Weisman for me," George said—giving her permission to run away, which somehow only made her feel guiltier for the fact that she wanted to flee.

"Right! Will do!" Charlotte chirped, bright and cheerful—as if chipperness could gloss over the awkwardness of the last five minutes.

She grabbed her bag and practically ran from the room.

She'd made the right choice—if these last two weeks had shown her anything, it was that her views on love and relationships were all out of whack and she needed some time to sort them out—but the look on George's face...That I'm-trying-not-to-let-you-see-that-I'm-hurt look. It killed her.

He couldn't have *really* been serious about asking her out. Right?

She was striding up the walkway to Vivian Weisman's adorable little patio home before she remembered she'd planned to check what time her first official appointment was before she came down here. Oh well. No going back now.

She knocked on the front door, knowing Vivian was as much of an early riser as she was, and waved at the Ring camera. A second later, the lock clicked and Vivian's voice came through the speaker. "Come on in, Doc."

Charlotte grinned. She loved when Vivian called her Doc—probably because most of the residents at the Estates preferred to make Doogie Howser jokes about how she was too young to be a doctor.

"Good morning, Vivian!" she called, slipping off her shoes in the little entry. "How's the knee?"

"Annoying," Vivian complained from her reading chair, where she had her foot propped on the ottoman with a pillow supporting her knee. "I hate getting old."

She tapped a button on the remote beside her to relock the door behind Charlotte—a habit carried over from a lifetime in Manhattan before she retired to Pine Hollow.

"Let's see how you're healing," Charlotte suggested, coming over to take a look.

"Slowly," Vivian announced. "At this rate I'm going to

have to learn how to play bridge just so I have some excuse to get out of the house."

"The bridge ladies do have the best gossip," Charlotte commented absently, focused on examining Vivian's knee.

"And their average age is ninety-two," Vivian grumbled. "I'm not that old yet."

Charlotte smiled at Vivian's grumpiness.

The residents at the Estates ranged in age from 62 to 104. Charlotte had found that her patients generally fell into two categories—the old guard looking for hip replacements and a way to get around a little better as they were getting along in years, and the more active seniors who tended to be younger and suffering from golf and pickleball injuries.

Vivian fell distinctly into the latter category—and she was chafing under the inactivity forced on her by her sprained ACL. Charlotte could absolutely relate, since she also found it impossible to sit still, but the body needed time to heal.

"We'll get you back on the court," Charlotte promised, frowning when Vivian hissed in pain. "But it looks like it's going to be another couple weeks of babying it. Have you been wearing your brace?"

"Whenever I'm not parked in this chair watching my ass get bigger."

Charlotte snorted. She loved the residents at the Estates, many of whom had declared themselves too old to give a damn—something Charlotte could stand to learn—and Vivian was quickly becoming one of her favorites, though she'd been slow to adjust to life at the Estates since she arrived.

"You know you could still go up to some of the social events at the main building," Charlotte suggested. "I could write you a prescription for a scooter if it's too far for your knee. There's always the singles' happy hour."

"No, thank you. I'm too old for that nonsense." Vivian picked up the paperback she'd set aside when Charlotte entered. "One of the physical therapists slips me romance novels. This is all the singles' night I need."

"You're never too old to fall in love," Charlotte insisted.

"Says the woman who swore off men at what? Twenty-six?"

"Twenty-nine." She resisted the urge to add "and a half," lest that undermine her point. "And I know you think my Puppy Pact is silly, but it's been really good for me." That awkward moment this morning with George had been the first time in weeks that she hadn't felt righteous and powerful because of her plan.

"I don't think it's silly. I think it's a mistake."

Charlotte laughed. "Don't hold back now."

"Oh, I won't," Vivian promised, smiling, but there was an edge to it. "Is this what you want?" She waved at the adorable little patio home. "To be alone in your golden years? No kids. No one to grow old with. Maybe a niece or nephew that feels obligated to visit you once a year, and a plaque in the lobby of the company you spent your whole life prioritizing—that sound good to you?"

"You aren't at the end of your story, Vivian. You could still meet someone—"

"I'm too old to build the life I might have wanted. Those opportunities are behind me now. I'm not looking for matching scooters and someone to help me with my blood pressure medication. I've come to terms with the choices I made in my own life, but that doesn't mean I don't have regrets. That doesn't mean I don't think about what might have been if my life had taken a different path. You always think you have plenty of time, but you don't. And it just seems to me you're awfully young to be closing the door on something I think you secretly want."

Charlotte narrowed her eyes. "So are you," she countered.

Vivian smiled cagily. "So if I go to one of these singles' nights, are you going to find a nice boy to date?"

Unbidden came the memory of George asking her out.

Something must have shown on her face because Vivian's eagle eyes caught her and she leaned forward. "What happened? Did you meet someone?"

"No." She blushed. "George sort of asked me out as a joke, but he didn't mean it."

Vivian gave her a which-one-of-us-are-you-trying-to-convince look. "Charlotte. A man doesn't ask a woman out as a joke."

"He thinks of me like a sister! He told me so." And she would hold on to that fact. He hadn't *meant* it. And of course it had been awkward after—even if he hadn't really wanted to date her, it still sucked to get turned down.

"Uh huh. So are you going out?"

"Of course not. I'm perfectly happy being single."

"That's a shame. If I were forty years younger, I'd take him off your hands."

Charlotte flushed... and an idea sank into her brain.

She might be swearing off men, but George deserved someone awesome.

She should find him someone awesome. And then she'd stop feeling this awkward guilt, and get back to feeling powerful.

He just needed a matchmaker.

Chapter Eight

A man does not recover from such devotion of the heart to such a woman! He ought not; he does not.

—*Persuasion*, Jane Austen

George was still kicking himself that afternoon as he walked into the rec center for the first meeting of the talent show committee.

Why had he asked Charlotte out in the most awkward way humanly possible at the worst possible moment? She'd just finished telling him how glad she was to be single and so he thought, what? She was going to leap into his arms and tell him she'd loved him all along?

He'd known it was the wrong thing to say, but he still hadn't been able to stop the words from coming out of his mouth. In that moment, it had felt like he was already too late and he needed to ask her *now* because he would never have another chance.

Well, he'd been right about one thing. He wouldn't have another chance. Because he'd royally screwed up that one.

"George! Good, you made it." Lois Dwyer appeared in front of him, beaming. She thrust a thick, paper-filled folder into his hands. "Here you go."

He glanced down at the folder and all the papers threatening to spill out. "Would you like me to pass these out?"

"Oh, no, dear, those are yours. Just to get you started. Some flyers to put up around the Estates with the audition dates, a hardcopy of the sign-up sheet, which you'll need to keep synced with the online page as it fills up, a schedule of our meetings, and a recommended timeline to follow as you're organizing the Estates acts and helping them practice for their auditions. You'll want to start on that right away—"

George interrupted—since Lois showed no sign of stopping for breath. "Isn't the show still five months away? That seems like plenty of time."

"You have no idea how fast it will go!" Lois exclaimed. "And trust me, you'll want every second. You don't want the Estates acts to be at a disadvantage."

The barrage of emails had given him an inkling, but he was starting to understand Charlotte's *be careful what you wish for* warning. "So I put up the flyers—"

"I'll explain the whole process once everyone has arrived. Why don't you take a seat?" She bustled away to greet a new arrival, and George turned to scan the small cluster of chairs facing a lectern where Lois apparently planned to deliver the gospel of the talent show.

Most of the folding chairs were unoccupied—George tended to get everywhere early—but Mac, the owner of one of the best restaurants in town, was sprawled lazily on one of them. George headed in that direction.

Mac looked up from his phone as George approached and grinned evilly, red curls going in every direction. He looked like a cheerful ginger Lucifer in a *Hadestown* T-shirt. "Lois got you, huh?"

George flopped onto the chair next to Mac. "I thought 'Cute little town talent show—how hard can it be?'"

"That was your first mistake. Just say no. Once they find out you're a sucker, you'll be on every committee from here to doomsday."

That doesn't sound so bad. "Says the sucker sitting right next to me."

Mac held up his hands innocently. "I'm just here taking notes for my grandmother. She's been on this committee since Jesus was a baby, and if she tells me to go check up on Lois Dwyer, I go check up on Lois Dwyer. That woman terrifies me."

"Lois?"

"My grandmother. She runs the old inn."

"The Pine Hollow Inn?" he guessed.

Mac groan-laughed. "God, no. And don't say that in front of her—the so-called historic Pine Hollow Inn is actually a hundred years newer than *the* Inn at Pine Hollow. Hers is the giant white one that looks like it ate all the other inns. Just don't try telling her bigger isn't always better—or that you can't come to a completely meaningless talent show committee meeting because you have your own business to run. She even lied about the time so I wouldn't show up during the last five minutes, grab her papers, and go. Machiavellian."

George chuckled sympathetically, playing the part of the unwitting volunteer, but frankly he was glad to be here. It felt like a sign that the town was finally welcoming him in as one of their own. Even if he was a sucker and this was more elaborate than the little community talent show he'd envisioned, it still felt like a step in the right direction.

And after his giant step in the wrong direction with Charlotte this morning, he needed that.

Lois Dwyer clapped her hands. "All right, everyone! Shall we get started?"

~

"I think you should go out with George," Charlotte announced, dropping her bag and throwing herself onto a stool.

Magda frowned, her hands never pausing as she whipped something that looked and smelled like chocolatey heaven.

They were in the kitchen of Magda's Bakery during what was supposed to be her lunch break. When Magda, Kendall, and Charlotte had all moved back to town, they'd promised one another that they'd make time to have lunch together at least once a week, no matter what, and they kept to that.

Though sometimes when they got busy, having lunch together consisted of eating standing up in Magda's kitchen at two-thirty on a Friday afternoon while Magda worked and Kendall and Charlotte squeezed in ten minutes between appointments.

One of Magda's multitude of nieces and nephews was currently manning the bakery while they hid in the back, waiting for Kendall to arrive with the food.

"I thought we were swearing off men," Magda said as the alley door opened and Kendall burst in, carrying a bag of burritos.

"Sorry I'm late. There was a line at the food truck—but Jamie gave me extra guac because it took so long."

"Jamie gave you extra guac because he wants to sleep with you," Magda corrected, setting aside the whipped chocolate batter to accept her burrito.

Kendall made a gagging face. "He's a toddler. I used to teach him in ski school."

Magda arched an eyebrow. "He's not in ski school now."

Kendall was unimpressed by this logic. "Didn't he date one of your cousins?"

"If we eliminate everyone you've taught in ski school, or who has dated any member of my stupidly gigantic family, we've eliminated the entire town."

"Exactly. There's no one dateable in this town."

"Actually, there is one extremely dateable man in this town, who is both age-appropriate and not related to Magda in any way," Charlotte interjected.

Kendall frowned as she passed Charlotte a burrito and grabbed a stool to perch on. "I'm drawing a blank."

Charlotte began unwrapping the top of her bundle of veggie-bean goodness. "I think Magda should go out with George."

"And I thought we were swearing off men," Magda countered.

"Yes, but George isn't most men. He's worthy. And hot. Have you noticed the dimples? The man is made of boyfriend material," Charlotte argued, before taking her first bite and groaning at the spicy deliciousness.

"So why aren't you dating him?" Kendall asked.

Charlotte took her time chewing and swallowing before pointing out, "We work together."

Except they didn't. Not really. Not in any way that would be a conflict of interest. They worked at the same locations, but she wasn't his boss. They just occasionally treated the same patients, or she would refer her patients to him for PT.

"Also, I'm a relationships hand grenade. We all know I would only blow it up, and I like him too much to do that to him. But he's perfect for Magda," she insisted. "You're both super nice and generous and kind."

"Thank you." Magda toasted her with her burrito. "Though I still don't see how this doesn't violate the whole swearing-off-men-and-getting-puppies thing."

Charlotte waved away the argument. "George practically is a puppy. He's sweet and loyal..."

Kendall paused with her burrito halfway to her mouth and arched an eyebrow. "So we're adopting him now?"

"No, I just..." Charlotte mentally flailed, trying to explain the logic that had seemed so obvious to her when she had the idea.

Magda frowned. "Didn't you already set him up with Kendall?"

"She did," Kendall answered before Charlotte could. "And, if I'm honest, she's not entirely off base that he could be good for you. He was a little too, I don't know, accommodating for me—like he might agree to go bungee jumping with me, but only because I loved it. He would never push me to be more, and I want *more*, you know."

"We know," Charlotte confirmed. Kendall was notorious for her ability to find a reason a guy was all wrong for her in three dates or less. Sometimes the reasons made sense, but more often it was Kendall's overdeveloped defense mechanisms activating. Though after Kendall's nasty divorce, Charlotte certainly couldn't blame her.

"But he wouldn't be terrible for you," Kendall admitted, pointing at Magda. "If we weren't swearing off men."

Kendall didn't need to swear off men—she needed to swear off the serial dating where she never gave someone a chance to get under her skin. Two weeks ago, Charlotte had drunkenly rationalized that the Puppy Pact would help Kendall cut back on work and allow herself to get attached to another living creature—even if it was a canine one.

"Look, I think we can all agree that the man detox thing was more necessary for me than for you guys. I'm the biggest dating disaster," Charlotte admitted. "But I still think we should all get dogs, and Kendall should work less, and I should date less, and Magda—you're perfect, do whatever you want. But I think you could be good with George. He deserves someone awesome, and so do you."

"Honestly, I was kind of enjoying the swearing off men thing," Magda said. "It made my singleness feel like a choice rather than a failure. And once I made that choice, I started thinking about what I really want, and I'm not sure I want to date right now." Her face flushed as she admitted, "I think I want to audition for *The Great Cake-Off*—and if I'm going to do that, I need to be actively working to broaden my repertoire so I won't have any weaknesses."

Charlotte blinked, all thoughts of matchmaking kicked to the curb. "Mags, that's awesome. I love that show. You should totally audition. You'd be amazing."

"Well, it's not just cake. I'm not very good at biscuits and breads," Magda hedged. "But my pastries are strong. Donuts, muffins, and cookies—I think I've got those."

"They're the best *I've* ever tasted," Kendall said.

"I need to practice chocolate sculpting and sugar work. I've been watching videos online." She bit her lip uncertainly. "I just don't think I want to think about men right now."

"No, of course," Charlotte assured her. "I'll find someone else for George. You focus on winning the *Cake-Off.*"

Magda smiled, small and pleased. "I have to get in first."

"You will. No one can do what you can do." Charlotte took another bite of burrito, but then couldn't resist adding, "But you should still get a dog."

Kendall and Magda groaned and trotted out their excuses—no time, no space, health inspectors—before the conversation devolved into a discussion of what Charlotte should name her puppy. But Charlotte's thoughts were only half on the conversation.

Magda wasn't the right fit, but she was going to find someone perfect for George. He really was the sweetest guy.

And Charlotte didn't give up easily once she had a plan.

Chapter Nine

A lady's imagination is very rapid; it
jumps from admiration to love, from love
to matrimony, in a moment.

—*Pride and Prejudice*, Jane Austen

That evening, George was still marveling at Lois Dwyer's unbridled passion for all things talent show—and trying his hardest not to think of that excruciating moment this morning when he'd asked Charlotte out—while he walked Duke along the greenspace at the back of the Net-Zero Village complex.

A row of solar panels lined the patch of grass, part of the eco-friendly sales pitch of the condos—all the amenities you could ask for, none of the environmental impact. George had picked the condo for the views. The mountains of the nearby ski resort curved around him on all sides to make it feel a little more like home—though the fact that the "mountains" around here never got above the tree line still made it hard for his Colorado heart to call them anything other than hills.

Duke thoroughly sniffed each of the solar panels in turn, making sure they smelled exactly the same as they had the night before.

George tipped his face up to the massive full moon and took a deep breath of the crisp March air. It was noticeably warmer than it had been even a couple days ago. It had been flirting with fifties all week, then descending into the teens overnight, but tonight there was a lingering warmth in the air, as if spring might finally be arriving in earnest. The forecast called for a gorgeous weekend—sunshine and clear skies. Maybe he'd take Duke for a hike—

The thought broke off as George caught sight of a figure running toward him from his block of condos. It was dark, but he immediately recognized the bounce in her step—and the voice shouting, "George!"

His heart rate kicked into overdrive. Charlotte wore an oversized gray hoodie, tiny denim shorts, and flip-flops— so apparently she'd decided it was spring as well. His logical brain fixated on her bare legs, worrying that she must be cold—even as the emotional part of his nervous system swamped his brain in stupidity chemicals and made his mouth go dry with a single, ringing question.

Had she changed her mind?

"I'm so glad I spotted you," she said, as she came to a stop in front of him, bending at the waist to greet Duke, who had abandoned his daily inspection of the solar panels in honor of the new arrival. "I need to find out what you're looking for in a relationship."

George blinked. Holy crap. "You do?"

She straightened from saying hello to Duke with a blindingly bright smile. "I'm going to set you up!"

His heart slammed down to his toes. "You are."

"I know what you're thinking."

I sincerely doubt that.

"I don't have the best relationship track record." Charlotte raised her hands in a *guilty as charged* gesture. "But I know everyone in town, and if you tell me what you're looking for, I'm positive I can find you the best girl. So what is it?"

George was too busy wishing for a sinkhole to open up and swallow him to process the question. Charlotte wanted to pity-matchmake for him. "Um…"

"What are you looking for? What do you want? When you picture your future, what do you see? Because shared goals are very important. Trust me. I've learned that one the hard way."

"Charles, you don't have to…"

"I know! But we're friends, and what kind of friend would I be if I didn't help you get everything you want?"

His gaze locked on hers. *What if I want you?*

"Come on," she coaxed. "At least let me try. I may be off dating, but I still think other people can have great relationships. Especially you. Let me help you find your person and renew my faith in happily-ever-afters."

He opened his mouth but had no idea what to say to that.

She cringed, her sunshiny enthusiasm suddenly retreating. "I'm being awful, aren't I? Elinor says I'm too bossy—always telling people what to do, acting like I know what's best for everyone. Just tell me no when I'm being obnoxious. You know you can do that, right? Mags and Kendall do it all the time. I'm not offended. Just say, 'Charles, piss off. My life is my life.'"

He smiled despite himself. God, she was adorable. "I like

it when you're pushy. I never have to wonder where I stand with you."

Her smile flashed, quick and almost relieved. "Yeah, I don't really contain unplumbed depths. What you see is what you get." She bounced a little. "So? You like direct girls? You want someone who won't leave you guessing?"

He refused to think about how much his sisters would be groaning if they saw this. "Direct would be good," he said—and Charlotte squeaked with delight.

"We are going to find you the *best* girlfriend," she enthused, and then cocked her head, eyebrows arching up. "Or...wife?"

"I do want to get married," he said. "Have kids. The whole thing. Though it feels weird and, I don't know, kind of desperate to say that before a first date."

"Dude, when a guy is emotionally mature enough to want commitment and responsibility, it isn't *desperate*. It's *hot*. Women are going to be bribing me to put in a good word for them." She fired off the next question. "How many kids?"

"More than three? I come from a big family, and I liked it."

Charlotte heaved a sigh. "It's such a shame Mags is taking a man break! She'd be so perfect. She's super domestic, and her family owns the Miller Dairy, all those huge barns south of town? So you know she has roots, and her siblings have popped out like twenty children between them, so clearly those genes are fertile."

"I don't need domestic. I can cook. I can clean. I can change a diaper." *I can load a dishwasher.* "I want my relationship to be a partnership."

Charlotte feigned a swoon, her eyes rolling back.

"Seriously, we should just auction you off for a good cause. We'd make millions. You are the dictionary definition of *too good to be true*."

And yet you don't want to date me.

"Do you want kids?" he asked.

"Oh." Charlotte blinked, surprised to have the tables turned. "I don't know. I mean, I guess I thought I did. Someday."

"Hard to do if you're swearing off men forever."

"Not as hard as you think. Lots of women have kids without men. But that's not—this isn't about me. We're finding you a person." She began ticking off items on her fingers. "She's gotta be smart, obviously, and have a good sense of humor. Kind. Because you're, like, the nicest person on the planet, and I refuse to hook you up with anyone who is going to take advantage of that." That little head-tilt came again, the one that seemed to show up right before she ambushed him with an uncomfortable question. "Do you have a type? Like physically?"

Brunette. Gorgeous dark eyes. Full mouth. Athletic, with legs that go on for days. Force of nature. Sparkling and tempestuous and over-the-top self-absorbed, but also incredibly gentle and compassionate with her patients. Extravagantly loving. Impulsive and energetic.

"Not really."

She nodded, lost in thought. "Okay. Okay, I have my marching orders. Give me a few days to come up with some candidates."

"Charles. You really don't have to—"

"I want to!" she gushed before he could try to dissuade her. It would be bad enough for the woman he wanted to try to set him up with other women if he didn't strongly suspect she was doing it out of pity.

"Trust me," she urged. "You won't regret it."

The reminder of Beks's sentiments about regret gave him pause—and Charlotte moved on to chattering about Vivian Weisman's pickleball ambitions before he could argue any more.

Beks had predicted that he might crash and burn, but he was willing to bet even she hadn't predicted this.

Chapter Ten

What are young men to rocks and mountains?

—*Pride and Prejudice*, Jane Austen

Charlotte woke up Saturday morning brimming with glorious purpose. Her therapist would doubtless remind her that fixating on the problems of others was a classic tactic for avoiding her own emotional baggage, but Charlotte didn't have any baggage right now, thank you very much—and she preferred to think of it as altruistically putting the needs of others above her own.

Besides, George needed a wife. She could totally picture him as Super Dad, with half a dozen adorable mini Georges climbing all over him. Her chest squeezed a little at the thought. It was her duty as his friend to ensure he got that future.

She wanted to start right away—but it was seven in the morning on a Saturday, and she had a feeling it wouldn't endear her to George's future bride if she called this early. She needed to think, come up with some quality candidates, and Charlotte always did her best thinking in motion. Normally, she would jog into town, but it had warmed up this week, which meant some of her favorite mud-season hiking trails would be open.

Charlotte laced up her hiking boots, grabbed her water bottle, cell phone, ID, and keys and drove out to the South Shore trail. It wasn't a hard hike, just a two-mile loop around the edge of a mountain lake, but Charlotte loved the views—and the quiet.

The trail was empty. The birds were chirping. It was just her and the breeze and the feel of her muscles working as she trotted down the trail with too much energy to keep herself to a walk. Boards had been placed over the muddiest sections, and she sprang onto them, her steps quick and light. She normally hated hiking alone—it was too quiet, and her thoughts would kick into overdrive—but when she was working on a problem, there was nothing better.

And besides, she'd better get used to doing things on her own since she'd sworn off men. She didn't need anyone—

As if the thought had tempted fate, Charlotte bounded onto the next board and her shoe slid sideways.

She yelped as her foot slipped off the side of the board and dropped two inches to the muddy ground below. Her ankle rolled and Charlotte hit the ground, her hip squishing into the cold mud. "Aaagh!"

Charlotte groaned, muttering curses under her breath as she fished herself out of the mud with a sucking sound—and hissed out a few more choice words when she tried to put weight on her ankle. She crumpled onto the board that had taken her out—and irritably eyed the black ice she hadn't noticed before her foot found it, a deceptive little patch that hadn't thawed yet on the cool morning.

The trail was empty. Cell phone service was notoriously crappy around here. And she was half a mile up the trail with one good foot.

She groaned. "Perfect."

~

"The plan backfired."

"Which plan was that?" Beks asked, sounding distracted even though she was the one who'd called him. Given it was Saturday morning, she probably had at least one small child hanging off her as she tried to make breakfast.

"The one you guys have been badgering me about for the last two weeks?" George prompted. "Where I ask out the woman of my dreams—and then proceed to get my heart stomped on."

"Oh no. She said no?"

"The timing was awful," he admitted. "She'd just finished gushing about how swearing off men was the best thing that had ever happened to her—but I had it in my head that it was now or never, so I made some crack about how if she wanted to try dating a guy who couldn't be less like her beloved Mr. Darcy, I was available."

"Maybe she didn't think you were serious," Beks suggested, though she didn't sound like she believed it any more than he did. "You probably surprised her. Maybe if you give it time—"

"She wants to set me up. She sought me out last night to ask what kind of girl I'm looking for so she can play matchmaker."

"Oh." He could hear the cringe in Beks's voice. "Okay,

well, that's pretty definitive. But it isn't the worst idea. At least now you know she isn't feeling it and you can move on. She might hook you up with someone great."

"Yeah," he agreed, without much enthusiasm.

Beks must have heard his disappointment. "I'm sorry, George. I know this isn't the outcome you wanted. But maybe it's for the best."

Beks had never been a fan of him having an unrequited crush on a coworker who was in a relationship. His other sisters would tease him and egg him on, but Beks always looked worried when he talked about Charlotte. Probably because she'd seen this coming.

"You're right," he acknowledged. "It's better to know now so I don't spend my last months here mentally chasing after something that's never going to happen."

"Your last months there?" Beks's voice lifted. "You're really moving home?"

"I don't know. I mean, I might. Dave still doesn't know if they're coming back, but I haven't exactly found what I was looking for here."

A slight hesitation. "This isn't about her, is it?"

"I promise I'm not moving halfway across the country because one woman wouldn't go out with me." He wandered over to the patio door, looking out toward the parking lot and the road that led to Pine Hollow. "I wanted to build something here. Not only with a wife and kids, but to be a necessary part of the community, and that hasn't happened. I'll always be the new guy."

A blue hybrid crossover pulled into the parking lot— Charlotte's car—and George watched it, even as he told himself to stop being a stalker.

"I thought you were doing that talent show thing," Beks said.

"I am. It's just...it's little stuff." He tried to find the right words to explain, as the car door opened. "Like this thing with the inns."

Charlotte climbed out slowly, not with her usual gust of energy.

"What thing with the inns?" Beks prompted.

Charlotte tried to take a step toward her condo—and winced, tipping off balance and bracing herself against the hood of her car.

Shit. She was hurt.

"George?"

He didn't think. He just reacted. "Beks, I've gotta go. A neighbor needs my help. I'll call you back, okay?"

He barely heard Beks sign off. He was already running.

If there was anything more embarrassing than spraining her ankle on the world's easiest hike, it was needing to be rescued by the Knight in Bare Feet currently racing across the complex because she couldn't even make it between her car and her front door.

Charlotte was reasonably certain it was just a bad sprain, hopefully without too much damage to the ligaments, though she'd know more once she took off her boot.

She'd managed to limp back to her car without too much difficulty, but the drive back to her condo had given her ankle time to swell and stiffen. She'd figured as long as she didn't take off her boot, she could hobble back to her place, elevate, ice, and be good as new, but when she'd tried putting weight on it, the pain had sliced up her leg and she'd nearly fallen over again.

George must have spotted her from his place, because he was currently sprinting across the grass in bare feet, a white undershirt, and red flannel pajama pants, with Duke leaping excitedly at his side.

"What happened?" he called out as he got closer. "Are you all right?"

"I'm fine. It's nothing." She waved off his concern—but since she wasn't sure she'd stay upright once she stepped away from the support of her car, she was incredibly grateful to see him.

"You're covered in mud," George pointed out helpfully as he arrived at her side.

"I was hiking, and I slipped on a patch of ice. My ego's more bruised than anything."

"Duke, get back, don't bother her right now." The dog had been trying to brush her legs, but at George's words he retreated a few steps to watch and wait.

"I'm going to have to get you to help me train my puppy. Duke is the best-behaved dog I know." Charlotte gingerly tested her ankle to see how much weight she could put on it. The answer? Virtually none. She winced at the renewed jab of pain, and George caught her arm at her side, his other arm gently wrapping around her back to support her.

"Goldens are smart. You'll have no trouble," George assured her absently, assessing the situation. "It's the ankle?"

"Just a sprain, I think."

He frowned. "We both know sprains can be serious. Have you already been walking on it?"

"Only about a half mile."

He released an exasperated breath. "Why didn't you call me? I would have come to help you."

"No cell service. And it wasn't that bad at first."

"Uh-huh," he said without an ounce of belief. "Hold on."

She looped her arm around his shoulders, expecting to use him as a human crutch as she limped across the compound, but George's shoulders shifted as he bent and before she knew it he'd scooped her up in his arms and was carrying her across the grass.

Her face grew warm. "I can walk."

"Sure you can."

She pointed over his shoulder. "My apartment is the other way."

"And on the third floor. We'll triage at my place. I'm not carrying you up multiple flights of stairs if we're going to have to go right back out to get an X-ray."

"You don't have to carry me at all," she reminded him.

He grunted.

Charlotte had to stifle a smile. She'd never seen George go all grunty caveman before. It was kind of cute.

Oh no.

No no no. She wasn't feeling mushy feelings toward George because he'd come rushing to her rescue and was currently carrying her like some kind of maiden across the moors. She may have been brainwashed by too much Austen, but she was off men. She was *happier* on her own. And she needed to protect that happiness even from her own stupid weak-at-the-knee impulses.

George was a friend. He was being a particularly good friend right now as he shouldered his patio door open farther so he could get them inside without setting her down—or even breaking a sweat. She'd never realized before what good shape he was in. The muscles of his arms were rock hard as he cradled her gently—

No.

Friend.

She was finding him his own Miss Right, and it *wasn't her*, because she was in man detox. It had only been two weeks since Jeff. She'd be falling right back into her same old disastrous cycle if she got all starry-eyed now. And Charlotte was breaking the cycle. Even if George smelled good and his arms felt like home.

That was an illusion. That was her imagination running away with her—like it always did at the beginnings of her relationships, when she convinced herself the man she'd just met was her romantic ideal. She was far too good at casting new men as the romantic lead, even when they didn't fit the role, and she refused to fall into old habits.

She was Charlotte 2.0. And George was a *friend*. A really good one, who deserved a lot better than her brand of relationship chaos.

End of story.

Chapter Eleven

Could there be finer symptoms? Is not general incivility the very essence of love?
—*Pride and Prejudice*, Jane Austen

I t's not the worst I've ever seen."

George grunted. The massively swollen purple ankle wasn't the worst he'd ever seen either—but considering both he and Charlotte looked at injured body parts for a living, that didn't set the bar very high.

"Classic second-degree sprain," she diagnosed confidently. "I told you it wasn't broken."

"And that diagnosis is based on what? Your X-ray vision?"

"My years of experience."

He gently manipulated her foot—forcing himself to continue his careful professional assessment even when she hissed in pain and the sound jabbed right into his heart. "You're going to need PT," he said finally. "And you should still get it checked out."

She waved away his concerns. "I'll baby it this weekend, and if it gets worse, I'll have Jack look at it on Monday."

Jack was the founding partner at the sports medicine clinic—and a more arrogant orthopedic surgeon had never walked the earth, but the man was good at his job. And he loved his work almost as much as he loved fresh powder at the ski resort.

"I guess that'll have to do." George stood up from the couch, where Charlotte was laid out with her ankle elevated on a pillow. He set a bag of frozen peas on top of the purpling mess—and Duke immediately crowded closer to sniff at the peas and receive Charlotte's cuddles. "We should wrap it. I've got some Ace bandages."

He started toward the medicine cabinet, and Charlotte called after him, "Are you always this grumpy with your patients?"

He was never grumpy with his patients. George was an infinite well of calm and patience where they were concerned, but watching Charlotte in pain was bringing out the worst in him.

"Sorry," he said, returning with the bandages and a bottle of anti-inflammatories. "Out of the way, Duke." He gently nudged the dog away and perched on the edge of the couch near her foot. "I don't like thinking of you in the woods somewhere, hurt and alone."

"I was barely hurt," Charlotte said lightly—until he fixed her with a long look. She was so covered in mud, she'd insisted that he put a towel down over his sofa before she would lie down and elevate her damn ankle. "I don't usually hike alone—and in the future I'll have my puppy with me."

"Because puppies are notoriously good in a crisis."

She grinned. "I was planning to train him to be like Lassie. 'Go get help!' is going to be the first trick we work on."

He gently lifted her ankle to wrap it and kept talking to distract her from the pain. "Have you decided what you're going to name him yet? I'm guessing not Lassie."

"I can't decide! Kendall says I'm not allowed to name him Darcy."

"And why's that?"

Charlotte grimaced—but he was pretty sure it was from the topic and not from pain as he snugged the bandage around her ankle. "Kendall used to call the guys I dated 'the Darcys'—because they were all rich and kind of smug and generally pretty judgmental."

"Charming."

"Yeah, I'm not saying I had great taste in men. Anyway, Magda would always say when we broke up that they weren't *real* Darcys. They were fake ones. So Kendall called them the faux Darcys and I—stupidly—kept thinking that meant I just had to find the real one. That he was out there, and if I kept trying, I would get my big romantic love story."

"You don't want that anymore?"

"I don't want to want it." Charlotte sucked in a breath and he gentled his grip. "I wanted it too much. I was looking for it everywhere, ignoring the signs that a guy was wrong for me or just a jerk. I wasn't in love with Jeff—I'm not sure I even liked him that much—but it took me catching him in the act of dating another woman to actually break things off. I would cling and cling and tell myself all these reasons why he was really a good guy and our happily-ever-after was coming." She was staring at her ankle, watching him slowly wrap it. "I didn't like who I was in those relationships, but I didn't know that. I had to get out to see it. And now that

I'm out—I don't want to go back in. I don't want to be that person again."

"Or you could find a relationship where you can be yourself."

Charlotte made a face. "That's harder than it sounds. At least for me."

He wrapped her ankle in silence for a moment as the realization of exactly how serious she was about swearing off men sank in. She wasn't being impulsive or dramatic—both things Charlotte definitely had a tendency toward. This wasn't about disappointment fatigue—or not only that. She was genuinely trying to take a step toward a better life.

And he wanted that for her.

Much more than her refusal when he'd asked her out, this was the moment he realized they were only ever going to be friends. And that was okay.

Duke nuzzled her hand, and Charlotte ruffled his ears affectionately. "Would you believe I never dated a guy who had a dog?"

"Well, there was your first mistake," George teased lightly.

Charlotte grinned. "Anyway, Kendall's right. My baby is so not a Darcy. He's got this adorable earnest thing going on—kind of more of a Bingley vibe, all floppy and sweet. And if I name him Bingley, I can always tell people it's because I love hiking Bingley Falls and not because I have an unhealthy obsession with all things Austen."

"Bingley Falls?"

"A waterfall up near Stowe—great cliff-diving if you're feeling adventurous. You should go, once it gets warmer."

"I'll have to check it out," he agreed, his attention on securing the bandage.

"How did you decide what to name Duke?"

George finished wrapping her ankle and gently set it back on the pillow, replacing the peas—which were no longer quite so frozen. "My sisters named him. It's short for His Supreme Hotness the Duke of Leighton—a character in a book we were all reading when I got him." He stood, moving to the kitchen area of the open concept main room to see if he had any more frozen vegetables.

"The infamous sisters."

"Infamous?" he asked, eyeing the contents of the freezer. Cauliflower rice? That should work.

"Why haven't they come to visit you since you moved here?"

He shrugged, returning with the cauliflower rice. "It's easier for me to go there. There are so many of them—especially once you add in kids and spouses—and one of them is almost always pregnant. I try to go back as often as I can."

"Why did you leave? Why come to Pine Hollow?" She cocked her head as he swapped out the frozen food. "I can't believe I never asked you that before."

"I came here on vacation and fell in love with the place. And I needed a change." He headed back toward the kitchen to refreeze the peas.

"Ooh, was it an ex?" she asked, sitting up with excitement.

He pointed a finger at her. "Rest. Ice. Compression. Elevate."

She rolled her eyes, but lay back down. "It was an ex-fiancée, wasn't it? Half the guys in this town have ex-wife or ex-fiancée baggage."

"Can't say I ever got that close." She eyed him dubiously

as he noticed the onion sitting on the counter where he'd set it over an hour ago—before Beks called and he got distracted. "Have you had breakfast?"

Charlotte's smile was hopeful. "Are you offering?"

"I was starting to make an omelet earlier. You want one?"

"I never turn down food." She tucked an arm behind her head, twisting partially on her side so she could watch him work without lowering her foot. "Are you going to tell me about the One Who Got Away while you cook?"

He gathered his ingredients, ignoring her.

Charlotte shoved out her lower lip in an exaggerated pout. "Come on, George. Take pity on me. I'm in *pain*."

He snorted at the dramatics, but he sucked at saying no to her. "There wasn't a big dramatic One Who Got Away or heartbreaking breakup." He began to dice the onion, something pleasantly domestic about cooking for her, talking to her, having her in his space—even if they were just friends. "I'd dated some people. It had never worked out—"

"Were you the break-upper or the break-uppee?"

He paused his chopping. "Do you have to ask?"

"I was always the break-uppee," Charlotte said.

"Yeah, me too." He grabbed the eggs and began breaking them into a mixing bowl two at a time.

"The first time I ever broke up with someone was Jeff, and that seemed sort of inescapable. Very black and white—catch jerk cheating, break up with jerk. But without a clear-cut reason…"

"Yeah. Turns out I was the guy girls dated for a while because they didn't have a good reason not to and I was too nice to break up with—and then she'd meet someone exciting and there'd be fireworks and she'd realize she never actually loved me, she'd just settled for me because she thought she was never going to find the kind of love all the songs were written about and I was a perfectly nice guy so why not?"

"Ouch." Charlotte winced sympathetically.

"After that happened a few times, I started thinking maybe it was me."

"It *wasn't* you," Charlotte insisted loyally.

"Part of it was." George shredded some cheese while he waited for the pan to heat. "I was stagnant. I was never destroyed by the breakups—I was just disappointed. More attached to the relationships than I was to the women. And I realized I was settling too. I wasn't finding what I wanted in Colorado, so coming here was a way of shaking things up. I needed to change what I was doing, or I could never expect different results."

"Your own version of a Puppy Pact."

"Yeah, I guess. Sort of."

He focused on the omelets for a moment, until Charlotte asked softly, "Did it work?"

He met her eyes, and for a moment didn't know what to say. He was no closer to his ultimate goal—a family, a place where he belonged—but he wasn't stagnating anymore. He wasn't settling for a string of five-month relationships that were the emotional equivalent of treading water.

Had it worked?

He turned his attention back to the omelets. "When I first came to Pine Hollow," he said, eyes on the eggs, "I randomly met this older couple—the Johnsons—and talked with them for, I don't know, almost an hour. They were…they were exactly where I wanted to be in fifty years. A team. Still holding hands. Still so in love. And I thought—if I can just find what they have, I'll be happy. And I guess I thought maybe I'd find it here. It's part of why I took the job."

"But you haven't dated anyone seriously since you arrived."

He glanced over at her. "I guess this time I didn't want to settle."

Charlotte felt George's gaze seep into her like sunshine slowly warming her skin. Her mouth went dry as her cheeks began to heat, for some inexplicable reason.

This tightening in her body couldn't be chemistry. This tingle along her nerves couldn't be *awareness*. She'd sworn off men. And George was a *friend*.

"I'm going to find you someone great," she promised, hoarsely. "No settling."

He broke the eye contact, turning back to the skillet with a slight smile. "Thanks," he murmured.

And that girl was going to be lucky as hell. The man cooked!

The omelet smelled amazing as he plated it and brought it over to her, helping her sit so her foot stayed propped up. He grabbed his own omelet and stood leaning against the island, plate in one hand, fork in the other as he ate.

The omelet tasted as good as it smelled, and Charlotte groaned, closing her eyes on a bite of cheesy, veggie goodness. "Okay, this is amazing. You are officially allowed to cook for me anytime you like."

He chuckled. "Good to know." They ate in silence for a few minutes, giving the omelets their due devotion. George finished first and carried his plate to the sink, beginning to clean up.

"I should do the dishes. You cooked."

"You should stay off your foot," he reminded her. "Do you want me to help you get back to your apartment?"

She flushed. She was so comfortable she'd practically taken root on his couch—but just because she liked being here didn't mean she could take up his whole day. "I should probably get out of your hair."

"No, I didn't mean—" George looked at her, speaking over the running water in the sink. "I thought you'd want to get cleaned up."

"It's not so bad. It's sort of like a full-body mud mask," she joked. "But yeah, I should probably take a shower."

Though she wasn't looking forward to going home. She was going to go stir crazy, lying around all day. It wasn't in her nature to sit still.

Not that she couldn't veg out with the best of them, but it was always with company, and when there was a sort of goal to her laziness—like binge-watching an entire season of something.

"I don't suppose you want to…"

George set the pan on the drying rack. "Want to what?"

"Would you wanna hang out and binge something?" Embarrassment sent more words rushing out to camouflage how badly she wanted him to say yes. "You could bring Duke and we could order pizza later. Elinor says I'm constitutionally incapable of being alone or sitting quietly. But we could watch—have you ever seen *The Great Cake-Off*? The

British original is so much better, but the US version is still super charming. You just fall in love with the contestants. I bet we could get through most of a season today. But you probably have stuff to do. Or...I mean, do you?"

"Not a thing." George smiled, his one dimple flashing—and Charlotte's heart thudded happily. "I'd love to marathon a show with you."

Charlotte beamed. "Great."

Chapter Twelve

Ah! There is nothing like staying at home,
for real comfort.

—*Emma*, Jane Austen

"You see?" Charlotte waved a hand irritably at the television. "This! This is why women date assholes."

Charlotte flicked a piece of popcorn at the distinctly unsmiling face currently occupying the television, and Duke lunged to snap the kernel out of the air.

Charlotte had showered off the mud—while George sat in her living room trying his hardest to think wholesome thoughts—and then the two of them had made it through exactly one episode of the fifth season of *Cake-Off* before it had come to light that Charlotte had never seen *Ted Lasso*, and George had made it his personal mission to rectify that immediately.

He'd known she would love the show—but he hadn't anticipated the violence of her reaction to one of the central characters.

He tapped pause, since Charlotte appeared to be gearing up for a rant. "You don't like Roy?"

"I love Roy! That's the problem. He's a total Darcy. All grumbly and growly, and then he turns out to be a prince among men—which conditions women to think all grumpy bastards are secretly squishy adorable puppies under the surface, and then we spend years making excuses for men who were really bastards all along."

She was sprawled on her couch with her ankle elevated between them, wearing a clingy T-shirt reading IN MY DEFENSE, I WAS LEFT UNSUPERVISED and a pair of pink yoga pants so soft George had caught himself playing with the fabric when he'd used her foot-prop pillows as an armrest.

They were nearing the end of *Ted Lasso* season one, and Charlotte, he was discovering, had very passionate opinions about the romance plotlines. He could see where she was coming from—especially given what she'd said about the "Darcys" she tended to date—but he had to defend his man Roy Kent.

"I feel like you're missing the point of Roy."

"Oh really?" She folded her arms grumpily. "Enlighten me."

"It's all about style versus substance. About not judging a book by its cover. Jamie's all flash and ego, but Roy is the real deal. He's the hidden gem—even if he's gruff about it."

"Exactly. Total Darcy. I'm just saying in real life the Darcys don't always turn out to be Darcys."

"So date a Bingley."

"*I'm* not dating anyone. I'm fully focused on my role as your loyal matchmaker."

He lifted his beer in a toast. "May you succeed where others have failed."

"Have you been set up before? Besides by me, I mean."

"Frequently. Four sisters, remember. And I think there

was some kind of lottery when I got to the Estates—all the grannies wanted to fix me up with their granddaughters."

"That's right! There was a bridge tournament to determine who got precedence. You're very popular among the biddies."

He smiled as he thought of the battalion of octogenarians who had taken him under their collective wing. "I like them."

"Yeah. Me too." She cocked her head, showing no apparent interest in returning to the show. "So all the setups were duds? You can't take Elinor and Kendall personally—Kendall never lets anyone get close to her, and Elinor was still hung up on Levi. I was hoping dating you would snap her out of it, but I guess true love conquered good sense."

"It's not just them. Apparently I give off friend-zone vibes. At least that's what my sister Beks thinks. She tried to set me up with her friend Sophie in high school. I had a huge crush on her—and I think Beks could tell—but Sophie only saw me as a friend. And I thought maybe that would change, maybe she'd see me differently with time—but then I introduced her to my best friend, Dave. It was like…lightning. They've been together ever since. Married eight years. And I'm still going on first dates. I think I'm just not the lightning guy."

"Yes, you are," Charlotte insisted, something almost angry flashing in her eyes. "You just haven't met the lightning girl yet. George, you're awesome."

He met her eyes, seeing the ferocity there, and had to smile. Somehow today it didn't sting quite so much that she didn't want to be his lightning girl. "Thanks."

She flushed, her gaze sliding away from his and returning to the screen. "Should we...?"

"Yeah." He hit play and reached for another handful of popcorn.

His fingertips brushed hers in the bowl, and he glanced over, but she didn't even look his direction, focused intently on *Ted Lasso*. George retracted his hand, popping a few kernels into his mouth and tossing one for Duke.

He wanted this—the lazy Saturday afternoon on the couch where the hardest decision was what to stream next, with someone who made everything feel easy and natural. But preferably with someone who didn't pull back when their hands brushed in the popcorn bowl, and to whom he didn't have to apologize when he realized he was absently stroking her calf through the velvety soft fabric of her yoga pants.

That person wasn't going to be Charlotte.

But maybe she was the perfect person to help him find that lightning.

~

They made it through all of *Ted Lasso* season one and half of season five of the *Cake-Off* on Saturday. By Sunday night they'd watched the champion crowned on *Cake-Off* and binged the first six episodes of *Ted Lasso* season two. George only left Sunday night after making Charlotte promise she wouldn't sneak episode seven without him.

He'd waited on her hand and foot all weekend—which made her feel guilty, but not guilty enough to make him stop.

They talked about nonsense—debating whether or not

she should name her dog after one of the bakers on the show, arguing over whether Ted and Rebecca were soul mates (which they obviously *were*), groaning when one of the bakers used the wrong kind of flour—as if either of them had any idea what the different kinds of flour were.

At one point on Sunday, Duke decided she gave better cuddles than his owner and abandoned George in favor of curling up next to Charlotte—a betrayal George complained about so ridiculously that Charlotte couldn't stop giggling.

It was heaven.

Easy and relaxed in a way she wasn't sure she'd ever known how to be. It was hard to be stressed around George. But she did feel a little guilty—as if she should have found him his person already, and she was somehow preventing him from finding the future Mrs. George by monopolizing his weekend. She'd gotten so angry when he'd told her he wasn't a lightning kind of guy. She was going to prove to him that he was just as lightning-worthy as anyone else—as soon as she was back on her feet.

By Monday she was mobile, but still wearing a brace on her ankle—and favoring it enough that Jack insisted on checking it out as soon as she walked through the front door of the sports medicine clinic. After a thorough examination, Jack confirmed her self-diagnosis and prescribed the same treatment plan Charlotte had already been following—and reinforced George's recommendation for physical therapy.

George happened to be walking past Jack's office at that moment and gave her an exaggerated "See, you should always listen to me" look that had her snorting and shaking her head.

She went about her day, seeing patients as usual. When she sat down to check her emails, George nudged a stool over for her to prop her foot on. When she paused in the breakroom for a coffee, he handed her a cold compress for her ankle. Always with a perfectly bland expression. But he was somehow magically there whenever she needed something—and it wasn't just him. By Wednesday all her coworkers were doing it—both at the sports med clinic and the Estates.

It should have been silly. It was only a sprained ankle. But she kind of enjoyed the way they made it into a game. Racing to see which of them could get her a foot prop or a cold pack first. It was fun. And it was all thanks to George.

"You ready for this?" he asked her, poking his head into the shared office space where she was logging her notes after her last patient's departure. She'd had a cancellation, so the rest of the afternoon was free.

"Ready for what?"

"You should check your schedule."

Panic spiked. Had someone added a last-minute patient? Was she late? Charlotte *hated* being unprepared. She quickly pulled up her appointments for the day—and there it was.

3:30—Physical therapy with George Leneghan.

George leaned against the doorjamb. "Jack didn't think you would listen to him, so he scheduled it for you."

"I was going to schedule it," she protested.

"Uh-huh." George nodded without an ounce of belief. "Doctors are the worst patients. Come on. Time to suffer."

She grimaced, but she was finished with her notes and didn't have an excuse to delay. "Fine. I'm coming."

George, she discovered, took his work very seriously. He was still smiling and relaxed, his voice calm and patient, but his eyes missed nothing, and he wouldn't let her get away with half-assing anything.

"I barely sprained it," Charlotte protested as he showed her yet another exercise he wanted her to do every day.

"Then this should be easy," he countered calmly. "Humor me. Do you want full strength back so you can go wandering off into the wilderness by yourself again or not?"

She flexed her foot, performing the exercise he'd shown her. "It's not like I *want* to go hiking by myself. But I don't sleep if I don't get enough exercise, and nature's gorgeous. Mags and Kendall are always working, and Elinor and Anne despise hiking—"

"I could go with you. I love hiking. And I've never been good at sleeping in."

"Me neither! I don't understand how people do it. How can you just lie there? Isn't everything in your body telling you to get up and go?"

"Your dog is going to love that you're a morning person." George studied her foot position. "That's good. Now try this one."

Charlotte went through the next exercise, before that familiar feeling that she was asking too much, demanding too much, rose up and made her say, "You know you don't have to go hiking with me if you don't want to."

He gave her a look. "Has it occurred to you that I might want a hiking buddy? I'm still the new guy. It's hard to break into the groups who have been hiking together since elementary school."

He adjusted her position, his hands gentle but firm. He

wasn't flashy or showy about it, but the man was great at his job. There was something incredibly sexy about that—not that *she* was growing susceptible to his charms. She was simply filing them away for the girl she was going to set him up with.

"Did you hike a lot in Colorado?" she asked, her voice a little thin.

"A fair amount. My best friend—"

"Dave," she supplied, thanks to their weekend conversations.

He nodded, his fingers gentle on her ankle. "Dave. Loves to hike. He was the one who would get me out there. I kind of miss having someone to drag me out of bed and get me on the trails."

"You guys stopped hiking?" She hadn't gotten that part of the story on the weekend—she'd heard half a dozen random childhood stories about "my best friend Dave" but none of them mentioned a falling-out.

"He and Sophie moved to Western Australia. Harder to meet up for hikes now." His hands shifted on her ankle and she caught her breath.

"Was that another part of why you moved here?"

"It was a contributing factor. So if you wanna be my new Dave and drag me out on hikes, you'd be doing me a favor, Charles." He gently tapped her ankle. "*After* this heals."

"Deal." She grinned. "I'm going to be the best patient you've ever had. You're going to be amazed how fast my ankle gets better."

He eyed her skeptically. "Just don't push it."

"Be honest, I'm your favorite, aren't I?"

George shook his head. "You know I've heard that about you—that you call all of your patients your favorite."

"Only the ones that are."

"They can't all be your favorite."

"Why not? Favorite should be a tier, not a singular item. Why should you have to have *one* favorite food or *one* favorite person? Why are we only allowed to have one *best* friend? Why does everything have to be ranked all the time?" She waved a hand like a queen issuing a proclamation. "I reject the entire fallacy of the favorite! If you love it, *really* love it, then it's your favorite. I always have at least two favorites, so I never have to worry about running out."

"So when you said this weekend that the *Cake-Off* was your favorite show…?"

"Oh, I have, like, twenty-seven favorite shows."

"And if you had to pick just one to watch…?"

"It would depend on my mood. Isn't everyone like that?"

"But if you had to pick one to watch for the rest of your life and it was the only thing you could ever watch again—"

"Why would I have to pick that? All these crazy desert island scenarios where you have to pick the *one* food you would eat for the rest of your life or the *one* show you would watch forever—*why*? And it doesn't matter what you pick! You would get sick of it. There is no food or show or person or anything that wouldn't get annoying if you were trapped with it forever."

"Spoken like a true romantic."

She rolled her eyes. "So just because there's no one I want to be trapped with for all eternity, I can't be a romantic? You honestly think it would all be sunshine and roses if you were stranded somewhere with your future wife and you only had each other *forever*?"

"I wasn't saying that. And I'm genuinely not sure how we got on this topic."

"You wanted me to pick a favorite, and I'm trying to prove that the entire idea of *one* favorite is an artificial construct and clearly wrong."

George's dark gaze was filled with humor as he nodded once. "Consider me convinced."

Charlotte narrowed her eyes at his capitulation. "Are you making fun of me?"

"No, you made a good argument."

She eyed him skeptically. "Really?"

George grinned, arching his brow. "Did you not want to convince me?"

"No, I did. I just…people don't usually concede."

He shrugged. "I guess I'm extraordinary. Does that make me a favorite?"

She narrowed her eyes, studying him. "Not yet. But you're on the path, my young padawan."

"We should marathon those next," George suggested, turning his attention back to her ankle. His callused fingertips brushed her skin, and she suppressed a shiver.

"*Star Wars?* Like, all of them?"

"After we finish *Ted Lasso* and *Cake-Off.* You shouldn't hike for a couple more weeks. I take my duties as Distractor in Chief very seriously."

She grinned. "I appreciate your diligence, but I actually have plans tonight."

He looked up from her ankle. "I wasn't thinking tonight. I have to go out to the Estates as soon as we're done here. Preliminary meeting for residents who want help getting their audition pieces ready for the talent show. But unless your plans consist of elevating your ankle, you might want to cancel."

"No can do. Kendall and I have tickets for *Hamilton* in Burlington. She got them months ago. I'll elevate my ankle every chance I get, but I am going to that show. No force on earth is going to stop me. I'm sick of being the only member of my family who hasn't seen it live." It was rare that she could pry Kendall away from work for even one night, and she wasn't going to miss this chance.

"You've never seen *Hamilton*?"

"Med school is time consuming. Don't judge me."

He shrugged innocently. "No judgment. I mean it's no *Ted Lasso*..."

She grinned. "We still have to finish season two. Tomorrow?"

"You're on."

"Excellent. And good luck with the biddies tonight. Talent show stuff can get intense." She wrinkled her nose. "You aren't mad at me for putting your name forward as a volunteer, are you? You had no idea what you were getting yourself into when you said yes."

"I didn't, but I did say I wanted to be more involved in the town."

She met his eyes and they both spoke at the same time, "Be careful what you wish for."

Chapter Thirteen

None of us want to be in calm waters all our lives.

—*Persuasion*, Jane Austen

Be careful what you wish for.

George was haunted by those words that evening when he was listening to his second consecutive hour of discussion about best practices for scheduling rehearsal times and practice auditions for the talent show.

Last year, apparently, there had been factions, and the residents of the patio homes had been edged out of rehearsing in the main auditorium by the residents of the towers, who had snatched up all the available slots and saved them for one another. George had finally determined that no one was allowed to reserve a second coveted auditorium slot until everyone who wanted one had scheduled their first, and that anyone who forfeited their slot gave it back to the scheduler—George—and was not, in fact, able to auction it off to their friends.

Another lengthy debate ended with George declaring

that each *group* could only reserve one spot at a time, not each *member* of a group, so the marching band would only be eligible for one slot and not twenty-seven. And that each participant was only allowed to reserve space for a single act—so people auditioning as soloists and as members of multiple groups could still only reserve one slot.

George was patient. It was his superpower. But even his patience was being tested by what felt more like arbitrating for a bunch of squabbling children than it did coordinating the charitable efforts of senior citizens.

"Ever wonder why last year's coordinator didn't volunteer again?"

George glanced over as a man with laughing blue eyes and a neat gray beard leaned over from the chair to his right. Both of his hands were stacked on top of the cane propped between his legs.

"I did, but I don't anymore," George admitted. "I don't think we've met."

"Never needed physical therapy." The man took his right hand off the cane and extended it to George, a tattoo peeking out the bottom of his sleeve. "Howard Fullerton."

"George Leneghan."

"I know. Lots of folks talking about the new guy."

George groaned internally. "I have been here for a year and a half."

Howard shrugged. "You'll be the new guy until someone else is. I'm not from around here either. Moved up six years ago to be closer to my daughter. Took, oh, two years before people stopped calling me New Howard—when another, newer Howard moved in."

Raised voices on the other side of the circle caught

George's attention, and he returned his focus to his job as an amateur treaty negotiator. It was ultimately agreed that no two acts would sing the same song—apparently the cause of the Great "My Way" Debacle of 2017—and that a random lottery would determine the order in which the acts claimed their musical selections.

George's brain felt like it had been through a blender by the time he noticed more than one of the residents around the circle nodding off and called an end to the meeting. He promised to post the official rules, along with a sign-up sheet for the song-selection lottery, and a separate sign-up sheet for auditorium rehearsal times within the next week.

Considering all the bickering, he was more than a little surprised when the residents burst into applause at the end of his little speech—rousing those who had dozed off. They began a shuffling progression toward the doors, a stately parade of walkers, scooters, and canes. Two of the women who had seemed most contentious with each other were now smiling and walking with linked arms—hell, for all he knew they'd only been shouting because they both had hearing aids.

George bent his head and scratched notes into the margins of the prep sheet Lois Dwyer had given him, trying to make sure he remembered all the rules and addendums that had been agreed upon.

One of the oldest residents paused and patted him on the shoulder as she was waiting for an electric wheelchair to whir by. "Don't worry, honey. You're doing great," she assured him.

"Thanks," he murmured, noticing that Howard Fullerton

was still next to him, watching him with his cane braced between his legs and his hands stacked on top. He met Howard's slightly smiling gaze with a wry smile. "They sure take this seriously."

"Course they do. Everyone's trying to get something back. Fountain of youth."

The room had nearly cleared out, but Howard made no move toward the door, and George didn't immediately stand up either. A bemused smile curled his lips. "Fountain of youth?"

"I have a theory." Howard raised one gnarled finger, keeping his hands stacked on the head of his cane. "When you're young—like little-kid young, not like you're young—you think anything is possible. You could be anything when you grow up—it's all in front of you. You're Frank Sinatra and Hank Aaron and whoever else you wanna be. It's all play. All pretend. All possibility." He pointed that finger at George. "But then you do grow up. And it's work and stress and the disappointing realization that you aren't actually Frank Sinatra. But then you *retire*. If you're lucky, to someplace like this. Then there's no longer any pressure to become something—you're already at the finish line—and you get to play again. You know you aren't going to be Frank Sinatra—no one's Frank—but you can remember what it felt like when you genuinely believed you would be. When you were young, and anything was possible. You can stand on that stage and sing and be whoever you dreamed you would be before you were tired and life was hard." He shrugged. "Fountain of youth."

George studied the man with the deep, persuasive voice. "What did you do before you retired, Howard?"

"Professional student of human nature." His smile was dry. "I taught sociology."

"That makes sense. Are you going to enter the lottery? Try to be the first act to claim 'My Way'?"

"Oh, no, I'm not Frank." He tapped his throat. "Can't sing to save my life. I'm just an old guitarist in search of a blues band."

"I know the feeling," George commiserated. He'd never been much of a musician, but he missed being in a band. "I bet you could find a few other musicians around here."

"You'd think. Not so much luck yet. I put an ad on the bulletin board and got a drummer, but somehow the songs aren't the same without the vocals."

"Is that why you came today? Searching for more talent?"

Howard chuckled. "Oh, no, I just came to watch the show. This is better than *Hawaii Five-0*, watching everyone get so worked up."

George laughed. "Howard, I have a feeling you're an instigator."

"Who me?" He levered himself to his feet, waggling his bushy eyebrows, and George laughed again.

"I'm glad you came. And good luck finding the rest of your band."

"You should save that good luck for yourself, young man." Howard chuckled darkly, and headed methodically toward the door, calling over his shoulder, "You're going to need it."

George gathered up his notes, tucking the folder into his bag, and headed out of the multipurpose room he'd reserved for the meeting. He'd thought Lois was overzealous with her proposed meeting schedule, but now he was figuring he was going to need to reserve every time he could get.

The meeting had felt like it lasted for hours, but it was still only a quarter past six when George climbed out of his car at the NetZero Village complex. Charlotte's car was still in the lot, but she'd said Kendall was driving them to the show—they were probably long gone.

The sun wouldn't set for another hour, but it had dipped behind the mountains, casting the complex in an early twilight as George crossed the courtyard.

He unlocked the door to his place, expecting Duke's usual eager welcome, but the Berner was nowhere in sight. "Duke?"

The condo wasn't huge. It only took a moment for George to spot the dog—and for his panic level to skyrocket.

Duke lay beside his dog bed instead of on top of it, his breathing labored.

George dropped his bag, hitting his knees beside the dog. "Hey, buddy, what's wrong?"

Duke tried to stand up, staggering, and immediately retched, but nothing came out.

"Okay, buddy, you're okay. We're gonna get you to the vet. You just lie down." His thoughts racing, George coaxed Duke onto his dog bed. Bernese mountain dogs were susceptible to bloat, a condition where their stomachs filled with gas and twisted. It could be fatal if they didn't get immediate medical attention—and the nearest emergency vet was an hour away. But he wouldn't let himself think about that. It wasn't bloat. It was probably just something he ate. Duke was going to be fine. No other alternative was acceptable.

George propped open the door and scooped up Duke and his dog bed, grunting at the weight and staggering a little as he hefted the awkward bundle. The dog bed was bulky, but George was hoping it would help support Duke's weight more evenly and keep him from putting pressure on his stomach—or anything else that might be hurting.

"Come on, buddy," he murmured, keeping up a steady monologue of soothing nonsense as he twisted to squeeze through the door without jostling Duke.

He was halfway across the courtyard, focused completely on getting Duke to the car, when a familiar voice penetrated his fear.

"George? What's going on? Is Duke okay?"

"I don't know," George managed, not wanting to say what he was afraid it was.

Charlotte didn't wait for answers he didn't have, moving in front of him to open the back door of his SUV. "Are you taking him to the emergency vet? It's okay, baby. You're gonna be okay," she soothed Duke as George settled him as gently as he could in the back of the car.

He pulled out his keys, and Charlotte took them from his numb fingers.

"You ride in back with him. I'll drive."

George looked at her—full makeup, hair curled and twisted to one side, a sexy little black dress beneath her bright blue wool coat. She was dressed to go out. To go to *Hamilton*.

"What are you doing here?" he asked. "Aren't you supposed to be in Burlington?"

"Kendall was running late. I'll call her from the car. She can take Magda. Or anyone." She turned him toward the back seat. "Get in. You're in no state to drive, and I know these roads like the back of my hand. Come on."

George slid in next to Duke, but as Charlotte pulled out of the parking lot, the flash of the bracelet on her wrist caught the light, and he felt a matching flash of guilt. "Your show..."

"Don't worry about that. Magda will love it. And I'll catch it next time the tour comes around."

She said it so simply. As if she hadn't said this afternoon that no force on earth was going to stop her from seeing it.

"Your ankle..."

"Is not the foot I'm driving with. You look after Duke. I've got this."

George stroked Duke's silky head, muttering comforting nothings—and was incredibly glad he wasn't alone.

Chapter Fourteen

Surprises are foolish things. The pleasure
is not enhanced, and the inconvenience is
often considerable.

—*Emma*, Jane Austen

The waiting room at the emergency vet had the same
sterile hush as hospital waiting rooms everywhere.
The vet techs had taken Duke into the back as soon as
they arrived, promising to be back with updates as soon
as they knew anything. The dog seemed about the same
when they arrived, and Charlotte was choosing to take
comfort in the fact that he wasn't any worse.

She sat next to George, his hand clasped tight in hers.
She wasn't sure he was even aware he was gripping her like
a lifeline. She'd already said variations of *he's going to be
fine* and *everything's going to be okay* a thousand times, even
though they both knew it was nonsense and she had no way
of knowing that. But it was the kind of nonsense that sometimes it was nice to hear someone say—as if the faith that it
would turn out okay might somehow tip the scales.

People had said stuff like that to her all the time when her mom had cancer. *I'm sure she's going to beat it. She's a fighter. She'll pull through.*

And she always had. Until she hadn't.

Charlotte hated hospitals when there wasn't anything for her to do. The helplessness was wretched. The *waiting*. Her heart ached for George. The least she could do was try to distract him.

"How was the talent show meeting?"

George looked over at her, brown eyes worried behind his glasses. "What?"

"The meeting today? At the Estates? Did it go all right?" The waiting room was cold, and she tugged at the hem of her skirt. George caught the gesture and released her hand to shrug off his coat, spreading it over her lap like a blanket.

His brow furrowed as he studied her outfit. "I can't remember if I closed the door to my apartment."

Charlotte immediately pulled her phone out of her clutch. "I'll text Levi. He'll go by and make sure everything's okay."

"Thanks." He shook his head ruefully. "I'm usually good in a crisis. But my brain just shut off."

"Hey. You got him here. That's what counts."

He nodded, and she took his hand again after sending the text, lacing their fingers together.

"My dad forgot me at a hospital once," she said in a bid to distract him, and it worked. His head turned immediately toward her—yanking his gaze off the doors he'd been staring at for the last ten minutes. "I don't blame him. My mom was sick, and he was dealing with a lot. I think that day was when they told him she was moving to hospice care. That there wasn't anything left to do."

"How old were you?"

"Eight. She died when I was nine. And she *loved* Jane Austen. The books. The BBC series. All of it."

"So that's why you and your sisters..."

"Are obsessed with all things Jane? Yeah. It's a way to feel like I know her, you know?"

His hand squeezed hers. "Yeah."

She kicked herself. She was supposed to be comforting him, not the other way around. "Sorry. I was trying to distract you, not bring everyone down. We can always discuss the horrors of soggy-bottomed pastry. The things I never knew were unforgivable baking sins before I started watching *Cake-Off*."

"It's an education." His lips curled in an attempt at a smile—but whatever he was going to say next was lost when the doors opened and a vet emerged.

"Mr. Leneghan?"

"Yes." George stood and Charlotte came with him, her hand aching a little from the sudden tension in his grip.

"Duke's going to be just fine."

"Oh, thank God." George sagged beside her and she squeezed his hand, trying to pour her strength through it into him.

"It wasn't bloat. It looks like he shredded a purple rubber toy and ate all the pieces."

George paled. "His pig. Oh God. He destroys his toys, but he's never tried to eat them before."

The doctor nodded. "It happens. We got him to throw up several times, and we're not seeing any remnants in his system that he shouldn't be able to pass naturally, but you'll want to keep an eye on him for a couple days and bring him back in if you notice any of the symptoms we've listed on his check-out paperwork. But he should be good to go."

"That's it?"

"He'll be tired. We can give you some high-fiber dog food, and you should take him on extra walks over the next few days to help him pass anything still in his system. But yeah. That's it. He's a good dog."

"The best."

The vet shook his hand, and Charlotte squeezed his other one, her free hand gripping his biceps.

George's arm was asleep.

That was his first thought on waking, chased quickly by the realization that thirty-two might be too old to fall asleep on the couch, if the nasty crick in his neck had anything to say about it.

Then a soft form sighed and snuggled closer against his side, and George revised his stance on couch sleeping toward the positive again.

She was still here.

It hadn't been that late when they'd gotten home from the vet, and Charlotte had asked if it was all right if she came in to help him keep an eye on Duke. They'd curled up on the couch, the three of them, and watched *Cake-Off* until they fell asleep, but at some point during the night Duke must have abandoned the couch. He was currently sprawled on his dog bed, snoring softly—

And Charlotte was currently stretched out, half on top of George, along the length of the couch. His right arm was pinned beneath her—hence the lack of circulation—but he wasn't in any hurry to move her.

It had been good having her here last night. She'd somehow known exactly when to distract him, and it had been so comforting, as they were driving to Burlington, to know he wasn't alone. He was used to being the one who was there for everyone else. It had been a while since someone outside his family had been there for him, no questions asked.

She'd missed *Hamilton*. Without a second thought.

"Oh." Charlotte jerked, going from soft and pliable against him to abruptly awake from one heartbeat to the next. "Sorry. I didn't mean to fall asleep. How's Duke?" She scrambled off the couch, surging into the day with her usual burst of energy. "What time is it?"

George flexed his hand, working circulation back into it as he sat up and nodded to the clock on the microwave. "Just after seven."

Charlotte didn't seem to hear him, crouched next to Duke, stroking his head as he groaned and stretched. "Hey, buddy. How are you feeling?" Duke opened his mouth in a massive yawn, and she grinned over her shoulder at George. "He seems better."

Something soft shifted in his chest at her smile. "He does."

For a moment their gazes held, before hers slid away. "I should go. I always visit Bingley before work, and I wouldn't want him to think I forgot him."

George stood, shutting off the TV and its carousel of Netflix ads. "You decided on Bingley, huh?"

"Kendall can tease me as much as she wants. He's a total

Bingley. Sweet and eager and happy all the time. I can't wait until next week when I can take him home."

"Last night didn't scare you off pet ownership?" He'd felt so guilty, so irresponsible for letting Duke have a toy that had hurt him.

"Not even a little bit." She was still in her dress from last night, her hair rumpled and makeup smudged, and she'd never looked better as she bent to collect the shoes she'd kicked off. "We still on for that marathon later?"

"Distractor in Chief at your service. Though I might have to spend some time at the Estates. This talent show stuff is a little more time intensive than I expected."

She made a face. "I should never have sicced Lois Dwyer on you."

"I think I might be glad you did. Check back in a week or two."

"Will do." She grinned. "Bye, Duke. See ya later, George."

"Bye, Charles. And...thanks."

She waved a hand as if she hadn't done anything, flashing him one last smile before closing the patio door behind her. He watched her cross the courtyard, favoring her ankle slightly, still barefoot and carrying her shoes, though the grass had to be cold. His heart squeezed at the sight.

"Come on, Duke." George roused the Berner, turning away from the view. "Extra walks for you this week."

Chapter Fifteen

It is well to have as many holds upon happiness as possible.
—*Northanger Abbey*, Jane Austen

Charlotte pulled into the Furry Friends parking lot on Friday afternoon and practically catapulted herself out of the car. She'd rushed here as soon as she finished her work for the day, feeling like a kid on the last day of school with anticipation a living thing, pulsing through her.

Bingley was coming home today.

Ally was putting one of the dogs back in his run after a walk and she smiled as soon as she saw Charlotte burst through the door. "Couldn't wait another second?"

"Is he ready? I'm not too early, am I?"

"Not at all." Ally waved her toward the puppy enclosure. "The Kowalskis couldn't wait either. They picked up their puppy an hour ago."

Charlotte barely heard her, since they'd rounded the corner and all her attention was on her precious baby. As soon as Bingley spotted her, he'd yapped his happy little puppy bark and climbed right over one of his littermates to take the most direct route to get to Charlotte. The other puppy didn't seem to mind, rolling over and pouncing on yet another littermate's tail as Charlotte dropped to her knees to receive Bingley's squirmy puppy kisses.

"Hello, baby! Are you ready to come home? You are going to love it so much! Yes, you are!" Charlotte promised him—which seemed like a reasonable thing to guarantee since Bingley seemed to love absolutely everything.

She'd brought him out to her condo a couple of times in the last week, to get him used to her place, but now he was finally old enough to come home for good. Fully, completely *hers*.

She wrangled him into his little puppy harness—which he now knew meant he got to go on an outing and made him so wriggly with delight that it took an extra two minutes to get him snugged into it.

She clipped on the leash, standing to face Ally and feeling a sudden, unexpected swell of nerves. "This is it." She fidgeted with the leash. "You don't have any more paperwork for me or anything?"

"No, we took care of all that last time, so you're good to go. Congratulations, Charlotte. You're now a pet owner."

"Thank you." Impulsively, Charlotte hugged Ally, who squeaked and squeezed her back—until Bingley began yapping and bouncing between them, wanting to be in on whatever was happening above his head.

Charlotte laughed at his antics, delighted by every delightful inch of him. "All right, buddy. Time to go!"

She'd set up a little nest for him in the passenger seat and clipped his harness to the seat belt so he wouldn't try to climb into her lap while she drove—a lesson she'd learned on their first attempted outing.

The drive to the NetZero Village didn't take long—thank goodness. She parked in the lot, and as soon as she unclipped him, he clumsily staggered his way across the gearshift and onto her lap.

"I know! I'm excited too," she told him as he wriggled and licked her chin.

She climbed out of the car—and realized she'd forgotten to ask Ally how long it had been since he'd done his business, so instead of heading up to her apartment, they detoured via the designated pet area at the back of the complex.

She beamed at Bingley as he cavorted at the end of his leash, excited by everything he saw. "Who's a good baby?" she cooed at him, ludicrously proud. When they neared the solar panels, he squatted to poop, and Charlotte was so besotted that even that made her coo with adoration. "Good boy! You're so smart. This is where you do that. Yes, it is! Who's a smart boy?"

He finished his business and stepped away—and Charlotte stared at the little pile. "Oh…" *Crap.*

She'd forgotten the poop bags. She'd bought a little roll that clipped to Bingley's leash, but she hadn't actually clipped it yet.

"I guess we'll come back for it?" she told Bingley, glancing nervously up at the nearest row of buildings, as if her neighbors might be watching and judging.

"Forget something?"

Charlotte spun guiltily toward the voice—and was instantly relieved that it was George. "I did get poop bags. They just aren't *here.*"

He looked down at Bingley, who had romped over to investigate the new arrivals, eagerly sniffing Duke, who returned the favor. "I see Netherfield Park has been let at last."

"A *Pride and Prejudice* reference. Be still my heart."

George chuckled and crouched to bring himself closer to Bingley's level, offering his fingers to the little nose, once Bingley had thoroughly sniffed Duke. "Hey, Bing. Remember me? We met at the parade. You were pretty little then." The puppy turned around and immediately began bouncing after Duke, who had moved toward the solar panels. "Yeah, Duke is more interesting." He straightened. "When did you bring him home?"

"Just now. I wanted to make sure he knew where to do his business, but I forgot the..." She trailed off, because George was already reaching into his pocket and pulling out a mostly gone roll of poop bags. He tore one off and bent to collect Bingley's pile.

"I can do that!" Charlotte stepped forward, nearly tripping herself in the leash she hadn't noticed was wound around her legs. "You shouldn't—"

"One-time service. Think of it as a welcome to the neighborhood for Bing."

She flushed, embarrassed that she was already coming up short as a pet owner—but at least it was only in front of George, who didn't seem to know how to hold anything against her. "Thanks."

Bingley trailed after Duke like a miniature shadow, sniffing everything that Duke sniffed.

"That ankle looks better." He eyed her feet as he fell into step beside her.

"Well, I have this amazing physical therapist."

He snorted. "You've actually been doing the exercises?"

"Where does this skepticism come from? I am a virtuous patient who follows every dictate to the letter."

"Oh, of course. My apologies. I never should have doubted you."

"Let that be a lesson to you."

He smiled, falling silent.

She hadn't seen much of George since their emergency vet trip. He'd taken a day off work to make sure Duke was all right, but then he'd been swamped at the Estates and they hadn't gotten their planned marathon. They'd had one more PT session, but that was it. Mags and Kendall had come over on the weekend, keeping her entertained with puzzles and a reality TV marathon—which had been awesome, but Charlotte had sort of missed George. He was fun—and he'd been totally sucked into his volunteer duties with the talent show.

"How goes the battle with the talent show coordination? Seems like you've been at the Estates nonstop."

He groaned. "It probably seems that way because I have. But hopefully now that we have the rules hammered out and the song lottery scheduled, they can rehearse on their own and there won't be anything else for me to do until we get closer to the actual auditions."

"I'm sorry, there's a song lottery?" Charlotte couldn't quite smother her smile at the idea.

"So we don't have eleven different renditions of 'My Way.'" He grimaced. "I just wish I could find a couple more volunteers to fill out Howard Fullerton's blues band."

"Howard...bushy eyebrows, great deadpan?"

"That's him. He comes to all the meetings, but he's a

guitarist and he hasn't had any luck finding a vocalist or a bass player."

Charlotte arched an eyebrow. She'd been pretty distracted the two times she'd been in his place, but she was sure she'd seen an electric bass on a stand beside his television. "Didn't I see a bass in your apartment?"

"Yeah, I mean, I used to play in college, but I've never done blues." His brows pulled down. "Why are you smiling like that?"

"Nothing, it just…somehow it fits." She could totally see him in a band, serenading the coeds.

"I'm not going to ask what that means, because I'm pretty sure I don't want to know." He shortened up Duke's leash when the Berner started to go behind one of the solar panels. Charlotte mimicked the action with Bingley's leash. Her puppy bumped up against the end of his leash and fell over, clambering clumsily to his feet and romping over to her.

"Even if I wanted to join Howard's band—which would probably break some talent show committee rule anyway— we'd still be short a singer."

"You should ask Mac."

George frowned. "Mac who runs the Cup? I ran into him at the first talent show meeting. He sings?"

"The fact that you didn't know he sings is a sign you've never seen him drunk. Didn't you come to Elinor's birthday last year? Karaoke?"

"Yeah, but I didn't stay long. Levi kept glowering at me, and it was hard to focus on the singing when I was fearing for my life."

Charlotte waved a hand. "That's just Levi's face."

"Is it?" he asked skeptically.

"Okay, he might occasionally think of burying your body in a ditch somewhere, but he would never actually *do* it. He's a good guy when he's not being irrationally jealous of Elinor. But don't tell him I said that. As his future sister-in-law, I reserve my right to give him a hard time. But the point I was trying to make is that Mac *loves* to sing. He'll break into show tunes at the drop of a hat. I don't know if he's ever done blues stuff, but that's sort of Broadway-adjacent, right? You should talk to him."

"He sounded pretty busy with the Cup."

"Talk to him," she insisted. "He loves the town stuff almost as much as you do."

"How do you know I love the town stuff?"

"I've met you, George. You love it here. You might be new, but you're Pine Hollow to the core."

Something moved across his face, something she couldn't quite identify.

"C'mon," she coaxed. "Do it for Howard."

Shrugging off his distraction, he smiled. "Okay. I'll talk to Mac." He jerked his chin toward the buildings. "We should get inside. It looks like rain."

She arched her eyebrows at him hopefully. "*Ted Lasso*?"

His smile softened. "Sure."

She bounced. "Excellent. And as an experienced pet owner, you can show me everything I've done wrong in setting things up for Bingley."

George sighed dramatically and looked down at Duke. "Typical. She only wants me for my puppy expertise."

"Well, *obviously*." Charlotte bumped him with her shoulder, grinning.

But the truth was that she'd missed him this last week.

Spending time with George was so easy. Kendall had asked, with a speculative light in her eyes, if the two of them hanging out was a violation of the Puppy Pact, but it wasn't like that. Charlotte was relaxed with George. There was none of that tension, that prickly awareness she felt when she was with a guy she was dating. He was a good friend. And it was always the right time to find another best friend.

~

The Cup was busy on Sunday afternoon—but then, the Cup always seemed to be busy. Though that might be because the tiny cafe felt crowded with only a handful of people inside.

George had learned quickly upon his arrival in town that the Cup was a Pine Hollow institution, though it had only been open a little over a decade. Tucked into the first floor of a historic building—as nearly every business in Pine Hollow was—it had some strangeness to the layout that either came from retrofitting the hundred-year-old space or from the fact that it had started out as an espresso bar before Mac began adding semi-permanent specials to the menu and turned it into *the* casual dining destination in Pine Hollow.

The food was great, but the sense of community was even better—there was always someone seated at one of the little bistro tables who wanted to chat about the latest town goings-on. If George hadn't liked to cook for himself so much, he probably would have been in here every day.

Mac was in the kitchen, but George managed to catch his eye through the open pass-through. Mac gave a little wave, indicating he'd be out in a minute, and George claimed one of the stools at the takeout counter.

"Picking up or placing an order?" A teenage waitress appeared in front of him, her voice impatient and tablet at the ready.

"I'm just here to talk to Mac."

The teenager frowned, her eyebrow ring seeming to glint menacingly as she furrowed her brow. "You aren't eating?"

His stomach growled. He'd worked all morning—some clients had a hard time making the weekday sessions—and grabbed a PowerBar for lunch between clients, but the smells inside the Cup were quickly reminding him that his body needed more fuel. "Actually, what's the special today?"

"Breakfast burrito—homemade chorizo, farm-fresh eggs, local cotija cheese, avocado, and Mac's secret sauce. Trust me, if you like spicy, you *want* the burrito."

"Sold."

"Here or to-go?"

"Here."

"Drink?"

"Just water."

The teenager nodded and moved away, tapping something into the tablet. Seven minutes later, Mac emerged from the kitchen, carrying a plate of heaven that he set in front of George.

"Hey," the diner owner said in greeting. Today he wore a T-shirt for *A Gentleman's Guide to Love and Murder* and a NASA baseball cap. "Was I mistaking the urgent look, or did you need to talk to me?"

"Not sure how urgent it is, but I was hoping to get a word. Do you have a minute?" He glanced toward the full dining area. "I naïvely thought three in the afternoon on a Sunday would be a quiet time."

"This is quiet. When it's just the tables, it's nothing. It's when the takeout piles up that we get busy. Let me finish up this last order and then I'll be free for a bit." He tapped the counter beside George's plate. "Enjoy."

Mac disappeared, and George spent the next five minutes wondering what the secret to Mac's secret sauce was—and why he didn't eat here for every meal. He was a pretty good cook, but this was nirvana.

By the time Mac returned, George had polished off the burrito and was debating the wisdom of ordering a second one to take home.

"Hey. So what did you need?" Mac asked, wiping his hands on a clean white rag. "Is this about the talent show? Because I'm not technically on the committee."

"It's sort of about that. This might sound weird, but someone told me you sing?"

Mac's auburn eyebrows bounced up as he laughed. "I'm surprised only one person told you that. I don't have a good off switch once I get going."

"I don't suppose you've ever sung blues?"

Mac grinned. "Only if you count very sad show tunes belted out while drunk—in which case ninety percent of my singing is blues. You forming a band or something?"

"I was thinking about it. One of the residents out at the Estates, Howard Fullerton? Apparently he's a guitarist. I think he'd love to have a band to perform at the talent show, but he's short a lead singer. Would you be interested? In at least giving it a shot? For Howard?"

Mac groaned. "Here I am, getting ready to tell you that I don't have time and then you have to bring out the please-do-it-for-the-sweet-old-man argument."

"I'm not sure how sweet he is."

Mac snorted. "Even better. I fully intend to be a very grumpy old man. It's never too early to take lessons." He shrugged affably. "Yeah, all right, I'll give it a shot. If I'm terrible you guys can replace me—no hard feelings. Who told you I sing, anyway?"

"Charlotte."

"Right. You two have been..." He lifted his eyebrows speculatively.

George shook his head. "Just friends. She's taking a break from dating."

Mac groaned sympathetically. "I've been there. Terminally friendzoned. Happens to the best of us. So when are we doing this Blues Brothers thing?"

"Let me talk to Howard and get back to you. Are there any times you *aren't* busy here?"

Mac leaned closer, lowering his voice. "You wanna know a secret? I'm not nearly as handcuffed to this place as I want everyone to think. I have good staff. I like to do all the prep work myself in the mornings—all the sauces and experimenting with specials—but the rest of the day? As long as I know in advance to schedule enough cooks and servers, I can pretty much escape whenever I want. That's the beauty of being the boss."

"So no scheduling conflicts I need to work around?"

"I've got a semi-regular Wednesday night poker game— you should come by. It's Levi, Ben, and Connor—though if you're hoping to get out of the friend zone with Charlotte, that might work against your cause."

George frowned. "Why would that mess things up with Charlotte? Levi's marrying her sister."

"It's not Levi. It's me. Charlotte is staunchly Team Magda. You can probably get away with fraternizing with the enemy for the talent show—playing the we're-doing-it-for-Howard card will get you off there—but poker night? I don't know."

"I think I can risk it." George studied Mac's smiling face. "You and Magda don't *really* have some big vendetta against each other, do you?"

Mac's expression grew melodramatically solemn. "We do not speak of it."

"But it's fake, right? Like a gimmick to drum up business? Or a rumor that got out of control?"

"Oh, no, it's real."

"But…" George frowned. "It's *Magda*. No one hates Magda. And you're one of the nicest guys in town."

"It defies explanation. And yet it's true."

George tilted his head, studying Mac. "Huh. So you guys really hate each other?"

"At this point we mostly avoid each other. And conversations like this when I have to talk about it."

"Sorry."

"Just embrace the inevitable contradictions of Pine Hollow," Mac advised. "It's easier that way."

George chuckled. "Will do."

"And let me know when and where to bring my vocal stylings for this band. I'm getting excited." He tapped the counter. "You need anything else?"

George glanced down at his empty plate. Charlotte would love it—and just because she was too loyal to come in and get one herself didn't mean she should miss out on Mac's culinary genius. "Another one to go?"

Mac grinned. "Coming right up."

Chapter Sixteen

Nobody, who has not been in the interior
of a family, can say what the difficulties of
any individual of that family may be.
—*Emma*, Jane Austen

Dad's being weird."

Elinor met her at the front door as soon as Charlotte walked into their childhood home on Sunday night. She had her Anxiety Face on, and her words were whispered ominously—but since over-worrying was pretty much Elinor's natural state, Charlotte didn't let it faze her as she hung up her coat. "Weird how?"

"He burned the pork."

That got Charlotte's attention. Their father took cooking *very* seriously. "Are you sure it wasn't supposed to be charred? Just because you smell smoke—"

"He was swearing in Spanish. And earlier he started freaking because some Hallmark movie he apparently wanted to show us had gotten bumped off the DVR."

Charlotte's worry was slower to rise but no less acute than Elinor's. "Do you think it's Anne?"

Their father had invited them all to family dinner tonight—just the girls, no significant others—which was odd, now that Charlotte thought about it. Their dad loved Levi and Bailey. He wouldn't exclude them. Unless there was bad news. Family news.

"It could be Abuela." Elinor twisted her hands together. "But Anne was my first thought, too."

Right on cue, the front door opened again and their middle sister entered, tugging off her cap and slicking a hand through her sleek, dark bob. "Hello, Rodriguez sisters." She smiled.

Neither Elinor nor Charlotte smiled back.

Anne had always been paler than Charlotte and Elinor. Thinner. With a delicate frame. Like a bird. Like their mother. But now Charlotte found herself studying her sister with a clinical eye. Was she thinner than normal? Paler? Had her dark hair lost some of its luster?

"Anne…" Elinor started, but Charlotte cut her off.

"Are you okay?" she demanded. "Is it you?"

"Is what me? I'm fine."

Relief sliced through her, quick and leaving a tingling chill in its wake, as if the grim reaper had come just close enough to scare them all again. Charlotte inhaled, reminding herself to breathe again—as Elinor took a deep breath at her side.

So much of their lives had been overshadowed by cancer. First their mother's illness, starting when Charlotte was so young she could barely remember a time before that first diagnosis. Her slow decline. The treatments that bought them time, but eventually failed to save her. The grief. The feeling of slowly pulling themselves out of that abyss—only to have it all start again, all that fear rushing back when Anne was diagnosed.

Anne had beaten it. She'd been cancer-free for over six years now. But that fear was always just below the surface. The awareness that it could come back and steal her from them.

But if it wasn't Anne...

"Dad's being weird," Elinor explained.

Anne frowned, accepting her assessment without questioning. "Abuela?"

"You're sure you're fine?" Elinor pressed.

"I had a checkup last month," Anne assured them. "I'm good. Bailey's good. Things are great. We've been driving all over, checking out wedding venues."

Elinor turned her worried frown to Charlotte.

"Don't look at me. I'm better than ever. I just brought my puppy home on Friday."

Elinor's frown grew even darker. "It's not me. I'm actually great. I was going to—but that's not important."

"Things are okay with Levi?"

"We're not to the venues stage yet, but so far the wedding stuff—" Elinor broke off. "Do you think it's money? Anne and I both just got engaged. He could be worrying about the expenses."

Anne shook her head. "Bailey's parents want to pay for everything. She's their only daughter, and they're rolling in it."

"Did you tell him that? Levi and I don't want anything big—I think he'd just as soon go down to the courthouse—but I haven't told Dad that. What if he's thinking we both want big white weddings and you know how he worries, holding everything inside—"

Just like Elinor. The worry apple hadn't fallen far from the worry tree in their family.

"Elle, I'm sure it's fine," Charlotte soothed. "And freaking out about it before we know what's going on isn't going to help. Maybe it's nothing. Maybe he just burned the pork."

Her sisters gave her identical dubious looks—but their father opened the door to the kitchen before Elinor could go off on another worry rant.

"Good! You're all here. Dinner is a catastrophe. I'm sorry. But come, we still have to eat." His accent was thicker than normal—as it got when he was excited. Or anxious. And he definitely seemed nervous.

Charlotte trailed her father and sisters into the kitchen, braced for the worst. She thought she was ready for anything—but she was still completely caught off guard by her father's announcement three minutes into a dinner of blackened pork and strange, lumpy potatoes.

"There's no point beating around the bush." He set down his fork decisively. "You can all see I'm not myself today." He waved at the food—which was, admittedly, horrible.

Charlotte had felt guilty for eating an entire breakfast burrito only two hours before she came over, but now she was grateful for George's gift. Usually even when their father was dissatisfied with his creations, they were delicious, but tonight, that could not be said.

"What is it, Dad?" Elinor asked, tension in every line of her face.

Their father sucked in a breath and blurted out, "I've met someone."

Charlotte's jaw fell. "What?"

"Papa!" Anne squeaked. "That's great! Who is she?"

His cheeks flushed above his neatly trimmed beard. "She's not from Pine Hollow."

"I didn't even know you were thinking about dating," Elinor said.

"I wasn't. I got on one of those dating apps—for the older people—and I was just going to see what was out there, what it was like. I didn't think I would actually meet anyone."

"But you did." Anne sighed happily.

"Her name is Avita. She lives in Barre. We meet in the middle so the whole town isn't watching me. She taught school, but now she's retired—just this year. She is a widow too. She never had any children, but she'd like to meet you, if you'd like that. I'd like that. For you to meet her."

They were meeting her already? "How—how long have you two been...?" Charlotte couldn't quite wrap her head around it.

She'd told her dad he should start dating again—their mom had been gone for twenty years—but she'd thought she'd see it progress in stages. He'd tell them he was thinking about it. She'd help him make a profile. They'd discuss his matches and give him advice on what to wear on his first date, what to talk about.

For it to be presented as a done deal...

"About three, maybe four months. We talked on the app thing for a couple weeks before we met."

"So Christmas. You've been dating her since Christmas."

Charlotte had been with Jeff then. Had she missed the signs? Too preoccupied with her own drama to see what was going on with her father?

"That's so great, Dad," Elinor said—shooting Charlotte a look—and Charlotte quickly echoed the sentiment.

"Yes. It is. I'm super happy for you." She was just shocked. And there was something else swirling beneath the shock. Something she wasn't quite sure she wanted to look at too closely.

The conversation continued, and Charlotte mostly listened, because she knew her enthusiasm sounded off whenever she opened her mouth, and she didn't want her dad misinterpreting her hesitation. It wasn't that she didn't want him to date Avita. She sounded great.

It was that something foundational in her life felt like it was shifting, and change like that always rattled her.

They were serious. She could hear it in her father's voice. He didn't say it, but she wouldn't be surprised if Avita moved in. If they got married. Would her father move to Barre? Sell her childhood home? There was nothing stopping him. He had a new future now.

And she didn't.

Charlotte cringed internally. There it was. The truth she hadn't wanted to look at.

She was happy with the Puppy Pact. Happy she'd chosen Bingley over the frustrations of love. But seeing her father trip into another perfect love story, like the one he'd had with her mother, the second he even thought about looking, made her feel like even more of a romantic failure.

She'd wanted that. She'd wanted it with a keen desperation that had always made her therapist make that worried little frown. For her entire life, for as long as she could remember, she'd wanted to be the center of someone's world. The same way her mother had been the center of her dad's.

She'd undoubtedly romanticized their love story, but all

that love, all that pain, it had carved out a definition of what love was that she'd never been able to achieve.

She knew herself. She knew she was impulsive and extravagant and greedy for attention. She knew she needed more than most people—more validation, more affection, more *time*—but she'd always hoped there would be someone out there who would be able to fill the stupid, yawning well of that need. If she was just good enough. If she just became a doctor and helped enough people. If she just made herself shiny and perfect enough on the surface. Then she'd deserve it. Even if she was still needy and desperate at her core.

She needed to schedule another session with her online therapist.

She'd felt so powerful since the Puppy Pact. So certain she'd changed. She hadn't been fazed at all when Vivian Weisman had painted a picture of her future without a man. But all it took was her father falling in love to send her sliding right back again.

She was actually jealous of her father. Not jealous of the woman who would suck up his time and attention. But jealous that he had what she wanted. That it was *easy* for him.

"Actually, since we're sharing news, I have some," Elinor said, fiddling with her unused knife.

"Did you set a date?" Anne asked.

"Are you pregnant?" Charlotte added.

"What?" Elinor yelped. "God, no. I'm not even sure we want—it's my book. Someone wants to publish my book."

Shock dropped Charlotte's jaw again. Then she screamed—the sound echoed by Anne as they both leapt up and tried to hug Elinor at the same time.

"My sister's going to be famous!" Charlotte bellowed.

Elinor laughed and shoved her off. "Writers aren't famous. And it's just one tiny contract. Don't get carried away."

"I plan to be incredibly carried away, thank you very much," Charlotte insisted.

Elinor laughed as Charlotte tackle-hugged her again, and begged her for all the details.

After a while, the conversation turned to weddings—both Anne and Elinor telling their father about their preliminary plans, in case he did have any worries about the costs. Charlotte fell silent again, smiling, listening—and trying to keep from sinking into the shadowy pit that stealthily opened up beneath her the longer they talked. Those feelings of change and being left behind...

"You were quiet tonight," Elinor said as Charlotte was heading toward her car later.

They were alone in the front yard. Elinor lived just down the street and had walked. Anne was still inside, discussing wedding plans with their dad, who was smiling at everything and happier than he'd seemed in years.

"Just processing," Charlotte said. "Lots of news."

"Are you okay?"

Charlotte smiled at the familiar worry in her sister's voice. "You don't have to worry about me, Elinor."

Elinor held up her hands in surrender. "I know. And I'm not trying to mother hen you. I'm just asking."

"I'm great, actually," Charlotte said—the words feeling true and false at the same time. "You should come see my puppy. He's adorable—did I tell you I named him Bingley?"

"You did." Elinor eyed her, still in worrywart mode.

"I'm a little nervous about leaving him alone for the first time tomorrow when I have to go to work."

"He's not alone now?"

"I left him with George. I wanted him with someone familiar so he could get used to the idea of me leaving and coming back."

Elinor's brows arched up. "He's familiar with George?"

"Don't do that," Charlotte gave Elinor her most implacable look. "We're friends. We hang out. We live in the same complex, and Bingley adores George's dog. I'm still sworn off men, remember?"

"So you're sticking with that. The pact thing."

"Puppy Pact," Charlotte supplied. "Yeah. Why wouldn't I?"

She asked the question knowing it was loaded, challenging her sister to come out and say that Charlotte got all her self-worth from men and would never be able to keep up the swearing-off-men part of the pact.

"You don't really like being alone," Elinor reminded her gently.

"I'm changing. I'm growing. I'm focusing on me. That's what you wanted, isn't it?"

"I want you to be happy."

"And I am." *Mostly.* "I just need to go get my dog." And then everything would be exactly like it was supposed to be.

As long as she didn't look at the gaping maw of negative emotion that seemed to be looming beneath her, waiting for her to slip.

Chapter Seventeen

We are all fools in love.
—*Pride and Prejudice*, Jane Austen

I'm sorry, I must have heard you wrong, because it sounded like you said you're puppy-sitting for the woman who told you she would rather be alone than be with you."

George frowned at the uncharacteristic bite that was back in Bekah's voice. Duke and Bingley were curled together on Duke's dog bed, snoring softly. "I thought you liked Charlotte."

"I never liked Charlotte because I've never met Charlotte," Beks corrected sharply. "I didn't have a problem with her when she was the unattainable coworker you had a harmless crush on, but when you asked her out and she shot you down and then proceeded to take advantage of your feelings for her to get you to do stuff like watch her dog, I started to have a problem."

"It isn't like that. I offered. And she isn't taking advantage—"

Bekah cut him off with a scoffing huff. "You're too nice."

George frowned. He couldn't tell if this was overprotectiveness or if something else was going on. "I like doing things for people."

"She isn't people. She's a fantasy. A stupid fantasy you're stupidly clinging to when you could be building a real relationship and a real life—"

"With who?" he demanded.

His doorbell rang, and both dogs jerked awake from their naps, hurtling toward the door in a barking rush. "I'm sorry, Beks, I've gotta go."

"She's there, isn't she?"

"She isn't a fantasy. She's a friend, okay? I'll talk to you later." He hung up while Beks was still muttering and headed for the door.

As soon as he opened it, Bingley rushed out, and Charlotte fell to her knees. "There he is!"

The puppy tumbled clumsily over her knees, trying to climb her so he could lick her face, and Charlotte giggled. "Hello, baby. I missed you too."

Okay, she might also be the fantasy.

Because he wanted her to say those words to him.

Then she looked up, her big brown eyes locked on his, and the look in them slayed him. She did look almost as happy to see him as she was to see the dog. Or maybe not happy. Almost relieved. Like he could see her relaxing before his eyes.

"How was he?"

"No trouble at all," George assured her. "He played with some of Duke's old toys—which made Duke suddenly interested in them again—but he wore himself out pretty fast and then he fell asleep half on top of Duke. I texted you a picture." He offered her a hand to help her to her feet—because her ankle was still healing, not because he wanted to feel the softness of her skin against his.

"I saw. Thank you." Charlotte's hand slid into his and she straightened.

"Do you want to come in for a minute?" he heard himself asking, without any conscious direction from his brain. He wanted her with him a little while longer, to stretch out the moment.

Maybe Beks was right and he was being an idiot.

"You don't mind?" Her voice lifted on such a hopeful note that he knew his impulse to ask her inside had been the right one. No matter what Bekah's disapproving voice in his head might think.

"Come on in."

She stepped across the threshold, toeing off her shoes on the mat—and Bingley promptly attacked them, growling his tiny puppy growls.

"Make yourself at home," he said, heading toward the kitchen.

She'd been in his place before, but both times had been under extraordinary circumstances—first her ankle and then Duke. She looked around the main room as if seeing it for the first time. His apartment was a mirror layout to hers—one kitchen/dining/living area, a short hall leading to a half bath, the guest room he'd turned into an office/gaming room, and, at the far end, the master suite.

Charlotte homed in on the bookshelves lining the wall behind the couch, moving closer to peer at the eclectic mix of titles. Her back had been to the shelves whenever they sat on the couch, but now she bent to snoop.

"You want something to drink?"

"Hm?" She glanced up from the books she'd been studying. "Oh, sure, if you're having something."

"All I have is boxed wine."

"I'm not fancy."

George grabbed two glasses, filling them generously.

"You have quite a few romance novels here, George Leneghan. Guilty pleasure?"

"Never really saw the point in feeling guilt about my pleasures. I like romance. And mystery. And sci-fi. And I watch *all* the cheesy Christmas movies. I like what I like." He shrugged, handing her a glass. "Straight from the box."

She sipped and arched her eyebrows appreciatively. "This is actually pretty good." She cocked her head toward the bookshelves. "It takes a very secure man to put the pastel pink romance novels out on full display."

"Or a smart one. You know what they call a man who reads romance."

She glanced over at him. "What?" She lifted her wine to her lips.

"Good in bed."

Charlotte nearly snorted wine up her nose, and George chuckled, leading the way to the couch. "How was your dad's?" He sprawled in one corner, Charlotte immediately taking her position tucked into the opposite one.

"Good." She made a face and stared into her glass. "Weird."

"Weird how?" He sipped his own wine.

Charlotte wrinkled her nose and took another drink before answering. "Well, for one thing, he's in love."

"Yeah?" George's eyebrows bounced up. He hadn't expected that.

"Some woman he met online. He hadn't even told us he was thinking of setting up a profile. Apparently they've been dating since Christmas."

Her voice was tight. George eyed her grumpy face. "And this bothers you."

"I'm not bothered! I want him to be happy."

George knew her too well to think it was as simple as that. "But?"

"But I'm jealous, okay?" she snapped. "Which is stupid and selfish and immature. Believe me, I know."

"It's understandable. Has he dated much since your mom?"

"Never. And I thought I was going to feel some kind of way about that—like he was replacing her, or she was really gone—" She shook her head sharply. "But it's not that."

"It's a big change. You guys have had him to yourself for years, and now he's going to be spending a lot of time with her—"

"I'm not jealous of that. I feel like that's what I should feel. It's just...Elinor is engaged. And Anne is engaged. And my dad is in love—and no, he didn't say it in so many words, but it was obvious he was, and here I am..."

"Being left behind?"

"Exactly!" She sat up straighter, pointing her glass at him. "And yes, I know I wanted to be single, and I still want that. I don't want to go back to *feeling* like I did, but I see them and I think, why not me? Why am I never going to be the center of someone's world? Because I'm a selfish brat."

"And kind. And caring. And funny and smart."

"I know myself," she said, as if she hadn't heard him. "I know I'm dramatic. I know I'm difficult."

"Who told you that you were difficult?" Anger irrationally at the thought, but Charlotte just waved the hand that wasn't holding her wine.

"Anyone. Everyone. I'm not a 'good' person." She wagged air-quotes around *good*. "Not like Elinor or Anne. Elinor almost became a doctor because she wanted to save everyone. I just wanted to be a doctor so people would listen to me, so they would *see* me." She looked over at him, making a face. "You know how I said my dad forgot me at the hospital? I felt so invisible when I was little." She shook her head slightly. "The doctors, they seemed to know everything and everyone listened to them. Respected them. *Saw* them. I wanted to be that person. The confident person everyone admired. The one who was never invisible or forgotten or ignored. That's why I went to med school. It was all ego."

"But you still help people. Every day."

"Not for the right reasons. I am this bottomless pit of all the ugly, greedy emotions. Elinor had some good news tonight—amazing news—and I was happy for her, but I was also *so jealous*. I don't want to be, but I am. Because people are going to praise her and celebrate her, and everyone thinks she's so amazing, and I have always wanted someone to see me like that. Elinor was this paragon—skipping grades and doing everything right, and everyone talked about how amazing she was, but as soon as I did the *exact same thing*, all anyone could talk about was how good those Rodriguez genes were and *of course* I was doing well because I was Elinor's sister and Elinor had *paved the way* and *shown me how*—like every amazing thing she did was because of her and every amazing thing I did was because of her too!"

George didn't even try to get a word in edgewise as

Charlotte gestured with her wine. "They were in *awe* of her, and it was just expected of me. So I became this person who likes to sing her own praises because I wanted someone to see what I had done. And it's petty and it's selfish, and I always felt guilty about how much I *needed* people to see me because there were such good reasons it couldn't all be about me. My mom and Anne—but it still hurt…"

"You're human. That's what that is. Even a non-MD can diagnose that one."

She rolled her eyes. "I'm not *good*, George. And it's never enough. That's why I'm always the one being broken up with. I'm needy and clingy, and I hold on too long. Because I'm so determined to make it work, so desperate to hang on. And I try to reel it in. I try not to ask for too much or *be* too much—I know I can be overpowering, so I pull back and I try so freaking hard, and it's never enough. I'm never enough. Or I'm too much. And I don't want to feel like that again."

"Maybe you were just with the wrong guys," George murmured, in a voice that sounded like a gravel road.

"No." Her answer was quick and certain. "It wasn't them. It was me. And I know what you're going to say. That the real love was inside me all along and I just needed to learn to respect myself before I could expect other people to respect me—but that's bullshit. I *love* myself. I know exactly who I am—and yes, I'm a lot, but I'm sick of feeling like I need to be something less or something more or anything else for someone to want me. I'm sick of *caring* if people want me. So I'm going to be by myself for a while. I'm going to stay single until I can learn how to hold out for the same standards of being loved as I have for loving myself.

And it's scary, you know, because what if you insist on what you deserve and you don't get it? What if you're always just going to be forgotten and overlooked?"

"It hurts," George said softly.

Charlotte's gaze landed on him, and she seemed to remember who she was talking to. Her intensity suddenly receded, and she stared at him.

The air seemed to tighten between them, the moment holding a beat too long. He could see the apology forming in her eyes. The understanding. The sympathy.

Whatever she was about to say—he didn't want her to say it.

"There is one thing I've been dying to ask you," he said.

Charlotte's eyes widened—almost like she was afraid he was going to ask her out again. As if his ego needed another kick in the teeth.

She wet her lips. "Yeah?"

"How do you know which inn people are talking about?"

A relieved laugh burst out of her, a little too loud.

"Seriously?"

"Seriously. It's driving me crazy. Locals call every single inn in this town 'the inn,' and I never know what anyone means."

She studied him, silent for a long moment before finally answering, "It's all context."

"Context," he repeated.

"Everyone knows everyone. We all know the same stories and the same history. So if Anne is talking about the inn, she means the one where she works. If Mac is talking about one, he probably means the one his family founded. If they're talking about going somewhere to eat, they mean the one with the fancy restaurant. If they're talking about the vandalisms from last year, they mean the one that got tagged. If they're talking about flooding, they mean the one by the river. It's all context."

"So I need to know everyone who works at each of the inns or is related to anyone working at an inn, and everything that has ever happened at each of the inns?"

"Yeah, pretty much."

George groan-laughed. "Well, I'm screwed."

Charlotte smiled. "Don't worry. You've got time."

Except he wasn't sure he did. His contract with the Estates was up in just a few months. Lately his boss, Eileen, had been saying she needed to talk to him, but they hadn't scheduled a time yet. She'd probably ask him if he wanted to stay on. He needed to have an answer for her. He needed to decide if he was staying or leaving. And tonight…tonight had shown him that he might need to leave.

He was always going to want to be here for Charlotte. He was always going to volunteer to look after her dog, or to listen to her troubles, or to lighten the mood when things got too real. He was going to bend over backward to make himself what she needed—but she didn't want him. Not in the way he still wanted her.

He needed to do what she was trying to. He needed to learn to insist on what he deserved. And he wasn't sure he was going to be able to do that if he stayed here.

Chapter Eighteen

You must be the best judge of your own happiness.

—*Emma*, Jane Austen

She'd said too much.

Charlotte knew that feeling well. She'd said *way* too much that night after dinner at her dad's house. She'd been babbling away about that hungry creature inside her, that bottomless pit for love and affection that could never be filled and how badly she wanted to be the most important person in someone's world—and there was George, sitting right across from her. Being too nice. Letting her impose on his kindness.

George, who had already asked her out once.

Not that he'd really asked. Most days she could convince herself that he'd been joking. Or if not joking, then at least not *really* serious.

But sometimes there would be a note in his voice, and she would look at him and there would be something in his eyes—as if he wanted her to see the truth and didn't want her to see it at the same time.

But then he would make a joke or change the subject and she'd tell herself she'd imagined it, that look, and the panic it inspired. Because when George looked at her like he might really want her, that was what she felt.

Pure, unfiltered panic.

If he asked her out again, she wasn't so sure she would say no this time. And it would be awful. If she dated him, she would mess everything up. Ask for too much. *Need* too much. She'd ruin their friendship.

She'd been so relieved when he'd changed the subject the other night. And so guilty that she'd been so relieved. And she'd told herself that she'd misread the moment. That he didn't want more, because they were friends. Like Magda and Kendall. The kind of friends that still accepted her, even after she'd word-vomited all her ugly inner thoughts all over them.

But she hadn't seen him since that night.

It had only been a few days—it wasn't uncommon for their schedules to be different enough that they missed each other for days at a time. She was officially done with physical therapy, her ankle only giving her the occasional twinge these days.

She took Bingley on long walks along the greenspace behind the complex, hoping Duke and George would come out while they were out there, but they never did.

Bingley seemed to be adapting well to his new routine. She'd left him in his crate on Monday morning with an old shirt of hers so he could curl up with something that smelled like her while she was away, and come home at lunch to walk him since the sweet baby had a tiny little bladder. He'd only had one accident since they started potty training, and she was determined to help him keep it that way with a regular routine.

He was so smart—and food motivated. She was signed up for a round of puppy training courses at Furry Friends starting next week, but her little genius was already catching on. He loved the training treats she'd gotten for him, and was already starting to figure out *sit*, though whenever she tried to get him to lie down he always seemed to end up climbing on her and trying to kiss her face.

He was such a delight. And she loved him so completely that it was hard to believe she'd only had him home with her for a week.

On Tuesday he stole one of her old sneakers and dragged it into his crate with him. She came home at lunch to find him fast asleep with his little puppy head buried inside her shoe.

On Wednesday she spent two solid hours just playing tug-of-war with him.

He really was better than any relationship she'd ever had. He was sweet and soft, and he'd curl up against her on the couch, gazing at her as if she had created the sun and stars just for him. Her heart was fully his. The Puppy Pact was working.

But she missed George.

Not in a big, dramatic way. Not like she was pining for him or anything. Just in a mild, I-wonder-what-my-friend-is-up-to kind of way. She wanted to invite him over again, have takeout Chinese, and binge another show, but she always asked for too much. She always clung too hard. So she watched a show with Bingley instead. And took long walks on the greenspace looking for Duke's fluffy black and white tail. And waited for a legitimate excuse to see her friend.

Or even an illegitimate excuse. Anything to bring him back.

~

George was inexplicably nervous as he stepped into the music room at the Estates on Thursday evening for the inaugural rehearsal of Howard's band. During the week there were choir practices and music therapy sessions in here, as well as periodic classes in every musical style imaginable with instructors brought in from all over the state, but tonight George had reserved the room and it was eerily quiet.

He was the first to arrive, and he flipped on the lights. Bongo drums were stacked on a shelf on one wall, and a piano on wheels had been shoved all the way to one side. George didn't know what the last class in here had been, but the chairs were arranged in a loose semicircle.

Should he rearrange them? George hadn't been in a band in so long he wasn't sure he remembered how. There was a drum kit in the corner—maybe he should cluster the chairs nearby? Those days in dorm basements practicing with his friends felt so long ago. This week he'd practiced the basic walking bass line for blues, but he was so rusty he wasn't sure this was going to work.

This was only a first meeting. They might not even play. Just a preliminary session to see if they hit it off and wanted to form a group for the talent show. For Howard. But George was as nervous as if he was about to walk out for a gig at the local pub back in college.

He was tempted to text Charlotte—to tell her that, thanks to her, he was in a band again—but he'd been putting a little distance between them since the night she'd come over after dinner at her dad's. Just reminding himself that he didn't need to be falling for her any more than he already was.

He took out his bass and began to tune. Should he warm up?

The door opened before he could start doing panic scales.

"George!" Howard boomed, beaming hugely as he walked into the room, carrying a guitar case and followed by a man with hunched shoulders and tufts of white hair sticking out from the sides of his head. "Have you met Bob?"

"Not yet. It's good to meet you, sir." George stood and shifted his bass to the side to shake Bob's hand. He reminded him vaguely of a Dr. Seuss character with his hair.

"Good manners, but none of that sir stuff. I'm just Bob."

Bob had a grip like a boa constrictor, belying the frailty of his frame, and he immediately beelined toward the drum kit. "Let's see what we have here," he muttered, pulling a pair of sticks out of his back pocket.

Howard had settled onto one of the chairs near George and flicked open the latches on his guitar case. George resettled with his bass on his lap, but before he could do more than thumb a note, the door opened again.

"Am I late?"

Bob looked up and gave a bark of laughter as Mac entered. "Mackenzie Newton, of the Pine Hollow Newtons," he bellowed in greeting. "I had no idea we were going to be playing with Pine Hollow royalty."

Mac laughed, crossing to shake Bob's hand. "Good to see you, Bob. How've you been?"

"Still kicking. You bring us any of those special grilled cheese thingies you make?"

"Not this time. But now that I know I have a fan, I'll bring 'em to our next rehearsal," Mac promised.

"Careful. He'll be shaking you down for free food every chance he gets," Howard interjected. "How are you, Mac?"

"Doing well, Howard. You?"

"Can't complain."

"So everyone knows everyone?" George asked, feeling that outsider feeling again. He'd thought Howard was relatively new to town as well, but he and Mac were shaking hands like old friends.

Mac nodded to Bob. "Bob here used to date my grandma."

"It was quite the scandal, back in the day," Bob announced proudly. "My kind had no business with those fancy Mackenzies. Then Rex Newton swept in and married Zella right out from under me. The great tragedy of my life."

"Funny. That's not quite how my grandfather told it," Mac said dryly.

"Don't believe a word he told you. Lies," Bob insisted, but they were all smiling, so whatever the sixty-year-old drama was, apparently it didn't bother them anymore.

"Enough of this gossip." Howard waved Mac toward a chair, taking command. "Let's get this show on the road."

"Full disclosure," Mac said as they sat down. "My only knowledge of blues comes from *The Blues Brothers*."

"That wasn't entirely blues, but Jake and Elwood were legends," Howard said with a grin. "And we are getting a band back together." He pulled a folder out of his guitar case. "Can everyone read music?"

"Afraid not." Mac raised his hand. "I just pick stuff up by listening to it."

"All right then, you know 'Sweet Home Chicago'?"

"Yeah, of course," Mac said.

Howard handed George a chord sheet. "You good?"

George quickly scanned the music, hoping he wasn't about to screw this up for everyone. "I'll do my best."

"Don't look so worried." Bob twirled a drumstick. "This is fun, remember?"

"No pressure," Howard said, running his fingers lightly over the strings of his guitar. "A pianist would be good, but let's see how we sound."

Howard lowered his head over his guitar—and proceeded to play the guitar intro to "Sweet Home Chicago" so perfectly that Mac and George both missed their entrances.

The guitar fell silent as he glanced up to find Mac and George gaping at him. "What?"

"Holy shit, Howard," Mac said.

"Who *are* you?" George asked.

Howard gave a wry smile. "I think you mean who was I. I used to gig some in Chicago."

"*Some,*" George echoed, meeting Mac's eyes to find him equally shocked.

"What? An old man can't rock his ass off? Paul McCartney's five years older than me."

Mac laughed. "Howard, I think you're my role model."

Howard snorted and lifted one bushy eyebrow at George. "You planning to play that bass or just cuddle it all night?"

"Oh, I'll play it, but I'm not sure I'm up to your standards."

"I just wanna play, kid. You ready?"

He ripped into the intro again—and this time George

caught his cue. Luckily, the bass line wasn't complicated. And luckily Mac could *sing*.

George began to smile.

～

"I haven't played like that in years."

Howard looked worn out, moving a little slower as he headed toward the door at the end of their rehearsal—but there was also something lighter about him. Happier. He'd freaking *communed* with his guitar.

Mac had a big voice, but it was Howard who was the real musician among them. He'd coached them each, giving tips, but he hadn't had to say much.

They sounded *good*.

They could all hear it. Right off the bat—well, maybe not right off the bat. Mac had been too Broadway, and George had hit a couple wrong notes in their first run-through. But by the third time, they sounded pretty damn good. Not at Howard's level, but there was real promise there.

"This talent competition is in the bag." Mac was energized—and carrying a list of songs he'd promised to learn by the next week.

"It isn't a competition," George reminded him.

Mac snorted. "That's what you think."

Bob and Howard said their goodbyes, Mac promising to bring snacks next time—including some special brownies, he told Howard with a wink.

"Farewell, oh you princes of Pine Hollow!" Bob called.

George waited until the older gentlemen had headed toward the tower elevators to their apartments, before turning to Mac with an arched eyebrow. "Prince of Pine Hollow?"

"I know. It's ridiculous. Pine Hollow doesn't have a king."

"But?" George pressed as they moved toward the exit.

"I'm the last scion of the original founding families. The Mackenzies and the Newtons. Our main claim to fame is that we haven't gone anywhere in two hundred and sixty-two years and we take up the most space in the cemetery over on Maple. My grandmother's very proud of our history. While I'm just trying to cook good food."

"Do I want to know what's in your special brownies?" George asked. "That was a lot of winking."

Mac laughed. "They aren't those kind of special brownies. Howard's trying to woo one of the ladies here, and he heard a rumor she has a sweet tooth. I've been trying out these new double-chocolate decadence brownies, and I promised Howard I'd bring some out for Vivian."

"Vivian Weisman?"

"Yeah. You know her?"

"She's one of the pickleball ladies." They were regulars at physical therapy, always trying to keep their joints in top shape.

"I'm sorry, pickleball?"

"It's kind of like tennis without all the running around. More finesse. It's very popular with the seniors here. They have a league."

"Lazy tennis sounds kind of awesome. Do they let the young whippersnappers play?"

George grinned. "Yeah, some folks come out from town to play. But be prepared to be trounced. They take it seriously."

"George! What are you still doing here?"

George turned to find his boss, Eileen, approaching with her usual harried expression. She was the therapy care coordinator at the Estates and never seemed to have enough hours in the day.

"Band rehearsal," he explained.

"I'm off." Mac waved and headed toward the doors. "'Til next time, Bluesman."

George glanced at a nearby grandfather clock as Eileen joined him. "You aren't still working, are you? It's after seven."

"I was on my way back to my office to get my purse, so I can go home and remind my husband what I look like. I don't suppose you have a minute to walk with me, do you? There's something I've been meaning to talk to you about, and I can never seem to sync our schedules."

"Yeah, of course." George fell in beside her. He had a feeling he knew what this was about, but he asked anyway. "What's up?"

Eileen opened the door to her office, waving him inside. "I know your contract isn't up until the end of the summer, but I wanted to give you as much advance notice as possible." She gestured toward the chair and George took it with his thoughts racing.

She was going to ask him to stay, and he still didn't know what he wanted to tell her.

"We love you here," Eileen went on. "The residents adore you, you're great at your job, and Jack can't say enough about the work you're doing over at the sports med clinic." She sighed, her smile gentle—as if she was about to break bad news, and George's whirring thoughts froze.

"I'd like nothing more than to be able to offer you a permanent position, but as you know, you were brought on to cover for Claudia while she was completing her PhD, and she's just let us know that she would like to return as planned. I'd love to be able to keep you both, but we simply don't have the space on the payroll. I've talked to Jack, and he doesn't have enough work to justify full-time either. We think, between the two of us, we can come up with enough work to keep you part-time after August, but I understand if that isn't viable for you. I'm sorry, George. You'll get only the most glowing references from us."

George opened his mouth, with no idea what to say.

He'd already been thinking of leaving, but this felt so much more final than his ambivalence. This felt real.

"I understand," he said. "Thanks for letting me know."

"We really will be sorry if you have to go," Eileen said.

He shook the hand she offered. "So will I."

And, as he thanked Eileen and headed toward the parking lot, he realized he meant it.

He didn't *want* to leave Pine Hollow. He wasn't sure how much of that had to do with Charlotte and a fantasy that was never going to come true, but there it was. He didn't want to start over again. But he either needed to find another job... or accept that his remaining time in Pine Hollow would be counted in months.

Maybe it was for the best. He could enjoy his time here without any expectation of a future. Which meant there was no harm in spending more time with Charlotte. No danger of getting too attached.

Right on cue, his cell phone buzzed with an incoming text.

How do you feel about spiders?

He felt himself smiling as he responded.

Is that a trick question?

Her reply was almost immediate.

My apartment is under arachnid attack. Save me?

He might be leaving in a few months, but that didn't mean he wouldn't take every excuse—no matter how trivial—to see Charlotte.

I'm on my way.

Chapter Nineteen

I do not know whether it ought to be so, but certainly silly things do cease to be silly if they are done by sensible people in an impudent way.

—*Emma*, Jane Austen

Okay, where is it?"

"The kitchen." Charlotte pointed George toward the Room of Doom, holding Bingley as George scratched his chin in greeting. "Bingley and I tried to hold the line until you got here, but then it launched an offensive, and we had to sacrifice the island."

George, to his credit, didn't laugh—until he got to the kitchen and spotted the eight-legged culprit perched smugly on top of her colander. "Charles," he said, his voice trembling with the effort not to laugh. "That's barely a spider. It's tiny."

He wasn't wrong, but she'd wanted to see him—and she had no problem making herself look ridiculous if it meant her friend was in her kitchen, laughing and calling her Charles.

"You don't understand. It was *on me*. It just walked up my shoulder, cool as can be. As soon as I can be sure it's dead, I have to shower for three days straight and set the security alarm."

She could see him fighting a smile as his eyebrows arched up. "Because security systems stop spiders?"

"You don't know that they won't."

George's lips were twitching madly now.

"You can laugh as much as you want, as long as you kill it."

"So no merciful relocation to a new home in the forest?"

"It needs to be made an example of. So its friends know this place is not for their kind."

George plucked a tissue out of the box on the end table and approached the Devil Spider.

"Be careful," Charlotte warned. "It might jump." Bingley squirmed in her arms, and Charlotte hitched him up a little higher.

George glanced back at her, and Charlotte pointed to the counter. "Don't take your eyes off it. That's how they escape."

His shoulders were shaking now. He reached out, quick as a flash, and the spider vanished into the tissue in his hand.

"Did you get it?"

"Yup."

"Is it dead?"

"Do you want to see?" He turned toward her, extending the tissue.

She backpedaled. "Nope, I'm good." She jerked her head toward the hall. "Will you flush it down the toilet?

Otherwise I'll have nightmares about zombie spiders climbing out of the trash to crawl on my face all night."

He disappeared down the hall, returning a moment later after the sound of a flush. "Done." He glanced at her and grinned. "Do you want me to check the house? In case he brought backup?"

She set Bingley down, now that the spider menace had been vanquished. "I know that I'm being ridiculous. In case you were wondering. I can kill my own spiders."

"I'm sure you can." He bent to peer under the couch. Bless him.

"I simply choose not to when there are other spider killers available." And when she was looking for any excuse to see him.

"I'm honored to be your spider assassin." He straightened, dusting off his hands. "All clear."

Charlotte leaned against the couch, going for nonchalance, as if a new idea had just occurred to her—and hadn't been part of her plan all along. "Have you eaten? Can I offer you Chinese takeout from Guiseppi's and a *Cake-Off* marathon as a reward?"

"I was at the Estates when I got your text. Duke hasn't been out yet."

Disappointment rose up, embarrassingly acute. Of course he didn't want to hang out. Last time he did, she'd word-vomited all sorts of emotional crap all over him. "Oh. Right—" She didn't get the rest of her retraction out before he was going on.

"I can bring him over, if that's okay. He can play with Bingley while we watch."

Charlotte felt herself lighting up like a Christmas tree that had just been plugged in. She was much too excited that he was coming over, but she tried for nonchalance. "Yeah, that'd be great. We have to see who wins season six."

"Tony. It has to be Tony."

"Oh please, Sharna is so much better than Tony!"

"The flan disaster? She barely made it through that week—"

"*One* bad week. And she overcame it! Tony's just so *smug*. He thinks he's better than everyone."

"Because he is. Is it arrogance if it's earned?"

"*Yes.*"

He grinned. "I've gotta go get Duke. I'll probably give him dinner, so we'll be a few minutes. You good?"

She was. So incredibly good. "Take your time. I'll call Guiseppi's. Extra egg rolls?"

George made a face. "That place is an unholy trinity."

"Yes. We've covered this. You object on principle to the pizza-Chinese-sushi hybrid. Do you want extra egg rolls?"

"Of course I do. They're amazing. I'll bring a box of wine."

Charlotte smiled as the door closed behind him and Bingley pawed at it, whining at the loss of his friend.

"Don't worry, he's coming back," she assured him.

She was a little too relieved about that fact herself.

She was still happily single—but being happily single didn't mean she had to be alone all the time. She liked people. She liked being with them. And if she wanted to spend time with George because he was awesome, that didn't make her codependent. And it didn't mean anything other than that she'd found a good friend. The Puppy Pact was working perfectly.

There was something about facing the wrath of the spider army together that really forged a bond. At least that was the excuse Charlotte was sticking with as to why everything seemed to shift with George after the Night of the Living Spiders. And yet nothing really changed.

They fell into a new pattern, hanging out whenever one of them wasn't busy. He became her default person, and she became his.

It wasn't constant. Bingley's training classes started, George was busy with his blues band rehearsals, book club, and poker nights, and Charlotte still hung out with Magda and Kendall whenever they could make their schedules line up. But the rest of the time, she and George watched every season of *Ted Lasso* and the *Cake-Off*, walked their dogs together, and explored all of Pine Hollow's—somewhat limited—takeout options, until George started coming over with groceries and cooking dinner instead.

The late April weather was miserable—rain-drenched days when all she wanted to do was curl up in front of a warm fire. But for once, Charlotte didn't mind the soggy weather. The rain didn't make her feel trapped this year. She could stay inside and play with Bingley, or visit Magda in the back of her bakery after hours to taste-test her new recipes, or binge-watch a new show with George.

She was still a strong, independent woman—but her puppy loved George, and even a strong, independent woman didn't have to spite herself just to prove how independent she was. George was fun. And he seemed to like all the same things she liked.

One night when they were watching *Rogue One*, Bingley stole one of George's socks and stashed it in the back corner of his crate with all his other treasures—his favorite squeaky toy, her ratty old running shoe, and the shirt that had started to come apart at the seams. When Charlotte explained that Bingley liked to cuddle with his treasures while Charlotte was at work, George insisted she let Bingley keep it and walked home across the compound with one bare ankle sticking out of his sneakers.

When April rolled into May and the weather turned gorgeous, George was the first person she texted when she wanted to go for a morning hike. He kept calling her dog Bing, but the nickname was starting to grow on her, just like Charles had. She'd started catching herself calling the puppy that as well.

Duke didn't even seem to be too jealous of all the attention the puppy was getting—probably because he was getting just as much. Whenever Bingley would steal his place in George's lap, Duke would climb onto Charlotte's lap and flop there with a long-suffering sigh, staring pointedly at his owner while Charlotte petted him.

Sometimes George would sit with his bass, working through fingerings as they talked, but no matter how much she goaded him, she could never seem to convince him to serenade her. He kept insisting that basses weren't serenading instruments.

It was a good routine. A comfortable one.

He was just so *kind*. He even offered to come with her for moral support when it was time for her to meet her dad's girlfriend. And he didn't even make her feel like she was being ridiculous and overreacting when she stood paralyzed by nerves on her father's doorstep.

"Is it cowardly to admit I was hoping it would rain and the barbecue would be canceled?" she asked, staring at the front door she'd walked through countless times.

Her dad had decided a big backyard barbecue would be the least stressful way to introduce Avita to the family—though Elinor had already met her. Because Elinor was perfect and emotionally mature, while Charlotte was considering having a mild panic attack on her dad's front step.

"You think your dad isn't prepared to move everything inside?" George asked lightly.

Charlotte waved a hand. "Don't distract me with logic. I'm having an emo moment."

He chuckled. "Sorry. My mistake. But you know it's gonna be fine, right?"

Did she?

"Elinor told you she was nice, didn't she?"

"Yes. Nice and super quiet. Which makes me wonder who carries the conversations in her relationship with my dad, since he's not exactly a talker."

"Nice is good."

"I *know*." Charlotte looked up at George, willing him to understand. And he did.

"But you don't want to meet her."

"It's not that I don't want to meet her. I do. And I'm not, like, worried about her trying to be my mom or anything. I just…"

She couldn't quite put her reluctance into words. There was no rational reason for it. It was just a feeling. A dread. Which was completely illogical, and she *knew* it was completely illogical, but it was there and it was *real* and—

"What if she hates me?"

Something unspeakably gentle entered his eyes. "Charles. She isn't going to hate you."

"But what if she does? My family has to love me because they're my family, but she doesn't have to."

"People don't only love you because they have to. Look at Kendall and Magda."

"Yeah, but they've known me a million years. Love is a function of time. Even obnoxious people become endearing with enough of it."

His dark eyes were still so soft behind his glasses. "I'm not sure that's how it works."

She bit her lip. "I just don't want her to hate me."

George didn't touch her all the time—they weren't cuddly except for random times when they fell asleep on couches or were offering support—but now he reached out and braced his hands on her shoulders. "Dr. Charles Rodriguez. She's gonna love you. Everyone loves you."

Her breath caught at the look in his eyes—but reality prompted her to argue. "Your sisters don't."

He blinked. "What?"

"When Beks called you while I was at your place and you handed me the phone because you had to look for that paper with that phone number—"

"I remember. You talked for two seconds."

"She doesn't like me. It was in her voice."

George sighed. "She was just being protective. You know how older siblings are."

Her chest squeezed. She hated the idea that George's sister thought he needed to be protected from her.

"Look, don't worry about Beks. She's been testy for weeks. Your dad's girlfriend—"

"Avita."

"Avita is going to love you. And if she doesn't, it's her loss."

The worry that squeezed her throat refused to release. "She could make my dad see me differently."

George groaned. "Come here." He pulled her against his chest for a hug, enveloping her in warmth and comfort. He smelled like fabric softener and spice as she gently slipped her hands around his waist. "You're an adventure, Charles," he said against her hair, "and not everyone knows what to do with you right off the bat, but no matter what anyone else thinks of you, no force on earth is ever going to make your dad love you any less. Am I wrong about that?"

"No." Her back expanded beneath his hands on a deep breath. "I'm okay."

He released her then, taking a step back and taking his warmth with him. Charlotte looked up at him, still nervous, but at a bearable level now.

"Thank you," she said. "For coming, and for that."

Something shifted in his eyes and even though he didn't move, she felt like he was pulling away. "What are friends for?"

Chapter Twenty

There is no charm equal to tenderness of heart.

—*Emma*, Jane Austen

How long have you and George been dating?"

Charlotte's face flushed and she resisted the urge to frantically shush her sister. She and Anne were beneath the tree where their old tire swing used to hang, setting up the backyard jumbo Jenga set while everyone else crowded around the grill. Avita was as nice as advertised, actually reminding Charlotte slightly of George, though she couldn't put her finger on why.

"We aren't dating," she insisted, keeping her voice low so it wouldn't carry to the rest of the party. "We're just friends."

"Oh. That's a shame."

"That we're friends?"

Anne shot her a look. "You know what I mean. He's nice. Unlike the guys you usually date."

Charlotte looked at her sister sharply, forgetting for a

moment that she was supposed to be stacking oversized blocks. "You've never said you didn't like a guy I was dating. Elinor was constantly picking at me, but you never said a word."

"Would you have listened?"

"I don't know. Maybe." Though if she was honest, she probably wouldn't have. She'd been too busy trying to prove to everyone—especially herself—that everything was perfect. That she was winning at love.

"I just like the idea of you with someone nice." Anne glanced over at her fiancée, who was currently chatting with George. "Nice can be *very* sexy."

Charlotte flushed. "Yes, he's very attractive. It's just not like that with us."

"Can't blame me for trying." Anne grinned as she reached for more blocks. "I mean the man quoted Austen to me. If he weren't male and I weren't madly in love, I might have to fight you for him."

"Ha-ha."

Anne just smiled. "Speaking of Austen, do you think you'll have time to help me organize the tea this year? I'm only asking because Bailey hinted she'd like to do it with me, but it's always been a family thing. Elinor's already said she's going to be too busy with edits for her book, but I don't want to edge you out."

The Austen tea at the Bluebell Inn where Anne worked had started as a way to remember their mother on her birthday one year and evolved into an annual event. Charlotte liked to help Anne with the planning when she could, but she also wanted Bailey to feel like she could be a part of their family traditions.

"Bailey should absolutely help with the tea if she wants to. She's family. If you need someone to be a worker bee and put together the party favors, I'm your first volunteer, but I don't need to be involved in all the decision making if you guys want to run it this year."

"Thanks. You should invite George," Anne suggested with a speculative light in her eyes. "Since he's so fond of Austen."

"If I invite him, it won't be a date. Because we *aren't* dating." This friendship between them was so much better than dating. She couldn't risk that.

"Okay. I'm just saying you could do a lot worse. And you have."

Charlotte smiled. "Duly noted," she said, as their father announced the food was ready.

~

"I hereby call the May meeting of the Leneghan Family Book Club to order and open the floor to new business. Beks?"

George frowned at his computer screen. "Okay, who gave Maggie a gavel?"

It was pink. And bedazzled.

Lori raised her hand. "Petition for the court, your honor?"

George groaned, dropping his head onto his hands. "Why are we encouraging this?"

"The petition shall be heard." Maggie regally inclined her head.

"Petition for an update on George and the Hot Doctor situation."

"All in favor?"

"Are you kidding me?" George glared at his sisters as four *aye*s echoed through his speakers. "I hate you all."

"Petition passes. *George?*"

"There is no update. We're *friends*. End of story."

"He's still seeing her. He went with her to her family barbecue today," Beks—the traitor—spilled.

"Ooh! A date!"

George shot daggers at his sisters through the web cam. "It wasn't a date. I was only there for moral support. She was nervous about meeting her father's new girlfriend."

"See?" Beks said—and his other sisters all nodded.

"Definitely in too deep." Maggie shook her head.

Lori sighed. "You always do this."

"Excuse me," George protested. "I always mess up my relationships in new and special ways, thank you very much."

"So you're admitting there's a relationship."

He groaned. "Do we have to talk about this?"

The chorus of yeses was deafening.

"What happened at the barbecue?" Lori asked.

Nearly at the same time, Beks said, "If you aren't dating her, what are you doing? Getting in too deep on an imaginary relationship?"

"Nothing happened at the barbecue," George insisted, ignoring Beks's words—and the acidic bite in them. "It was just a barbecue."

Charlotte's father's new girlfriend had been quiet, as advertised. When George had a chance to chat with her, she'd seemed more nervous than anything—and she'd smiled shyly when Charlotte bounded over to her to invite her to play one of the lawn games the family loved.

It had all gone well.

Though his sisters weren't the only ones who mistook him and Charlotte for a couple.

George had become friends with Charlotte's sister Elinor last year after Charlotte tried to set them up, but they didn't hang out together all that often—largely due to how busy Elinor was with her job and her fiancé and her quest to become the next big young adult author—but when they did spend time together, it was always comfortable.

He'd never told Elinor about his feelings for Charlotte—since, to be fair, he hadn't even acknowledged them to himself until recently—so she didn't realize she was salting the wound when she sidled up to him at the barbecue while Charlotte was playing lawn Jenga to tell him it was about time the two of them realized they were perfect for one another.

He should have known what her family would assume when he came with her to a barbecue that was all family and significant others, but he hadn't been thinking of that when he offered to be her moral support. He'd only been thinking of Charlotte and making things a little easier for her.

"She doesn't see me that way," he'd explained—and then, because that made him sound entirely too pathetic he'd added, "And I'm probably leaving Pine Hollow at the end of the summer anyway."

Which he hadn't meant to blurt out. He hadn't even told Charlotte about his probable move back to Denver. His job situation was still up in the air, but he really didn't want to go. Not now when things felt…

Shit. Beks was right.

He was in much too deep on this imaginary relationship. These last few weeks, he'd been playing an idiotic game with himself, using the fact that he *might* leave as an excuse to let himself get close to her, but avoiding actually telling her he was going, as if it wasn't real until he did and he could still change his mind if she suddenly decided she loved him.

He knew what he needed to do. To commit to going. To just *do* it.

So he pulled the ripcord and interrupted his sisters' ongoing debate about what he should do about his non-relationship to announce, "I'm probably not even staying in Pine Hollow."

It was like dropping a lit match in a dry haystack. The inferno of curiosity was instantaneous.

"Wait, you're leaving?"

"George! Are you moving back home?"

"When? Why haven't you told us?"

Only Beks remained silent, but only Beks had already known. She watched him intently.

"I'm telling you now." He had to speak over his sisters to be heard, and they all shushed one another. "And I'm not sure yet what I'm going to do. The Estates can't afford to keep me full-time after my contract is up, but I haven't started looking for jobs either here or in Colorado…"

"But your contract isn't up until September, is it? So you have time to look."

"You could always look both places, and then when you find something, let that make your decision for you," Evie suggested, always practical.

"You know your old job would take you back," Lori added.

George held up his hands for silence. "I'm still weighing both options."

"Because of her?" Beks asked.

"Oh my goodness," Maggie gushed before George could answer, "if you came back, we could put you on that app! The one where your friends and family get to pick your person for you!"

George's eyebrows flew up. "Like an arranged marriage?"

"No, like a setup! It's like those dating apps, but instead of you picking your person, we pick them for you! That would be so much fun!"

"We could put you on now," Evie offered eagerly. "So you can start seeing what the options would be."

George cringed. "No, thank you. I'm not ready for that."

"Because you're busy playing house with the girl?" Beks asked. "She isn't into you, George."

"Ouch." He tried to meet his sister's eyes through the camera, but Beks turned her face away.

"I've gotta go," Beks said.

"But we haven't even talked about the book," Evie protested.

Beks waved away the objection. "You guys go ahead. I didn't have a chance to read it anyway."

Before they could offer any more arguments, her window disappeared.

"That was weird," Lori muttered.

"Didn't Beks pick the book?" Evie frowned.

"Do you guys know if anything's going on? Is she okay?" George asked. He hated the distance between them. Hated not knowing what was going on with her.

Maggie waved him off. "She's been kind of moody, but Beks is always moody. It's probably nothing."

George frowned. He told himself he shouldn't be worried

if Lori and Maggie weren't worried—they were right there. They saw Beks all the time. But the worry didn't want to leave.

"Are you sure you don't want us to put you on that app?" Maggie asked, reverting back to their favorite subject lately—his love life, or lack thereof. "We could always set it for Vermont. Find you someone there."

George groaned. "No. Thank you. But no."

He didn't want to be set up. He didn't want anyone else. No matter what he'd told himself or his sisters or Charlotte. He had to face the truth. He had been "playing house," as Beks put it, because on some level he'd been hoping that Charlotte would wake up and realize she wanted to be with him. That they were more than friends.

And even though he knew it was pointless and probably unhealthy, he wasn't ready to give up that hope yet.

He'd been waiting. He'd been giving her time. He'd been giving her space to get over her last relationship and decide on her own that she was ready, that she wanted more. And that hopefully that *more* would be with him. He'd been wooing her, on some subconscious level. But at some point he was going to have to do something. He couldn't wait forever.

He had to tell her he might be leaving.

Tomorrow. They were supposed to go hiking. To some lake Charlotte loved. Either it would be romantic, or it would be the end. And he would cut the string on this foolish hope.

Tomorrow.

Chapter Twenty-One

To wish was to hope, and to hope was to expect.
—*Sense and Sensibility*, Jane Austen

The weather was perfect.

This hike ranked among her all-time favorites, and Charlotte had done it dozens of times, but she wasn't sure she'd ever seen it on such a gorgeous day. Sunlight filtered through the trees, and there was the slightest breeze in the air, cooling the sweat on their skin. After an hour of thumping happily through the tall trees with George and Duke and Bingley, they stepped out into the clearing, where a mountain pond lay pristine and crystal blue in front of them and the purple mountains in the distance seemed to curve around them in the perfect backdrop.

"Ta-da!" Charlotte flung out her arms. "Behold the majesty of nature!"

"Not bad," George acknowledged, as he slid his pack off his back. He'd been quiet on the hike, lost in his thoughts, but she didn't mind that in a hiking partner.

"Not *bad*?" Charlotte scoffed. "How gorgeous is this?" She spun in a circle, her arms raised to take in the magnificence. Duke struck a majestic pose while Bingley flopped down on his belly and instantly fell asleep—but he was still a baby, and this had been a big hike for him, so he could be forgiven for failing to appreciate the awe-inspiring scene.

"I mean, it's no *Colorado*," George said dryly. "Your mountains are pathetic."

Charlotte gasped in horror—as she did every time they had this argument. "How dare you malign the splendor of Vermont? Your Rockies are upstart babies compared to the seasoned wisdom of the Green Mountains."

"Your mountains are older. I'll give you that." George sat down on a granite boulder, and Duke trotted up to him with a stick in his mouth. "Ancient...worn down..." He took the stick, flinging it into the water.

Duke went plunging after the stick as Charlotte dropped down beside George. "We can't all have perky young mountains in our backyard. I think the view holds up pretty well."

George tipped his chin back, considering the landscape, and smiled, almost wistfully. "It is stupidly gorgeous here. Like a postcard everywhere you look."

Charlotte followed his gaze to the lush greens of the trees up against the robin's-egg-blue sky, all of it reflected by the crisp clear waters of the lake—from which Duke was emerging, hauling a stick that was significantly larger than the one he'd gone in after.

"Does he know he's supposed to bring back the same one you threw?" Charlotte asked, as Duke trotted over proudly, bringing what seemed like half of the lake water with him.

"He hasn't mastered the finer points of fetch yet." George tried to keep the dripping dog at arm's length as he accepted the new stick and flung it back toward the lake. "At this point I've given up trying to teach him. He loves it and it gets him exercise, so we work with what we've got."

Bingley stirred himself enough to pad over to Charlotte and curl up against her leg. She reached down to pet him up as he settled his head on her lap, heaving a big sigh for such a little guy as she gently stroked his silky fur. Bracing one hand behind her, she leaned back, tipping her face up to the sky.

God, it was perfect. The day. The company. This feeling. She felt *so good*.

Duke emerged from the water with another still-bigger stick and trotted back to George with his offering.

"I will miss this."

Charlotte almost didn't catch the words, then what George had said penetrated and she opened her eyes to frown at him. "Why would you...?"

He met her eyes, searching her face as he explained. "My contract's up in September. I might go back to Colorado."

Everything inside Charlotte went still. Even the birds seemed to stop chirping. "Oh."

"I thought Elinor might have told you."

"You told Elinor?"

"Yesterday," he admitted. "It just sort of came up."

She shouldn't feel hurt that he'd told her sister first. She really shouldn't. But it was there, mixed in with the chaotic swirl of *no* and *why* and *no really, why* that was tangling in her thoughts.

"They can't afford to keep me full-time when Claudia comes back," he explained.

"But there are other places you can work. Jack has contacts all over the state. It might be a longer commute, but I'm sure someone with your qualifications..."

"Yeah, I might be able to scrape something together, but it seems like a good time to go back if I want to."

He wanted to go? "Right. Okay."

He must have heard something in her voice, because his gaze searched her face again.

"I don't know for sure yet," he said, softly. "It's just something I'm thinking about. The original plan was for me to try this out for two years. See how it went. So I'm taking this as a chance to think about where I want to be."

"Right. Yeah. That's smart. You should do that." Then a desperate thought popped into her head, something to make him stay. "What about the band? You guys have been practicing so much. You can't just leave them."

"I'll still be here for the talent show. And I'm not exactly irreplaceable. I'm an amateur among professionals in that group."

"But everyone's going to miss you." *I'm going to miss you.* But that was the selfish thing. That greedy, hungry, wanting-what's-best-for-me thing. She couldn't say it.

George took the latest stick from Duke and stood facing the lake. "It just feels like it's a chance to reassess." He looked over his shoulder at her and she couldn't read the expression on his face. "Think about what I want."

And what he wanted might not be here.

Her throat tightened.

But if he found what he wanted, maybe he'd stay.

She'd completely fallen down on the job of setting him up with the perfect girl. No one she came up with ever seemed to be quite right. And, if she was completely honest with herself, she'd also been selfish, enjoying his company for herself. But that wasn't fair to him.

As George stepped forward to throw, the sun hit his hair, catching blond tones she'd never noticed among the sandy browns. After he released the stick, he took off his glasses, absently cleaning them on the hem of his blue Henley, and Charlotte was struck by the angle of his jaw, the straight line of his nose. She saw him so often, he was so familiar, that sometimes she forgot how handsome he was. Then it would hit her in the strangest moments.

She looked away, busying herself by digging in her pack for the collapsible doggie water dishes—though Duke seemed to have plenty of water, and Bingley was now fast asleep.

George was a catch. She needed to find him a girl. But whenever she tried to think of someone to match him up with, there was always some reason that girl wasn't good enough for him.

She needed to refocus her efforts. Immediately.

"You're going to Elinor's birthday party, right?" Elinor's birthday had been weeks ago, but they'd pushed back the party because she'd been swamped with the first round of edits for her book. Her sister's karaoke birthday parties were legendary. Half the town would be there. Including several eligible women.

George glanced at her with a slight frown. "I'll be there," he confirmed, flinging Duke's new stick and sending him romping back into the water. "But don't expect me to sing. I'm more of a background vocals guy."

"Right. No, that's fine. I just wanted you to come."

He looked at her, holding her gaze, the air filling with unspoken words—until Duke emerged from the lake dragging a stick nearly as big as he was and breaking the tension.

"Seriously?" George demanded of the dog, and Charlotte laughed, a soft, almost relieved burst.

Duke paused at the water's edge to get a better grip on the stick so he could half-carry, half-drag it back to George.

"He has more faith in your throwing arm than I do," she said, forcing lightness into her voice. Trying to prove she wasn't still wobbling inside, like a Jenga tower with the wrong piece yanked out.

"Oh yeah?" George challenged. "Just for that, I'm gonna show you how manly my throwing arm is." He took the massive branch from Duke, tossing it slightly to check the balance. His biceps flexed and Charlotte yanked her gaze off them just in time as he turned to look pointedly back at her. Cocky arrogance in every molecule of his body, he reared back and flung the "stick" end over end into the lake.

Her mouth went dry—just because she'd sworn off men didn't mean she wasn't *aware* of an attractive man when he was standing right in front of her—but they were friends. Only friends. She was a gaping maw of desperation and need when she got in relationships. She would ruin this if she let it be anything more.

So she slapped on her most just-friends smile as she applauded his manly effort. "Bravo!"

George sketched a bow in her direction. "Thank you."

Duke seemed to have lost track of all the sticks that had gone into the water and now paddled happily in circles, so

George dropped back down beside Charlotte, his shoulder brushing hers.

Bingley's paws began to twitch in little puppy dreams, and Charlotte kept her attention on the puppy—a tangible reminder of the Puppy Pact. That she was working on herself. That she was better when she wasn't a needy mass of want.

She would find George the perfect girl at her sister's birthday party. They would fall madly in love, and he would stay.

And she wouldn't ruin this friendship. Because no other alternative was acceptable.

Chapter Twenty-Two

If one scheme of happiness fails, human nature turns to another; if the first calculation is wrong, we make a second better: we find comfort somewhere.

—*Mansfield Park*, Jane Austen

We need to find a girl for George. Tonight," Charlotte announced as soon as she walked through the door of the Furry Friends indoor obstacle course, where Magda and Kendall were already waiting.

Elinor's karaoke birthday party was scheduled to start in two hours, but Mags and Kendall had agreed to meet her at Furry Friends beforehand so they could talk for what felt like the first time in weeks.

As if the weather knew George was thinking about leaving, it had started to rain as they were driving back from the hike on Sunday and had kept up a steady downpour all week. Bingley had been going stir-crazy, and since she knew he'd be cooped up all night, Charlotte had scheduled a session at the little indoor play room at Furry Friends. There was a larger agility course outside, with all the obstacles Elinor's Australian shepherd loved, but the indoor course was plenty big enough for little Bingley—who wasn't exactly known for his grace or agility yet.

When Charlotte unclipped his leash, he immediately bounded over to the two shelter dogs Magda and Kendall were playing with, leaping on top of the black lab.

"Here I thought we were going to hear all about your dad's new girlfriend," Kendall said, waving a tug-of-war toy and catching the attention of a scraggly tan mutt, who pounced on it.

"She's great." Charlotte flopped down beside them as the dogs played. "I was a little nervous going in, but George made me see how ridiculous that was—"

"Wait. I'm sorry. You brought a date to meet your dad's girlfriend?"

Charlotte rolled her eyes at Kendall's words. "It was George. George isn't a date. He's a friend."

Magda and Kendall exchanged a look.

"What?" Charlotte demanded.

"Nothing," Magda and Kendall said in unison. Kendall continued, "You're just spending a lot of time with your *friend.*"

"That's what I do. I spend time with my friends—when they aren't insanely busy like you two have been. But then on Sunday, George and I went hiking and he told me he's thinking of moving back to Colorado—which I know he's only considering because he hasn't found love here, so I need your help finding the perfect person. Someone who is going to appreciate a unicorn like George when they see one."

Kendall eyed her. "I feel like this is a trick question."

"What's that supposed to mean?"

"Nothing. I just think you might have a blind spot where he's concerned."

"I don't have a blind spot. I know he's great. Which is why I'm trying to fix him up with someone awesome."

"Have you considered looking in the mirror? Because you already seem like you're doing everything with him that you would usually do with a boyfriend, except sex."

"Our friendship is nothing like my romantic relationships."

"Because it's functional?"

"Because we're *friends*. And yes, if I were a better friend, I would have set him up already."

"Have you thought about what's going to happen when you do set him up?" Magda asked gently. "It's not like you're still going to do morning hikes and all-day Netflix binges when he's dating someone else."

"Of course I've thought about it. And I know I've been selfish to take so much of his time, but I'm trying to do better."

Everything would change when he found his person, and yes, if she was being honest with herself, Charlotte hadn't wanted it to change too fast. She'd been so happy lately. And part of that was *because* they were just friends. She'd carried around a low level of anxiety about her romantic relationships for years and now, with it gone, she felt like a new person.

"The Puppy Pact has been really good for me, and I don't want to screw it up, or screw up my friendship with George. But I do want to know why I'm the only one who's actually gotten a puppy," she said, turning a stern eye on Magda and

Kendall, who were so busy fawning over the shelter dogs that they didn't notice.

"You realize you can't bully us into getting dogs," Kendall pointed out.

Charlotte scoffed. "You know I would have stopped bugging you the second either one of you said you didn't want one. But all you've done is come up with bogus reasons not to do something that would make you ridiculously happy. I mean look at you." She waved her hand at them—both caught in the act of puppy cuddles.

Magda looked over at Kendall. "She makes a good point."

"Okay, yes, I want a dog," Kendall admitted. "But I need to work out a few things first."

Charlotte frowned at the stress in Kendall's voice. "What kind of things?"

"I just... I want to make some changes. I'll do it. But in my own time." She looked to Magda. "What's your excuse?"

"I'm processing," Magda said, a defensive note in her voice. "I don't make major decisions as quickly as you guys do."

"Except when you're mad," Kendall reminded her.

"Luckily I've only been that mad twice in my entire life."

Charlotte refrained from pointing out that both of those times she'd been mad at the same person—and her impulse decisions had actually worked out pretty well in the end, even if they hadn't quite gone the way she wanted at the start.

"I'm not rash," Magda insisted. "I like to think things through. I prepare. So I'm mentally preparing." She stroked the head of the dog curled at her side. "And even though I love this sweetheart, I have this feeling like he isn't *mine*, you know? I feel like when I meet the right dog I'll know."

Charlotte didn't mention that Magda had that same thought about meeting the right man, and it hadn't quite worked out the way she'd hoped. Instead she sighed melodramatically. "*Fine.* Take your time. You're just ruining my master plan for all of our puppies to be playing together and going on walks together."

"I'm not sure I want a puppy," Magda said. "The whole house-training thing doesn't sound ideal. Maybe by the time yours is grown and socialized, I'll get one that already is."

Across the room, Bingley tumbled sideways off the teeter-totter.

"Besides," Kendall added, "don't you already have George to walk your dog with?"

"Not for much longer. Not if we can't find someone who makes him want to stay."

Kendall stared at her. "I'm trying really hard not to say the obvious thing right now."

"Thank you. Now who can we hook him up with?"

"Lily Evans who runs the bridal shop? She's cute," Magda suggested without looking up from the black lab she was petting.

Kendall made a little growling noise at the dog who was currently hanging on the other end of her tug-of-war toy. "Isn't she dating that guy from out of town?"

"Right, so not Lily," Charlotte said.

"What about Suzie Keep? Didn't she and Eli break up last month? She's a total sweetheart and she works part-time at the Estates so they've probably bumped into each other a few times."

Kendall nodded pensively. "She could be good. Doesn't she teach those senior dance classes? She could teach George a few moves."

"Yes!" Charlotte latched onto the idea with more enthusiasm than she was feeling. "Suzie would be perfect. I'll talk to her tonight. Now who's our backup?"

Chapter Twenty-Three

One cannot have too large a party.
—*Emma*, Jane Austen

Are you aware that Charlotte's in the billiard room pimping you out to every unattached woman in town?"

George groaned as Mac appeared at his side with those words. At least he could stop craning his neck, trying to spot Charlotte in the crowd.

Elinor's birthday party was in full swing at the Tipsy Moose pub. The birthday girl was currently on stage, belting her way through a Kelly Clarkson song like it had been written for her—and her youngest sister was apparently in the billiard room playing matchmaker. Lovely.

"You've gotta tell her, man," Mac declared, slurring slightly—he was the happiest drunk George had ever met, but he was definitely three sheets to the wind, though George could swear he'd only had two beers. "Do it in song! Do you know *Dear Evan Hansen*? There's this one called 'If I Could Tell Her.' I bet they have it. I made Iain add more Broadway options to the karaoke."

George shook his head, smiling at Mac's enthusiasm, if nothing else. "What are you talking about?"

"Charlotte! Seriously, man," Mac said—or tried to say. The *s*'s got slightly tangled. "You gotta tell her how you feel."

"It doesn't matter how I feel if she doesn't feel the same."

"Didn't you say she gave up *Hamilton* tickets for you? That's *love*, man."

"No. That's Charlotte."

They weren't going to ride off into the sunset together.

That had become very clear on Sunday when he'd told her he was leaving. She talked about his work, the band, but never once had she mentioned that she wanted him to stay—and then she'd started talking about her sister's birthday party as if nothing had happened.

He'd hoped...well. He'd hoped for something that wasn't going to happen.

And then he'd come here tonight, half-hoping again that she'd made a point of asking him if he was going to be here because she wanted to make some big romantic gesture—like sing a song asking him to stay. That sounded like something Charlotte would do.

But apparently she'd only wanted to play matchmaker.

Mac looked out over the bar and sighed gustily. "The friend zone *sucks*. We gotta get you out of there. *Wooo!*" Mac flung up his hands and shouted as Elinor's song ended.

Anne took the stage next and the opening notes of "Paperback Writer" filled the bar.

"I think she secretly has feelings for you," Mac declared. "They do that sometimes."

"Uh-huh." He'd been hoping she did, but it was looking less and less likely. George took a long pull of his drink, taking his attention off his surroundings long enough for Mac to catch sight of someone and bellow.

"Kendall! KEN-DULL!"

Oh no. "Mac, don't—"

"What are you yelling at me for?" Kendall asked, glaring at both of them as if George was somehow responsible for Mac's outburst. "Don't you have a song coming up?"

Mac waved a hand. "Yeah, I gotta sing in a second. But first, is Charlotte secretly in love with George?"

"Christ," George muttered under his breath as Kendall's expression froze. "You do not need to answer that."

Mac forged on. "Because I think my boy here is freaking *awesome*, and she has been spending a lot of time with him."

Kendall met George's eyes, and the sympathy in hers was the worst part. "Honestly, I don't know, but if she has feelings for you, they are buried *deep* behind a firewall of denial. She really seems to need to see you as a friend."

"He is a stud!" Mac bellowed.

"She compared him to a puppy," Kendall told Mac—which at least shut him up.

Mac turned bleary eyes on George. "Okay, that's not great."

"Sorry," Kendall said to George. "Figured it was better to know."

He nodded. "Thanks."

Kendall departed back into the crowd—and George reminded himself that he had known. It wasn't like it was new information. Nothing had changed.

She thought he was a puppy. Because of course she did. He'd been holding his breath waiting for something that was never going to happen.

"Damn." This from Mac. He shoved his full beer at George. "Here. You need this more than I do."

An opening riff played over the speakers and Mac's head jerked toward the stage. "Crap. That's my song. Connor! Connor, take my song!"

"Go ahead," George said—it wasn't like there was anything Mac could do to help.

But Mac had already thrown his arm around George's shoulders and was steering him toward the front door. "C'mon. Let's go for a walk."

George didn't protest—he wasn't in the mood for a party anyway. It was still raining outside, only a drizzle, but Mac swore and ducked under the awning in front of Magda's Bakery for cover.

George leaned against the brick building and lifted the beer. "I don't think I'm allowed to have this out here."

"Levi's inside making lovey eyes at Elinor. He's not gonna give you a ticket tonight." Mac propped himself beside George. "You okay?"

"Yeah. I'm fine."

"Hey. You can talk to your feelings about me. We're *evolved*."

George cracked a smile at the garbled invitation. He and Mac had mostly talked about band stuff for the past several weeks, but there was a trust there. And, honestly, he was tired of pretending it didn't suck, being crazy about someone who had lodged him so hard into the friend zone.

"I'm just sick of being that guy," he heard himself admitting. "The one everyone likes and no one falls for because he's not the leading man. Steady, stable, easygoing George. No sparks. That's me." He drained half the beer. "And you tell yourself that it's not you, that you just need to find someone who *wants* a low-drama partner, but there's always that obnoxious little voice in your head saying you're not exciting enough. You're the boring choice. And no one wants boring."

"You're not boring," Mac objected, as if offended by the idea. "And boring is frigging great. Except in food. And in bed. Are you boring in bed?"

George laughed. "I almost wish that was it, because at least then I could get better."

More than one of his exes had told him he was hard to leave because he knew what he was doing in the bedroom. Which should have been a compliment, but also served as a reminder that it was his personality that was the problem.

"Makes no sense," Mac declared. "No reason you should be single if you don't want to be."

He didn't want to be. But he didn't want Charlotte matchmaking for him either. He just wanted *her*. And she saw him as a puppy.

He swore under his breath. "I'm probably moving back to Colorado anyway."

"Because of Charlotte?"

"No. It's not about her."

But it was cleaner this way. It made moving home easier. But no matter how many times he told himself that, it still sucked.

"We're friends. That's it, and I knew that was it."

But he didn't want her matchmaking for him. He needed to tell her to call off the search.

"Come on," he said to Mac. "We should get back."

"You should sing," Mac suggested, throwing an arm

around him. "This shit is why musicals were invented. When you feel too much to talk, you sing. That's how it works."

George smiled at Mac's earnestness. He would miss the diner owner. "I'll leave the musicals to you. Come on."

George found Charlotte in the billiard room, as advertised, wearing a bright red party dress and earrings that flashed like disco balls whenever she moved. Her face lit when she spotted him, and she bounced to his side. "George! Hey! You know Suzie Keep, don't you?"

"Hey, Suzie." George nodded to the woman who sometimes manned the front desk at the Estates, before turning to Charlotte. "Can I talk to you for a minute?"

"Sure!" she shouted over the opening bars of "Don't Stop Believin'" as Ally took the stage in the main room. "I need to freshen up my drink—why don't you talk to Suzie for a minute and I'll be right back!"

He lifted his empty beer bottle and raised his voice as the entire pub started belting out the lyrics in unison. "I'll come with you."

Charlotte looked like she wanted to argue. If he stayed put a moment longer, she would probably offer to buy him his drink so he had to stay and flirt with Suzie, so he turned and started threading through the crowd toward the bar.

He didn't look behind him, but as soon as he found a space against the well-worn wood, Charlotte appeared at his side. "You should've talked to her!" she said, leaning close to yell into his ear. "Suzie's great! And she's single now!"

"I don't want you to set me up."

"What?"

"I don't want you to set me up!"

A flash of something he couldn't read passed over her face and he leaned closer. "Can we just talk somewhere?"

He saw her mouth form the word *yeah* and she nodded, her eyes wide and nervous.

Abandoning their space at the bar, George caught her hand and tugged her behind him toward the patio door. It was always quiet out there—but he'd forgotten, until he stepped outside, that it had been raining when he was outside ten minutes ago.

The rain had stopped, but the air was still cool and heavy with the possibility of another shower. Dark clouds made the night feel especially black, blocking out the stars as he turned to face her.

The door clanged shut behind her, leaving them—thanks to the recent rain—completely alone.

"I don't want you to set me up," he repeated, at a normal volume.

"I'm just trying to help," she said softly.

"I don't want you to."

"But why?" she pleaded. "You're the unicorn. The perfect guy. If you want to be in a relationship, why aren't you? It doesn't make any sense," she insisted. "Why is George Leneghan, the dictionary definition of too-good-to-be-true, still single?"

Because you're too busy throwing your friends at me to notice I'm standing right in front of you.

George knew what he should do.

He knew he should laugh it off. He knew she didn't

really mean the question. It was something people said when they thought they were complimenting you. When they wanted you to laugh and say, "It's a mystery!" or some other bullshit.

He knew exactly what to say—but tonight…

He just couldn't.

She thought he was a freaking *puppy*.

He felt the frustration bubbling up, and then the words were coming out and he couldn't stop them.

"Why the hell do you think?"

Chapter Twenty-Four

I think I am justified—though where so
many hours have been spent in convinc-
ing myself that I am right, is there not
some reason to fear I may be wrong?
—*Sense and Sensibility*, Jane Austen

W hat?" Charlotte's eyes grew huge.

A tiny, rational part of George told him to shut
up, but anger was in the driver's seat. "You tell me," he
snapped. "Why am I single? What am I doing wrong? Why
does every woman look at me and think, 'you know, he's
absolutely perfect *for someone else.*'"

"I . . . I don't know," Charlotte stammered.

"Well, if you figure it out, you be sure to let me know.
That's what friends do, right?"

Her eyes widened even more. "George . . ."

"Just don't set me up with anyone else. All right? I don't
need your pity."

"It's not—"

"Good night, Charlotte."

"*George,*" she called after him, but he was already crossing the patio to the side exit that let out onto the alley. He'd already wished Elinor a happy birthday, and he wasn't exactly in a party mood anymore.

"George, I'm sorry! It was a stupid thing to say!" Charlotte shouted after him, but he didn't slow.

Right on cue, the sky opened up as George stalked quickly down the alley, toward the side street where he'd parked his car. He hunched his shoulders, ducking his head against the rain dribbling down his collar.

He made it to his car, unlocking it and diving inside. It wasn't until he was sitting there in the darkness with the rain drumming on the windshield that the first glimmer of regret took hold.

He shouldn't have blown up at Charlotte like that.

It wasn't her fault that she didn't feel the same way for him that he felt for her. It wasn't her fault he'd foolishly let his imagination run away with him and built up unrealistic expectations in his mind. That he repeatedly *kept doing that* even when he knew it was insane. She'd always been very clear about where they stood—firmly in the friend zone— and he couldn't get mad at her for acting that way. Even if his pride was bruised.

He needed to go back. Smooth things over. Apologize.

His phone rang.

George twisted to dig it out of his pocket, hoping to see CHARLES on the caller ID, but it was Beks instead.

"Hey," he said, connecting the call. "What's up?"

Silence. A soft catch of breath.

"Beks?"

He heard a soft muffled sound then—almost a whimper—

as if she was crying and trying to get herself under control. *Beks.* Who never cried in front of *anyone.*

George instantly shifted into crisis mode, blind to his surroundings as his entire world narrowed to the voice on the other end of the phone. "What's wrong?" he demanded. "Is it the kids?" No reaction. "Is it Scott?"

Beks released a choked sob—and George's shoulders knotted with tension.

"Did something happen?"

"I think…" A high-pitched catch of breath. "I think he's having an affair, Georgie." Her voice cracked on *affair*— and George's fists clenched, itching to plant themselves in his brother-in-law's face.

"What happened?"

"I hacked his phone," she admitted. "I wanted to be wrong. But he's been acting weird—not all the time, but it's been driving me crazy wondering, so I took his phone while he was in the shower and figured out his code—he didn't used to even have a code. He's gotten all secretive—like he doesn't want me to see the screen when he's texting, and now it all makes sense because he's been texting *her*." A heavy sniffle. "They used to date. Before we met. I recognized her name. His friends—his stupid frat brothers—still call her 'the one that got away.' And he's been texting with her for *months*, George. Maybe even years! Little cute memes and flirty shit. I don't know if they're sleeping together, but he's been hiding this from me—why would he be hiding it if he'd innocently reconnected with an old friend? If he hasn't slept with her yet, he's obviously planning to." Her voice broke. "Maybe she wasn't even the first. Maybe there are others. Who knows what else he's hiding?"

"Have you said anything to him?"

"No." A sniffle. "I put his phone back and pretended I didn't know anything. Part of me is scared to know how bad it really is—because when I know, I have to do something, right? I have to leave him? Because I don't know if I can— and that makes me hate myself, because I should, right? If I have any self-respect, I should go—but we have three kids together, and I can't—why would he do this? I thought he loved our life."

"We don't know the extent of it." George fought to keep his voice calm and steady. "Maybe it's just texts—but whatever he did or didn't do, there is no 'should' here, Beks. No one can tell you the right way to react to this. Whatever you do, however you feel, I'm behind you, okay?"

"I can't talk to him yet," she whispered jaggedly. "I just need to—I can't think. I don't want to be alone, George."

George's response was instant. "I'll come home."

"You will?" Her voice cracked, but this time with hope.

"I have some vacation. I'll come next weekend."

"Oh. No, don't come now…" Beks sniffled, dragging herself together.

And he realized why she'd been so hopeful. She thought he meant for good. Moving back to Colorado. And why shouldn't he?

"You won't be alone," he promised. "You and the boys will always have me. I'll start looking for jobs in Colorado tonight."

"I can't ask you to do that," she whispered, but he heard the longing in the words, and felt that hook sink deep into the softest part of his heart. How could he say no when Beks needed him? Especially when no one needed him here, when his future here would only be more of the same, more of feeling like he wasn't enough.

"You aren't asking," he said. Firm.

"If you were here, I think I could . . ." She didn't finish the sentence, her voice wobbling as the tears returned.

"I'll be there, Beks. Always."

His sister sobbed—and George said soothing nonsense as he became aware of the steady drum of rain on the windshield.

He turned on the car, connecting the Bluetooth and starting back toward his condo as he consoled his sister.

Sometimes the universe gave you a sign. And sometimes it gave you a shove.

It was time to leave Pine Hollow.

Chapter Twenty-Five

She hoped to be wise and reasonable in
time; but alas! alas! she must confess to
herself that she was not wise yet.
—*Persuasion*, Jane Austen

George is mad at me."

Charlotte leaned against the counter in Magda's
bakery, watching her best friend make something sinfully
decadent out of dark chocolate, and stewed over the
same thing she'd been stewing over for the last sixteen
hours.

George was mad at her. And it had thrown her whole
world out of whack.

She'd ruined it.

She hadn't meant to. She'd been thinking how much she
was going to miss him and wishing that she'd already set
him up with some amazing girl who would convince him
to stay—and she'd said the stupid thing.

Of course he'd gotten upset with her.

But George never got upset with her. Which was notable

in itself. *Everyone* got upset with her. Except George. He just seemed to accept all her messy, ugly parts.

Only now she'd apparently found his limit. And she didn't know what to do to make it better.

He'd called her Charlotte. Not Charles. Charlotte.

She hadn't gone after him last night. She'd thought he needed to cool off and then he'd come back to the party, but he hadn't. Not when they all sang happy birthday to Elinor. Not when Mac and Magda took the stage for a very drunk, very belligerent rendition of "Anything You Can Do, I Can Do Better." George never returned.

She'd taken Bingley for a long walk around the complex this morning, lingering by the solar panels. She kept hoping that she would see George, and he would smile and all would be forgiven and they wouldn't even have to talk about it—but she hadn't seen him, and anxiety kept gnawing away at her, reminding her that he was still angry. At her. And she hated it.

"What did you do?" Magda asked as Kendall came sweeping in through the door to the front of the bakery, shaking off the rain.

"Why are there a dozen teenagers in your shop giggling and wandering in circles?" Kendall demanded as she stripped off her jacket.

"My nephew Dylan is manning the shop today," Madga explained. "He wants to be Ed Sheeran, and apparently the entirety of Pine Hollow High School thinks he's dreamy. They're 'browsing.'" She made air quotes with a white-and-dark chocolate swizzle stick.

"That explains it." Kendall frowned at Charlotte. "What's wrong with you?"

Magda caught Kendall's eye. "She's having angst because George got mad at her last night."

"About time," Kendall muttered.

"Hey," Charlotte protested. "Whose side are you on?"

"Can I be on the side of truth, justice, and the American way?"

"Like Captain America." Magda eyed Kendall. "I could see you as a superhero."

"Right?" Kendall struck a pose.

"I'm having a crisis here," Charlotte reminded them.

"You aren't having a crisis," Kendall said. "George isn't really mad at you."

Charlotte straightened, hopeful. "Did he tell you that?"

"No," Kendall admitted—and Charlotte deflated. "But I've seen you two together. I'm pretty sure he's not physically capable of being genuinely mad at you."

"That's what I thought. But you didn't see his face."

"You didn't tell me what you did," Magda reminded her.

Charlotte winced. "I asked him how he could still be single. Which, yes, wasn't the most tactful, but I was thinking of all the women he was set up with by the biddies at the Estates, and I couldn't figure out why none of them had snapped him up—it wasn't about *him*, but I said it wrong and he got pissed."

"Oh, God, *Charlotte*," Kendall groaned, dropping her head to the counter with a thud. When she raised it, her eyes were filled with pity. "He's in love with you."

"No, he isn't." Charlotte felt her face heating as she shook her head. "He only asked me out that one time as a joke— he said so."

"Wait." Magda held up a spatula dripping chocolate. "He asked you out? When was this?"

Charlotte waved away the look on her face. "It wasn't real. It was way back in March. Right after I dumped Jeff—right at the beginning of the Puppy Pact, and he knew about the pact so it was obvious he wasn't being serious."

"So let me get this straight." Kendall faced her, her eyes probing. "The second he knew you were available, he asked you out, you turned him down, he pretended it was a joke, and you guys have been platonic dating ever since?"

"We aren't platonic dating," Charlotte argued.

"Honey, no one goes to the drive-in as friends."

"Sure, they do," Charlotte insisted. "And we didn't go to the drive-in. We were just talking about maybe going this summer because he's never been to one. I invited you guys to come with us! How is that a date?"

"Did he suggest you invite us? Or did you invite us as a buffer after he pseudo asked you out again?"

"I don't need a buffer. We spend time alone together all the time."

Kendall feigned a cough that sounded like *"Platonic dating."*

Charlotte appealed to Magda. "Mags. Back me up."

Magda winced. "Sorry, Charlotte. He's completely in love with you."

Something sharp kicked in her chest, but she ignored it. "Did he tell you that?"

"No," Magda admitted. "I'm not even sure he knows."

"Then he isn't in love with me. You have to know to be in love."

"Do you?" Magda asked.

"Fine," Kendall acknowledged. "Don't call it love. Call it a crush or him *really* liking you or liking you *like that* or whatever high school phrase you want to grab from the teenagers giggling in Magda's shop—"

"Shoes." Magda grinned.

Kendall froze, losing her momentum. "Oh my God, I forgot all about shoes."

"Right?" Magda was beaming now, caught by the memory.

It had been their code when they were fourteen. Kendall had started it by admitting she had an *issue*, an unwanted crush on an unavailable boy, but Mags hadn't heard her correctly and thought they were talking about *shoes*. Once they'd cleared that up, shoes had become what they called those feelings they didn't know what to do with.

"I don't have shoes for George," Charlotte protested.

Mags and Kendall exchanged a look.

"I don't!" she insisted.

"Ignoring for a moment the matter of *your* shoes," Kendall said, "George definitely has shoes for you. And you need to decide what to do about the fact that you hurt his feelings by asking him why he's unbangable while simultaneously refusing to bang him."

"That isn't what happened!"

Kendall shrugged. "It's kind of what happened."

"I'm better single! You've all seen it, these last few months. I'm happier. I'm not angsting about being good enough. I'm becoming my best self."

"You're platonically dating George..." Kendall added.

"We aren't in a relationship! I'm a train wreck in relationships. I'm better alone."

"So you never want to have sex again?"

"Maybe I don't," Charlotte snapped.

Kendall sighed. "Honey. You never needed to swear off men. You needed to swear off assholes and this ridiculous myth of Darcy. That was never George."

"So what? You think I should go out with him?"

"I just think you should be honest with yourself about whether or not you want to."

Magda met her gaze, quietly reinforcing Kendall's words. "She's not wrong."

Charlotte tried to think about dating George, about *kissing* George—and fear stabbed into her chest.

The problem wasn't that she didn't like him, or that she didn't find him attractive. He was *George*—she knew his face so well that she never saw a hot guy when she looked at him; she just saw *him*. His warm eyes. His endearing smile with that one lopsided dimple. His sandy hair that was always a little too long, a little too shaggy—and made her want to push it back, away from his face, soft against her fingers, trailing them down his throat—

No. The problem wasn't that she didn't want him.

It was that she loved him.

As a friend. In that safe, platonic space. And anything that happened between them would put that at risk.

"What if we have no chemistry?" she asked. "What if we try and it's awful and it makes everything weird?"

"What if it's great?" Magda asked gently.

"What if I'm too much?" Charlotte argued. "What if I ask for too much and need too much?" *What if he leaves?* "I don't want to lose him."

"Hon," Kendall said softly. "You can't lose him. He isn't even yours. Not really."

She knew that. Of course she knew that.

But...she wanted him to be.

She wanted George.

Oh God. She wanted *George*.

She'd been in denial, pushing away everything she felt for him because she was scared. But now that she'd seen the truth she couldn't shove it back in Pandora's box.

Vivian Weisman had been right when she said Charlotte had been closing the door on something she secretly wanted with the Puppy Pact. She didn't want to be alone. She still wanted the fairy tale. She wanted it with George.

And she was going to have to do something about it.

Chapter Twenty-Six

Know your own happiness. You want
nothing but patience—or give it a more
fascinating name, call it hope.
—*Sense and Sensibility*, Jane Austen

Can we talk?

George stared at the text for the four-thousandth
time. There was something so ominous about the words.

He'd shot back a *Yeah, of course* and arranged to meet
Charlotte at his place after his band rehearsal. It should have
felt normal, meeting up to hang out. They'd spent countless
hours in his apartment or hers over the last few months, but
anxiety still soured his stomach.

He needed to apologize for losing his temper. He would
have texted last night, but his focus had been elsewhere.

Beks had texted this morning and told him not to move
back for her. She'd insisted she was fine, she shouldn't
have asked him, and there was nothing he'd be able to do
anyway. He'd told her he already had a ticket to come visit
the next weekend, and she'd called him to insist he cancel

his trip. She didn't want him hanging over her, making her feel like she had to make a decision before she was ready. She said she would refuse to even see him if he showed up, so he canceled the ticket—but George still felt the ties of home pulling at him. He wanted to be there to be his sister's safety net, in whatever form that took.

And there wasn't anything for him here.

He'd spent all day applying for jobs and checking out apartments back in Denver. The cost of living seemed to have gone up again in the last two years, but he could make it work.

If Mac and Bob and Howard noticed that George was a little quieter than usual at rehearsal, no one commented on it. Mac talked about the new song they were considering for the talent show as they walked toward the parking lot at the Estates, and George managed to make affirmative noises in the right places, but his thoughts were on Charlotte's text again.

It felt like something was coming to an end.

Probably because he was going to tell her tonight that he'd started applying for jobs back home. He'd finally done it. Given up on the fairy tale of them and settled into the reality that he belonged back in Colorado.

He'd apologize first, for losing his cool the other night, and then he'd tell her.

When he got back to his place, he took Duke out, and then tidied up the living room—which was already perfectly neat—as he waited for Charlotte.

She was right on time.

She hadn't brought Bingley—which only exacerbated his nerves. She'd stood on his front step in a soft red sweater, snug dark jeans, and heeled boots. Her hair was twisted up in some fancy knot—even though he knew it bothered her that way and she always automatically yanked it down when she got home and could relax. She was even wearing makeup and earrings. All the armor she put on when she was trying to impress someone. All the stuff she usually didn't need when it was just them.

She looked gorgeous.

And distant. Like all the effort she'd put into her appearance was a gulf opening up between them. He felt a pinch in the region of his heart.

"I'm sorry," he said, before she could get a word out. "I shouldn't have lost my temper last night. That isn't like me."

"No," she rushed to say on the heel of his words. "I deserved it. I shouldn't have asked—"

"It's not like I haven't wondered why not me—here, come in. Sorry." He realized she was still standing in the open doorway and waved her inside, shutting the door behind her and moving to the kitchen. "You want something to drink?"

"No, I—Yeah, sure. I guess."

George was already reaching for glasses, and he froze with the cabinet door open. "Are you sure? You don't have to..."

"No, I know, I want one." She stood awkwardly in the middle of his living room instead of making herself at home. No throwing herself on the couch like she belonged there.

Picking up on the mood, Duke moved from George to Charlotte and back, not sure where to settle.

George grabbed the glasses and shut the cabinet. "You hit

a nerve, but it wasn't your fault, and I shouldn't have gone off like that," he said as he filled both glasses with overly generous pours of wine. "I know—intellectually—that I'm *enough*, you know."

"Of course you are—"

He didn't let her get started with the friendly reassurances. "I just get frustrated sometimes. You see people who have what you want, and you think, why not me, right?"

"Yes, exactly—"

"And there's this nagging little voice deep down that you don't want to listen to, but sometimes you can't help but hear it telling you that it's you. That no one wants what you have to offer."

"George—"

"No. You don't have to say anything," he insisted, crossing to the living room and handing her the full glass. "I just wanted to explain why I went off like that. It wasn't you. It was that voice in my head telling me I'm single because I'm not good enough."

"George," she said fervently. "You are the *best* guy I know. You're the biggest catch in all of Pine Hollow and probably all of Vermont, and I was only asking my stupid, *stupid* question because it feels like one of the great injustices of the universe that you don't have everything you want."

And yet she didn't want him.

But somehow that realization didn't sting as much as it used to. It was a dull, familiar refrain now, without any of its previous bite. He smiled and sat on the couch so she would take the cue and relax as well. "Sometimes you remind me so much of my sisters it's scary."

"Right. Your sisters." Charlotte sank down to perch on the

edge of the couch cushion, still looking far from comfortable. Duke sat on the floor beside her, leaning his shoulder against her knee. She didn't even reach down to pet him, both hands wrapped around the wineglass she hadn't drunk from yet.

George kept talking, trying to reassure her that everything was normal with words, and his standard-issue steady calm. "They also can't figure out why I'm still single. They want to set me up on some dating app where your friends and family pick the person for you. I'm not sure why they think that would be any more effective than what I've been doing, but I know they only want to help. Like you."

~

Charlotte opened her mouth, but no words came out.

She'd come here with a plan. She'd dressed up like she was going on a date, only resisting the urge to put on a cocktail dress because that seemed a little formal for hanging out in his apartment. She'd psyched herself up to take things in a romantic direction, to tell him that she had feelings for him. Feelings she wasn't even sure she knew how to define but she wanted him to help her define them—

But then she'd arrived and he'd started apologizing, and she'd tried to stop him from apologizing but he kept talking, and when she'd finally told him he was *everything*, he'd said she reminded him of his sisters. Which was not the vibe she was going for with the makeup and the clingy red sweater, though she was probably being overly sensitive. She felt like an exposed nerve.

Then he'd started talking about his sisters setting him up and the idea that they might be able to, that they might introduce him to someone else, had sent a twinge of actual panic up her spine.

Yes, she'd tried to set him up too, but if she was honest with herself, she'd never even wanted to. Because she wanted him for herself.

She'd thought she only wanted him for herself platonically, but the longer she looked at him, sitting across from her, his leanly muscled body, his smile, his *hands*—why had she never noticed how much she loved his hands before now? Why was she such an idiot that she'd completely missed how incredible he was?

"Charles?" George prompted gently when she was silent too long. "You okay?"

"I don't want them to set you up," Charlotte blurted.

George smiled, teasing and light. "Because no one can do as good a job of it as you can?"

"I came here to tell you something," she announced.

George sobered, nodding. "There's actually something I need to tell you too."

"Me first," she insisted. The words were bubbling up inside her now, everything she'd been practicing saying as she put on her makeup and tried on three different outfits.

"Okay." George's eyes were so open. Like there was nothing she couldn't tell him.

So she told him.

"It's been really good for me. Being single. These last few months." He nodded and she went on, the words starting to run together as she built momentum. "I thought I was so happy because I wasn't trying to be something for someone else or put on a show. I've had a lot of for-show relationships. We'd go places, and my boyfriend's friends would talk about how crazy he was about me and how perfect we were together—but that was just how it looked on the outside. Inside my relationship it would feel different, it would feel like I wasn't there yet, like I needed to do more, be more for him, and if I could just be enough then we'd get past this imaginary threshold in my head and we'd all live happily ever after like they do in the books. Like my parents did. And then I would *feel* like I was the center of his world."

She swallowed thickly, willing him to understand. "I was always chasing that feeling. And I hated that Elinor didn't believe the for-show version of who I was in those relationships, because then I couldn't believe it, you know? And I wanted to believe it so badly. I tried so hard, but I was picking all the wrong guys. I thought if I was nervous around him and I felt like I had to *earn* something from him, then when he decided he loved me it would prove something about me. I'd be good enough. But it was exhausting."

She hadn't meant to blurt all that out. She'd only meant to say she'd been happy with him, but now that she'd started she didn't seem to have control of her words anymore. Charlotte met George's understanding eyes and kept going down the rabbit hole.

"I was always tired when I got home from dates or spending time with my exes. I'd been working so hard to put on the show, to make them like me, to be what *they* needed—and I'd be drained. That was what I was used to. It was what I thought dating was. So when you and I started hanging out and it was easy with you and I was never tired afterward, because I wasn't trying to be anything else and we could just recharge together—I didn't recognize that."

A slight frown pulled between his eyebrows.

Charlotte swallowed a sudden bolt of nerves, and forged on. "It wasn't fair to you. I haven't been fair to you…You went with me to meet my dad's girlfriend just because you knew I was nervous. None of the Darcys would've ever done that."

The ice machine thudded off, leaving a sudden silence in its wake.

"Kendall told me I was using you for platonic dating," Charlotte confessed, "and I have been, and that wasn't right. You deserve…" Her throat closed, and she forced herself to take a breath. "You're so great—and I told myself you didn't really mean it when you asked me out and you liked being friends and this was all you wanted, so I didn't have to think about what *I* wanted…"

George was fully frowning now, his wine forgotten in his hand.

"I've been so happy, these last few months. And I told myself it was because I needed to be single. Because I needed to swear off men and get a dog…" She met his eyes. "But I think it was you."

He still didn't move, and her heart felt like it was about to beat out of her chest.

"Maybe you don't…maybe, um…" God. Did he not feel the same way? Had she completely misread the situation? Why had she listened to Kendall and Magda telling her that he loved her? She was ruining everything—

"You mean as friends."

Charlotte jerked a little, startled by the sound of his voice, the rough tone of it. "What?"

"You're so happy because we're friends."

Charlotte stared at him, at the almost-angry challenge in

his eyes, the hard set of his jaw. George. Who never got angry with her.

She could just say yes.

She could chicken out. She could say she'd been so happy because of their friendship and nothing else. She could run and hide and be safe. She could retreat back to the safety of the Puppy Pact and pretend her entire speech had been about why she valued their friendship...

Except she couldn't do that.

Not to George. And not to herself. If there was even the slightest chance that he felt for her the way she felt for him, she had to know. She had to drop a grenade in the middle of their friendship and deal with the fallout.

"No," she breathed. "Not as friends."

His frown didn't clear. If anything it got darker. And her heart tried to escape her chest up her throat.

He set down his wine and stood suddenly—and she did as well, not sure whether she was moving to meet him or running toward the door until she was on her feet. And her feet were moving toward him.

It wasn't far, the distance between them. And then he was standing right in front of her, somehow taller and stronger than all her memories of safe, comfortable George, but still *George*.

He lifted his hands to her face, his fingers slipping into her hair as his eyes searched hers. "Are you sure?"

No. She was terrified. But she'd never wanted anything so much. "Do you think you could kiss me?" she whispered.

A flare of heat fired in his eyes a fraction of a second before he lowered his head. Eagerly, she went up on her tiptoes—and was suddenly off balance in her high-heeled boots, tipping forward. Charlotte squeaked, catching herself against George's chest.

He chuckled, curving an arm around her to steady her against him. "Shall we try that again?"

With anyone else she would be mortified. With George, it somehow made the moment better. All her nerves and her worries that they wouldn't fit, that it wouldn't be good, they all dissolved into the glint in his eyes and the heat on her cheeks.

Then his lips brushed hers, her lashes fluttered closed—and she almost shoved him away as all the fears came rushing back.

This was *George*. What if this ruined everything? There was no going back now and that was *terrifying*.

His lips coaxed hers, tentative and sweet. He was a good kisser.

And he might as well have been kissing a two-by-four.

He lifted his head after a moment. "Is this okay?"

At least he noticed she wasn't with him. That was a plus, right? "I'm freaking out," she confessed.

"Okay." He started to pull away and she clutched at his arms, her nails digging into his shirt.

"No, I'm sorry."

"Charlotte, we don't have to—"

Oh God, now he was calling her Charlotte. She was supposed to be Charles. It was supposed to be playful and easy. "I'm ruining this," she groaned.

Everything in his body was leaning away from her, even though his arms were still around her. "I don't want you to force yourself."

"George, that isn't what's happening. I just…" She

sucked in a breath and stared straight into his eyes, willing him to see the truth. "You matter more than anyone I've ever kissed." His arms tightened minutely around her, more a flinch than a conscious movement. "And what if it isn't what you thought it would be? What if you had this vision of how it would be with me and it isn't, and then you don't know how to tell me because you don't want to upset me and you always give me what I want—and what if you don't even want to kiss me, but you're only doing it because you think *I* want to kiss *you*—"

His lips crashed down on hers, stealing the rest of her words and slamming a lid over her panic. One hand thrust into her hair, holding her in place. He wasn't tentative now. There was nothing questioning or cautious—and her fears flew away as her hands tightened on the firm, familiar muscles of his shoulders.

This was *George*. And it was *hot*.

His teeth nipped at her lower lip, tugging gently, and a jolt of liquid heat shot straight down to her core. Charlotte made a low, needy sound in her throat and pressed closer. She stretched onto her tiptoes, trying for more contact, more *everything*, and his arms were instantly there, lifting her. She wrapped her legs around his hips, the kiss deepening, until it swallowed up all her thoughts, all her sensations, her existence defined by the stroke of his tongue against hers.

He spun them around—the world seeming to fly in all directions—until her back settled firmly against the wall and he settled firmly against her front, and it was like a lock clicking into place. And she needed *more*. She'd never known it was possible to want like this, for it to feel this *right*—

Until Duke barked at them.

George lifted his head, his pupils so large his eyes looked nearly black. "He's probably wondering what the hell we're doing." His voice was gravel.

"I'm wondering why the hell we haven't been doing this all along," Charlotte replied, her own voice throatier than she'd ever heard it.

George didn't seem to mind. His eyes grew darker, and his smile more wicked.

It was almost too much, too real. "To think it all began over puppy poop," she murmured, trying to lighten the moment.

George's eyes went darker still. "That isn't where it began," he growled.

A thrill shot through her at the possessive edge to the words. She knew exactly what he meant. It felt like this thing between them had stretched out forever—impossible to mark the exact moment it had started.

And she needed to know where it would go. She needed to chase this tension to its destination. Even if it was rash and impulsive. Even if they were rushing in. She wanted to be reckless. To feel the thrill of it racing through her. The thrill of him.

"Bedroom?" she requested.

George hitched her up higher, both of them catching their breath at the contact, and she locked her ankles at the small of his back, holding on tight, not letting go for a second as he navigated them through the small apartment. He shut Duke out of the bedroom, and Charlotte tuned out the whine of protest from the dog—the only thing that mattered in her world at this moment was George.

The feel of him. The taste of him. And the perfect reckless rush of chasing each sensation into the next.

Chapter Twenty-Seven

Why not seize pleasure at once? How often is happiness destroyed by preparation, foolish preparation!

—*Emma*, Jane Austen

I slept with George."

"That was fast." Kendall's voice came through the phone without missing a beat. "Was it awful?"

"Why would you assume it was awful?" Charlotte demanded, walking quickly across the courtyard toward the stairs to her apartment.

"Basic deductive reasoning? You texted Mags and me to wish you luck because you were going over to talk to him at eight. It's currently ten-thirty. If he was any good, you'd be spending the night."

"I left Bingley at my place," Charlotte explained, defending George's honor. "I need to take him out one more time before bed. George is going to meet me at the greenspace with Duke, and then we're going to come back to my place after."

Kendall hummed knowingly. "So this is an illicit best friend check-in during the break between bouts of wild monkey sex. Gotcha."

Charlotte glared at her phone. "I don't know why I called you." She would have called Magda—who was always the more empathetic of her friends—but it was late, and Magda woke up so early. She didn't want to wake her up for a worry that felt so... vague. And vulnerable.

"I don't either," Kendall replied cheerfully. "If it were me, I'd be conserving my energy for the sex. So what's up?"

"Nothing's up." She unlocked the door to her apartment and cooed a greeting to Bingley, who immediately began wriggling in delight in his crate. "Hi, baby."

"I take it that's Bingley and not George." Kendall paused while Charlotte grabbed the leash and petted Bingley hello, but she'd never been known for her patience. "So you and George talked, the sex was good enough for a sleepover... What's wrong?"

"Nothing's wrong," Charlotte insisted, clipping on Bingley's leash—but not immediately moving toward the door and the greenspace where George would be waiting with Duke, even as Bingley tried to drag her in that direction.

"Then why the stealth call the second you got away from him? C'mon, Char." Kendall paused, and when she spoke again her voice was uncharacteristically gentle. "Are you regretting it?"

"No. Of course not. I just..."

She was scared.

But she didn't know of what. Scared that it was too good to be true? Scared that it was too real? Scared that she couldn't trust it?

She hadn't been scared when she was with him, when they'd been cuddling and planning where to spend the night and everything had felt warm and perfect and lovely. It was only when the door to his apartment had clicked closed behind her that her nerves had kicked in. She felt…exposed. In a way she wasn't used to feeling after sex. She usually felt powerful, buzzy and energized—and she did feel that, just, this anxious *softness* too.

"So you guys are, like, together now?" Kendall asked.

Charlotte didn't have an answer to that either. "Yes?"

"Is that a question?"

"We haven't exactly defined our relationship. We've been dating for like fifteen seconds."

"Okay." She could hear Kendall moving, the clink of ice. "So maybe you go meet up with George, and you define it. Or you don't. Not everything has to have a label. Especially when it's new. Maybe try turning off that big brain of yours and living in the moment."

"Just go with it." Skepticism coated her words.

"Not one of your strengths, I know. But maybe try it on for the night. Go with the flow. And then meet Mags and me for lunch on Monday and tell us everything."

"Monday?"

"I figured you guys wouldn't want to interrupt round one of your sexual marathon until you have to for work."

Her face heated. She'd never been embarrassed talking about her sexscapades with Magda and Kendall before. They were a part of her. Telling them things felt like telling herself. But George was different…It felt more private. Or maybe it was only that she was scared talking about it too much would jinx it. Make it go up in smoke.

"What if I ruin it, Kendall?" Charlotte asked, her biggest fear poking through.

"You won't. Just relax."

"What if he doesn't want me now that he has me?" That had happened so many times. The Darcys had loved the chase so much more than they'd ever loved her. "You said yourself he's been in love with me for a while—what if the idea of being with me was just some fantasy and he doesn't like the reality?"

"Then he's an idiot," Kendall declared. "But I don't think he's an idiot."

Bingley whined at the door. "I've gotta go. Bingley needs to go out."

"Go," Kendall commanded. "Have fun."

"Thanks."

"Hey, Charlotte?" Kendall said before she could disconnect the call.

"Yeah?"

"You deserve this, you know? You deserve to be happy."

Her throat tightened. She didn't know why those words should be so hard to hear. "Thanks. Love you."

"Yeah, yeah. Now go break your headboard."

Charlotte snorted a laugh as she disconnected the call—trust Kendall to retreat from the mushy love stuff—but also to be exactly what she needed.

She took a deep breath, pocketed her phone, and opened the door for Bingley.

~

The universe had a sick sense of humor. The sonofabitch waited until he'd mentally committed to moving back to Colorado—even applying for jobs there—and then it had thrown the mother of all monkey wrenches at his heart.

The metaphor didn't make sense, but George wasn't feeling very logical at the moment. He stood on the greenspace behind the complex, waiting for Charlotte and watching Duke sniff the solar panels.

Tonight had been unexpected, to say the least.

She'd told him she was happy with him—which was good. She'd told him she didn't want to just be friends—which was *very* good. And they'd gone a little crazy, rushing from first kiss to multiple orgasms—which had been fricking amazing.

His stupid heart wanted to race straight from there to happily-ever-after—but they hadn't even been together one night, and Charlotte hadn't said anything about the future. He couldn't let himself get carried away.

And then there was Beks.

She needed him, and he wanted to be there for her. He'd promised. How could he turn around and stay in Pine Hollow now? Especially when he didn't even know if that was what Charlotte wanted. She'd said she didn't see him as a friend, but that didn't necessarily mean forever.

And either way he had to find a job.

His life had suddenly gotten a lot more complicated. But he couldn't regret it. His muscles felt loose with a relaxation that was born out of contentment as much as multiple orgasms. Tonight had felt like he was finally getting that lightning.

He needed to talk to Charlotte, to make sure they were on the same page, but it was still so new. He didn't want to kill this fledgling thing between them with too many questions.

She'd said it wasn't *fair to him* at one point, and his brain kept snagging on that phrase, replaying it. Had she only slept with him because she felt like she *owed* him something? So it would be *fair*? The thought turned his stomach, but he didn't think that was the case.

She'd been enthusiastic in her consent every step of the way—but they'd moved fast. Too fast? It had felt like this tension was building up inside him for months and it had finally been released—but if she'd *just* decided she wanted him, it must have felt sudden.

And yes, her foot had been on the accelerator even more than his had, but he didn't know why. Because she wanted him? Or because she just wanted him to stay and this was what it would take?

He saw her across the complex, moving toward him with Bingley, and felt his spine straighten instinctively at the sight, everything in him pulling him toward her.

She wasn't smiling, but there was something almost hopeful on her face. Nervous anticipation?

"Hey," he said softly, as she and Bingley came into range.

"Hey," she replied as she stopped in front of him, her voice breathy, with a hint of a question.

The impulse to put her at ease was too strong to resist. George felt himself smiling self-deprecatingly. "So that happened."

She laughed—the sound more relieved than entertained. "We did kind of jump in with both feet, didn't we?"

"No half measures." He met her eyes. "Do you want to talk about..."

"We don't need to define it, right?" The words rushed out. "We can just play it by ear."

Disappointment shafted through him, but he shoved aside the feeling. Of course she wasn't ready to rush straight to happily-ever-after. "Yeah," he assured her, keeping the slight, easy smile on his face. "Absolutely."

Maybe it wouldn't be so hard to move back to Colorado after all. If this was just a summer fling…

"Just go with it," she reiterated.

"That sounds perfect," he agreed. Because he always wanted to give her what she wanted, even when that wasn't forever with him.

It was too soon to think that way, anyway. Too soon to start changing his life around, or even think about with-drawing the job applications in Colorado.

Charlotte took a small step toward him. "You still want to sleep over?"

He wanted to grab her and kiss her, but he contented himself with taking her hand, rubbing his thumb over the soft skin on the back of her wrist. "I'd like that. If that's what you want?"

She met his eyes, something teasing and confident *finally* reentering hers, centering him, making him feel like himself again. "I'm not done with you yet, George Leneghan."

Thank God.

Now all he had to do was figure out how to salvage his heart on the day when she decided she *was* done with him. Because he had a feeling that before long it was going to be entirely hers—and he wasn't sure he was going to get it back in one piece.

Chapter Twenty-Eight

I have no talent for certainty.
—*Mansfield Park*, Jane Austen

One week later, George found himself fixating on Charlotte's hand resting on the gearshift of her car. To hold or not to hold, that was the question—and he had a sudden affinity with Hamlet because he couldn't make up his damn mind.

They were headed to Summer Movies in the Square—their first time together in public since That Night—and even though they'd spent several nights together in the last week, he didn't know if they'd reached the casual-handholding-in-public stage yet.

They hadn't defined their relationship, still playing things by ear. Though once the town realized they were together, their relationship was going to get defined for them, whether they wanted it or not, so maybe he shouldn't hold her hand tonight.

Charlotte seemed cheerfully oblivious to the implications of their first public appearance as a...a what? A couple? A summer fling? Friends who slept together?

Duke rode in the back seat with his head out the window and his tongue hanging out the side of his mouth, while Bingley stretched his nose desperately toward the cracked window on his side, still too small to reach it.

George hadn't applied for any more jobs, either here or in Colorado. He'd wanted to see how things played out. Give it a little time. He still felt like he needed to go to Colorado for Beks if there was no future for him here, but he didn't want to put pressure on Charlotte to decide whether she wanted a future with him.

Another Hamlet question—to go or not to go.

He'd talked to Beks a couple times this week. She hadn't been thrilled to hear he was seeing Charlotte, though he'd assured her it was just casual. Beks still hadn't confronted Scott about the text messages. George wanted to tell her to rip the Band-Aid off, that the truth wasn't going to change as she waited and dithered—but he wasn't exactly one to throw stones about dithering at the moment.

"Here we are!" Charlotte parked not far from the square and hopped out to release the dogs and get the picnic gear from the back. George moved more slowly to follow her.

He'd thought that as soon as she kissed him everything would change, like the end of a rom-com where once they both admitted they wanted one another everything was resolved and they lived happily ever after. Tom Hanks kissed Meg Ryan and the hard part was over—he hadn't even had to kiss her in *Sleepless in Seattle*. Just take her hand. And here George was, overthinking whether he was supposed to be holding Charlotte's hand in public.

In the end, all his mental gymnastics were for nothing.

Charlotte loaded him up with two folding chairs and a

cooler, taking a backpack and a picnic basket for herself. With each of them wrangling a leash as well, there were no hands left over to hold.

She bounced a little, beaming at him. "Let me know if you see a good spot," she said, leading the way toward the square, where a large screen had been set up in front of the bandstand.

She wove through the groups already claiming their places around the square, calling out greetings to various townspeople. Bingley zigged and zagged in every direction, nearly tripping her in his eagerness to see everything.

It was still hours before the movie was due to start. The sun was high in the sky, and the show couldn't start rolling until after dark, but the summer movies were a whole event in Pine Hollow, and the square was already packed with people picnicking.

Mostly couples.

Picnic blankets and cuddling seemed to be everywhere he looked.

Though that made sense. The movie tonight was *Casablanca*. Inherently romantic. Charlotte wouldn't have suggested attending if they weren't going public as a couple, would she?

One of her sisters called out to her, and Charlotte lifted a hand in a wave but didn't head toward her family. The Rodriguez crew had set up in the shade of a tree with their dogs—Elinor and Levi, Anne and Bailey, and Charlotte's dad and his girlfriend.

It looked like a couples retreat.

"We aren't sitting with your family?"

"Hmm?" Charlotte mumbled absently, her gaze still

scanning the green for the perfect spot. "Oh, no. Dory gets Bingley so wound up. He'd be a monster all night."

The little golden was four months old now, and still an adorable fluffball, but one with a lot more energy and a *lot* of curiosity. Charlotte had been working with him on his training, but he was still a baby, and it was a work in progress.

"I'm hoping he'll settle down for the movie. He's usually pretty worn out after his training class," she said, continuing to search with a little frown on her face.

"Are you looking for Kendall and Magda?"

If they sat in a group with her friends, he'd have his answer about what kind of vibe they were supposed to be giving off for the town.

Charlotte shook her head. "Kendall might make it for the movie, but she had some work to finish up, so she's gonna skip the pre-movie picnic today. And Mags said she didn't want to get eaten by bugs to watch a movie she's seen a million times—speaking of, there's bug spray in the cooler—don't drink it."

"You put bug spray in the cooler?"

She shrugged. "It was where there was room. Bingley's treats took up way more space than I planned in the backpack."

George glanced at the bag slung over Charlotte's shoulder—it did seem to be straining at the seams.

"Don't worry—there's also wine chilling in there," she assured him, nodding toward the cooler in his hands.

Wine was a good sign, right? And if she wasn't looking for her friends, maybe she was looking for the perfect space where they could be alone...

"Oh, there's Vivian Weisman!" Charlotte declared, doing her best to wave with her arms full. "We should see if she wants company."

Charlotte took off, making a beeline toward the elegant, silver-haired woman from the Estates, sitting alone and reading a book as she waited for the movie to start.

Vivian Weisman. The only person in the entire green sitting by herself. Who they both knew in a professional capacity—so no one would think anything of them sitting together if they were both sitting with her.

Looks like he had his answer.

Charlotte had just found them a chaperone.

~

George was being weird.

Charlotte had been jittery about making their Pine Hollow debut as a couple. This last week had been lovely, just the two of them holed up in his condo or hers, enjoying being together. Kendall and Mags knew, of course, and she'd told her sisters that she was spending more time with George, but once they went Pine Hollow Public the news would spread like wildfire, and the entire town would know by morning. They might even be an item in the next town newsletter.

It wasn't that she didn't want people to know. She did, which was why she'd picked *Casablanca* as their first public date, but ever since they'd arrived at the square, something had been off.

She'd been looking for the perfect place to set up when she spotted Vivian Weisman sitting by herself. As someone who hated being alone, Charlotte hadn't been able to stand the idea of walking away from Vivian if she wanted company. But as soon as she and George joined the older woman, he'd started acting strangely.

Charlotte was used to the men she dated acting differently in public, but usually they were *more* affectionate, playing the part of the perfect boyfriend to enhance their own image—but George was acting *less* like he wanted her.

It was like he'd gone into Super Friend Mode.

He struck up a conversation with Vivian, chatting with her about the book she'd been reading—and Charlotte realized that George must be the physical therapist who had been slipping Vivian romance novels—then he spotted Mac and excused himself to go laugh with the diner owner across the square. When he returned, he brought Mac and Howard Fullerton with him—and volunteered to run back to the car to get more collapsible camp chairs so they could all sit together.

Since Howard seemed *extremely* interested in taking him up on the offer and Vivian blushed every time Howard looked at her, Charlotte certainly didn't mind the additions to their party, but she would have felt better about it if she hadn't had the creeping suspicion that George didn't want people to know they were together.

Charlotte loved big groups. She loved making everyone feel warm and included, and she *loved* matchmaking. She should have been in heaven.

Vivian might say she wasn't looking for romance, but Charlotte had literally never seen her without a romance novel close at hand, so she couldn't be *entirely* opposed to the idea of happily-ever-afters. And from the way Howard was smiling at her as he leaned on his cane, he was very interested in being her prospective love interest.

George and Mac headed off to get the chairs, and Charlotte popped out of hers. "Howard, why don't you take my chair? I'm gonna walk the dogs before the movie starts. Why don't you two open the wine? I brought way too much for just George and me."

Howard didn't have to be asked twice to take the seat next to Vivian. Charlotte left the two of them chatting about their favorite varietals and took Bing and Duke on a circuit around the edge of the square, giving herself a little pep talk about not being paranoid.

When she returned, George was back with the extra chairs, and Mac was nowhere in sight. Charlotte internally perked up at the double-date feeling of it, taking the seat next to George. His hands were busy unpacking all the food she'd brought—and keeping Bingley from stealing any of it—so she didn't think anything of the fact that he wasn't being overly physically affectionate.

Until Kendall arrived and he practically levitated out of his chair.

"Here! Kendall, take this one," he insisted, pointing her friend toward his chair next to Charlotte, and moving to the one that had been set up on the other side of Vivian and Howard.

Charlotte opened her mouth to protest, but no words came out.

Kendall flopped down next to her with an exhausted sigh. "Wine me," she demanded, and Charlotte focused on filling a cup.

"You okay?" Kendall asked as she accepted the wine.

"Yeah, of course. Why?"

"You're quiet. You're rarely quiet."

"I'm just being paranoid," Charlotte said, inadvertently glancing over at George.

Kendall followed her gaze, a little frown pulling at her brow. "Trouble in paradise?"

"No. Just forget it."

Kendall lifted her eyebrows, but didn't push. "Okay."

Charlotte was trying to take Kendall's advice from last week, trying not to overthink things, to play it by ear—but that wasn't really her natural state. Charlotte overthought *everything*. And her brain kept swirling with doubts as dusk grew heavy around them and the start of the movie grew closer.

Mac came back, bringing more townspeople with him and turning their little cluster into a party. Charlotte put on her brightest, most effervescent smile, playing the perfect hostess. She smashed all her insecurities down beneath sparkling energy and a desire to make everything fun and light and perfect.

Because putting on a good show was what she did when she was afraid she wasn't wanted.

She'd just never thought she would feel that way with George.

He wasn't ignoring her. There was nothing pointed. But he stayed on the other side of the group—even as the screen lit and the entire green cheered the first flickering shots of *Casablanca*.

Around the square couples cuddled, and she couldn't even see his face.

Charlotte tried to focus on the movie. Vivian and Howard bent their heads together, whispering through the familiar scenes, and Kendall made periodic anti-romance comments under her breath. The evening wasn't *bad*. It just wasn't at all what Charlotte had been envisioning. The dissonance between what she had wanted it to be and what it was kept her from being able to enjoy herself.

This always happened. It was her expectations that got her into trouble. Wanting things that weren't there.

By the time Bogey was telling Bergman that what he wanted didn't amount to a hill of beans, Charlotte had nearly convinced herself that she didn't care if she and George went public.

As soon as the credits rolled and applause rippled through the square, Kendall surged to her feet. Bingley and Duke perked up at the movement, and Kendall grabbed the leashes, shoving one at Charlotte.

"Come on," Kendall said in a tone that was more command than request. "Let's see if the dogs need to pee before you take them home."

"I can take Duke," George started to offer, but Kendall waved him away.

"We've got this." She linked her arm with Charlotte's, nearly dragging her away from the small cluster of chairs and picnic blanket they'd set up. Around the square, the townspeople began gathering up their things.

Charlotte looked behind her, but other than a frown, George had no reaction as he moved to help Vivian and Howard.

"Okay, what's going on?" Kendall demanded when they were out of earshot. "Are you guys dating or what?"

Frustration sharpened Charlotte's tone. "How would I know? You're the one who told me to play it by ear."

"I didn't *tell* you to do anything," Kendall argued, stopping beneath a big oak tree. "I was just trying to get you out of your head when you were spiraling. Are you saying you haven't talked to him about what he wants?"

Charlotte gave her a look. "We talk about what we want."

Kendall rolled her eyes. "Outside of the bedroom."

At that, Charlotte couldn't hold Kendall's gaze, turning her attention instead to the dogs, where they were sniffing for good spots to do their business. "I don't want to screw it up. I always push too fast. This was probably too soon to go public."

"Honey." Kendall groaned. "You always do this when you like a guy. With everyone else in your life, if you have any issues, you can't blurt them out fast enough, but the second things get romantic, you get all cagey and weird. Like the more you like someone, the more you hold yourself back."

"I'm not the one who's being cagey and weird. He's avoided me all night. Ever since we got to the square. It's like he doesn't want to be seen with me."

"I know it's a novel concept, but you could always ask him why."

"I can't. What if—"

"Stop. No what if. No overthinking things. Just *ask* him."

"Ask me what?"

Chapter Twenty-Nine

If I could but know his heart, everything
would become easy.
—*Sense and Sensibility*, Jane Austen

Charlotte whirled toward the sound of George's voice, her heart suddenly racing.

"I think that's my cue," Kendall drawled. She handed Duke's leash to Charlotte, who took it with numb fingers, all her focus locked on George. "G'night, you two," Kendall singsonged while walking toward the edge of the square.

"I finished packing up, and Howard and Vivian just left," George said. "They said to tell you good night."

He reached for the leash, taking it well below where her hand wrapped around the leather, so he wouldn't have to touch her.

Anxiety spiked again. He was going to break up with her. That was how this felt. That tenuous, awful feeling when she needed desperately to make things better because he was pulling away.

But instead of her usual need to be perfect, to pretend nothing was wrong and prove that she was worthy so he wouldn't leave her, she heard herself blurting out, "Are you mad at me?"

George's chin reared back, surprise flashing across his face. "What?"

"You haven't touched me all night."

He frowned, his brows drawing downward. "I thought—isn't that what you wanted? This town is made of gossip—you seemed like you didn't want people to know we were together."

Charlotte's chin jerked back. "You thought *I* didn't want to go public? I brought you. I suggested this."

"And as soon as we showed up you zeroed in on the only single person in the square like we needed a chaperone so people wouldn't get the wrong idea. Someone to use as a buffer. There were couples everywhere, and you went straight for Vivian."

"Because I didn't want her to be alone!" She realized she was raising her voice and glanced around. The green was thinning out, but it wasn't empty yet, and they were drawing curious looks. She lowered her voice. "I wasn't trying to avoid people thinking we're together. I just didn't want her to feel like no one cared. I hate being alone, and I didn't want her to feel that. But then you were so focused on her and running off to talk to Mac and bringing back Howard—which was brilliant, by the way. He clearly has a thing for Vivian, and it seems like they needed a little push, so I'm glad you did that, but it felt like you were avoiding me—and then when Kendall showed up, it was like you couldn't get away from me fast enough. And yes, she's my friend and I love her, and I'm sure you were being considerate or whatever, but I just wanted to be with you."

"You did?"

"Are you seriously questioning that? George. I *always* want to be with you."

She always asked for too much. She'd been trying not to drown him in her wants, but she never imagined for a second he thought she didn't want him.

"Really?"

"Foolish man."

She closed the distance between them—not overthinking, because at the moment she wasn't thinking at all.

Her hand curled into his shirt, yanking him close as she went up on her tiptoes and pressed her lips to his. She knew the taste of him now, the feel of him, but her heart raced as if it was the first time. His arms closed around her, and she felt the anxious tension of the night melt away as she sank deeper into the kiss.

God, he felt good.

If she'd ever worried that they wouldn't have chemistry, she'd been a total idiot. Electricity zipped across her nerve endings with every feather-light stroke of his thumb against the small of her back, where it had slipped beneath her shirt. His tongue gently stroked her lower lip, and she met him with the tease of her own tongue.

Only the crash of something falling over next to the bandstand jarred them back to reality.

They broke apart, both a little out of breath. George's warm brown eyes looked into hers, his thumb still absently brushing the small of her back and sending shivers up and down her spine. After a moment, his dimple flashed and he murmured, "I guess we've gone public."

"I guess so." She bit her lower lip. "Is that okay?"

"I didn't know if you wanted..."

She spoke before he could finish the words. "I was trying not to put pressure on you."

He groaned, laughing at himself. "I was trying not to put pressure on *you*. Play it by ear, like you said."

"I don't even know what I meant by that."

His eyes were so close to hers. So warm. "So we're together?" he murmured, that thumb driving her slowly crazy. "Officially."

"I'd like that," she whispered, forcing herself to be brave, to ask for what she wanted and not give in to the fear that it was going to be taken away from her the second she admitted she needed it.

It was dark in the square, but she could swear his eyes grew even darker. "Me too."

Her heart probably would have melted right into a pool of liquid happiness if Bingley hadn't chosen that moment to bark his adorable little puppy yap.

George pulled back slightly, his hand slipping from beneath the back of her top to brace her hip.

She'd completely lost track of what the dogs were doing while she was making out with George in the middle of the green. They both looked down to find Duke lying on his side, eyeing Bingley with put-upon patience as the puppy climbed all over him.

"We should get them home," she said.

"Yeah." George gave her hip one last squeeze before he stepped back, taking all his lovely warmth with him. "You want to load the dogs while I get the chairs?"

"Sure," Charlotte agreed, sinking back to reality as he handed her Duke's leash.

But right as her hand closed over the leather, George shifted his grip, catching her hand instead of the leash and tugging her toward him. He pressed his lips against hers, a quick surprise of a kiss that made her smile against his mouth and whisked her right back into the giddy perfection of the moment.

"Just marking my place," he murmured, his dimple winking down at her—and Charlotte felt like she could float right off the ground.

"I wouldn't want you to get lost."

He grinned and turned to gather the chairs, but Charlotte stopped him with an impulsive question. "How do you feel about teas?"

George cocked his head. "Like the beverage or the shirts?"

"The beverage—but more as an event. Anne hosts this fancy Jane Austen Tea at the Bluebell every year. You wouldn't want to go, would you?"

She'd wanted to ask him before, but it was still three weeks away, and that hadn't felt very playing-it-by-ear. She'd been trying not to ask for too much too fast and ruin this. But this was George. She had to keep reminding herself of that.

He met her eyes. "I'd love to. Is this a costume thing?"

"Costumes encouraged but not required." She caught her lip. "Are you sure? It's kind of silly—"

"Charles. I've read every Austen novel. I'd love to."

That air balloon of happiness was back. The one that threatened to lift her off the ground. "Great."

She needed to keep her feet on the ground. She needed to not get sucked back into all her bad dating habits. But right now…Right now, floating felt pretty amazing.

Chapter Thirty

A general spirit of ease and enjoyment seemed diffused, and they all stood about and talked and laughed, and every moment had its pleasure and its hope.

—*Mansfield Park*, Jane Austen

The parlor of the Bluebell Inn looked exquisite, like they'd stepped back in time—if you didn't notice the glossy lamination on all the Jane Austen quotes propped up on stands around the room. Anne and Bailey had outdone themselves...and they weren't the only ones.

Charlotte couldn't seem to stop grinning every time she looked at George. The man looked *good* in Regency wear. He'd driven all the way to Burlington to pick up a costume and, if not for the Clark Kent glasses, he could have doubled for Mr. Darcy. He'd even figured out how to tie a cravat.

She usually felt a messy tangle of things at the annual Jane Austen Tea—she'd smile and keep things fun and light, but the weekend of her mom's birthday was always an emotional minefield. But this year, her smile felt like it went past the surface and the reason for that was George.

These last few weeks had been *fun*, filled with hiking and Netflix binges and playing with the dogs—and great sex. They didn't talk about the future—as if they had an unspoken agreement not to rush this. She knew they'd have to talk about it eventually, but she loved this moment, when everything was new and shiny, and she wasn't ready for the honeymoon phase to end.

"I see you brought George," Elinor said as she sidled up to Charlotte at the pianoforte, lifting her delicate china cup for a sip. "And in costume, too."

Charlotte grinned, feeling like a true Austen character as her sister trolled for gossip in a great dress. "I can't believe you got Levi to come." He and George were on the other side of the parlor, in deep discussion with the town's former mayor, Delia.

"He wanted to," Elinor said. "He's been listening to all the Austen audiobooks—though sometimes I think he only reads them so he can provoke me. He keeps insisting they need more action sequences."

"I've often thought all *Persuasion* was lacking was a good chase scene," Charlotte drawled, just to rile Elinor.

"I'm not rising to the bait. I'm in too good a mood," Elinor said archly, sipping her tea. Over her teacup, she eyed Charlotte knowingly. "*You* seem to be in a good mood lately."

"Do I?" Charlotte smiled.

Elinor looked like she was dying to say something, finally blurting out in a rush, "You know I've been trying very hard not to meddle."

"And I appreciate it."

Charlotte had a tendency to meddle in everyone else's problems to avoid her own, but with Elinor it was more of a mother-hen reflex. She'd been the pseudo-mom figure in Charlotte's life for decades, but Elinor didn't always know how to turn off I-know-what's-best mode.

It was extra annoying because she was almost always right.

"I'm not trying to shove my nose in where it doesn't belong," Elinor said. "I just wanted to say, I really like George for you." Which was notable, since her oldest sister had never approved of a single one of her boyfriends. "You look really happy with him."

"I am," Charlotte agreed, which felt too good to be true.

Whenever she'd *looked* happy with someone in the past, it had been work. She'd been performing her smiles and paddling frantically beneath the surface to make it look natural and easy. This just *was*. And she wasn't sure she knew how to accept that it would stay that way.

"It's good to see," Elinor said. "You always seemed to have a disconnect between your experiential self and your narrative self before."

Charlotte eyed her oldest sister. "You just listened to a podcast about that, didn't you?"

"I did, but I really feel like it applies here."

"And I assume you're going to tell me about it."

"I don't have to."

Charlotte smothered a smile. "Tell me about the experiential self, Elinor." Last year the two of them had butted heads about Elinor's meddling, but now Charlotte found she didn't mind so much. She kind of missed Elinor in her business. Not a *lot*, but in a vaguely nostalgic way.

"Well, so, basically, the experiential self is your immediate self—what you feel in the moment. And your narrative self is the story you tell yourself when you look back on your day. And I always felt like your experiential self was miserable with those guys you used to date, but your narrative self kept insisting that you were blissfully happy and everything was perfect, even on days when you'd been miserable all day. And now they line up. Like you're happy *and* you're telling yourself you're happy."

Charlotte frowned. What Elinor said made sense in a way—she had been telling herself she was happy when she was miserable with those other relationships—but she wasn't so sure her experiential self and narrative self were lined up now either. It felt more like she'd taken her narrative self off-line, and she was only existing as an experiential self. Because she was scared to think too much about this feeling. Or the future.

"George is looking very Mr. Knightley today," Anne commented as she joined them.

Charlotte had come in costume, but Anne's pale pink outfit put hers to shame, and Anne's fiancée, Bailey, looked just as flawless in her white muslin dress. The two of them could have walked right off the set of a BBC miniseries.

"I always thought of him as more of a Bingley," Charlotte mused.

"Nope. Definitely Knightley," Elinor insisted. "There in the background quietly loving Emma all along when she was too oblivious to notice."

Charlotte frowned at her sister, something uneasy shifting inside her at the words. "That isn't..." she started to argue, but Anne had cocked her head.

"You are sort of an Emma."

Charlotte barely stopped herself from wincing. "Mom hated Emma."

"Which I never understood," Anne said. "It's a good book."

Charlotte grew quiet, thinking about their mom and the fact that she wasn't here for them to ask her why she'd had an irrational vendetta against Emma Woodhouse. Her sisters fell silent as well, all of them remembering the reason they'd picked this weekend for the Jane Austen Tea.

"I'm just glad you've found your Knightley," Elinor said finally. "I feel like Anne and Bailey are Bingley and Jane, and I have my Darcy." She gazed fondly across the room at Levi, who caught her eye and started toward them. He did indeed look very stern and proud, but Charlotte couldn't let that one go.

"He's not really a Darcy. More of a Wentworth. The whole carrying-a-torch-for-decades thing is very *Persuasion*."

"But Darcy does the heroically-saving-the-day-and-never-taking-credit-for-it bit. That's very Levi," Elinor argued.

"He could be both," Anne suggested.

"Not everyone is an Austen character," George said as he and Levi joined them.

All three sisters turned to frown at him and answered in unison, "Yes, they are."

George blinked. "Okay."

Levi clapped him on the shoulder. "Smart man to know when you're outnumbered." He slid his arm around Elinor.

George held up a hand in surrender. "I cede to the higher authority on all things Austen."

The conversation continued—but Charlotte was distracted, looking at George. He was at ease with her family in a way none of her exes ever had been. She'd been trying not to question or overthink things, but the comparison to Mr. Knightley kept bothering her.

Had George really loved her all along like Mr. Knightley loved Emma? Because something about that made her uneasy.

And Anne—always the intuitive one—seemed to know. When the others decided to investigate the tea sandwiches, Anne linked her arm with Charlotte's and asked her to "take a turn about the room."

Charlotte couldn't resist the chance to do such an Austen-approved activity and glided along at Anne's side. "Are you okay?" Anne asked softly, when they were out of earshot.

"Absolutely," Charlotte said, keeping her smile bright. "You look fantastic by the way. And the tea is gorgeous. You and Bailey did an amazing job—and I'm extremely jealous of your dresses."

Bailey had taken a seat at the pianoforte and was playing a classical piece from the Regency era. Anne glanced over at her as they walked, her smile tugging at Charlotte's heart. "Thank you." Then she turned her all-too-seeing gaze back to Charlotte. "Are you sure you're okay?"

"It's usually Elinor who worries about me."

"I do too. In my way." Anne studied her, her eyes gentle. "You just seem like you might be holding back."

Unease whispered through her. "I don't know what you mean."

"You usually throw yourself into things." Anne paused to regally nod at someone as they passed. Then, her voice light, she asked, "Did I ever tell you about the time I broke up with Bailey?"

"Wait, what?" Charlotte's head snapped toward Anne with a complete lack of Regency grace. "When did that happen?"

"Right when we first got together. We hadn't been dating long when I realized I was in love with her—and I also realized how much harder it would be if I got sick again. I kept thinking how that would hurt her, if we really let ourselves fall in love. We had talked about the cancer stuff before—but it was obvious to her it was in my past. I'd beaten it. But to me it was past, present, and future. It was this thing that felt like it was always going to be a part of me. I knew it could come back. I knew we might not have decades together. That I could be taken away at any time. So I broke up with her, thinking I was sparing us both."

"But you got back together."

"Yeah. After I cried a lot. I was so sure I'd done the right thing, but then I went and talked to Dad. About how he wouldn't have traded his time with Mom for anything. How you can't live your life trying not to get hurt without giving up the things that make life worth living. And I realized that I was giving up what I most wanted because I was scared it wouldn't last forever." Anne met her eyes. "I always admired you, did you know that? The way you went after things. How hungry you were. It was hard for me to want things like that. It takes a lot of courage to go after what you want when forever is never a guarantee. It's hard to really let people in when you know it can be taken away. But that's where the best stuff is. The stuff that's worth living for."

Anne's eyes went to George across the parlor.

It was easy to see what Anne was driving at. Charlotte hadn't been her usual all-in self. She'd been holding herself back—though she wasn't sure whether it was because she was afraid of pushing for too much and ruining it, or scared to let herself feel the big scary emotions.

"Just something to think about," her sister said softly.

But Charlotte wasn't sure she was as brave as Anne. And she wasn't sure she was ready to go all in. Especially this weekend. When everything felt a little more raw.

~

"So you're dating my little sister."

George paused in the act of filling a plate with tiny sandwiches when Elinor appeared at his side. He was a little surprised it had taken this long for her to seek him out.

"Is this when you tell me that you'll murder me and hide the body if I ever hurt her?"

"Of course not," Elinor said. "Levi will do it. He has all that law enforcement background, so he knows how to get away with it."

George smiled—though he wasn't entirely sure she was joking. "For the record, I have no intention of hurting her."

"I know," Elinor assured him. "And I love you two together. She seems really happy."

There seemed to be something hanging out there unsaid. "But?"

"I know it seems like Charlotte wears her heart on her sleeve—and she does, but not everything is on the surface. When her feelings get hurt or when she's sad, she can be secretive. She's always been that way, tucking everything inside.

She covers it up by being brash and loud, but she's the most sensitive of the three of us. So just... be careful, okay?"

"I will," he promised—feeling suddenly guilty for the job applications he hadn't told her about.

He hadn't talked about his possible move back to Colorado with Charlotte since the night of Elinor's party. He'd started putting in applications both in the Denver area and in Vermont—to keep his options open—but there had been more jobs to apply for in Denver. He was waiting to see what developed, waiting until he had some news before he talked to her, but maybe he should bring it up. Focusing on the present had started to feel like hiding from the future.

"And be extra careful this weekend," Elinor said, right when he was debating clearing the air with Charlotte tonight.

"She said she had plans."

"It's our mom's birthday tomorrow, and Charlotte's always had kind of a hard time with it. She usually goes off by herself. I just wanted to give you a heads-up."

"Thanks," George murmured.

But something about what Elinor had said didn't sit right with him.

Charlotte hated being alone. But she also didn't like showing people her less-than-perfect side. She never wanted to inflict herself on someone else when she was upset, but if he invited her, if he opened the door, she always walked through it.

Maybe tomorrow was different, but it continued to bug him for the rest of the day. Maybe she just needed someone to open the door.

Chapter Thirty-One

Her heart did whisper that he had done
it for her.
　　　　—*Pride and Prejudice*, Jane Austen

Sunday was awful.

Anniversaries and birthdays had always been hard for Charlotte. She tended to imbue days with meaning. Her therapist was fond of telling her that she created her own emotional obstacles—and yes, she probably did, but they were still there. They were still real. And they still had her waking up on a Sunday morning in June with her heart tight with anticipated pain.

She hadn't arranged to see George today. She didn't want him to know what a maudlin mess she became once a year, missing the idea of her mom more than the person, since the memory of her mother was so old and faded by time it no longer felt real, more like an old carbon copy that hadn't imprinted well.

She'd planned to self-isolate and watch old BBC adaptations of Jane Austen all day—but she was only halfway through *Northanger Abbey* when her phone pinged with a text from George.

I know you're doing your own thing today, but I have a surprise for you in the courtyard if you're up for it.

She thought of half a dozen dirty responses involving "up for it" and surprises, but his next text came before she could decide what to say.

I'll only take two minutes. Promise.

Which of course led to even more potential replies on how he shouldn't sell himself short—until a third text arrived.

Bring Bing.

Curiosity took over—and the fact that in spite of her resolutions to be maudlin on her own, she really did want to see him. Charlotte paused Felicity Jones and grabbed Bingley's leash—which immediately sent the puppy into contortions of delight. He yipped, bouncing in front of the door until she told him to sit—the one command he had a good handle on. His butt plopped down, still shimmying with the force of his wagging tail, and she clipped on the leash.

"Come on, baby."

As soon as she stepped out in the courtyard, she saw George. He was standing next to the pond, Duke seated at his side looking majestic with something that looked kind of like a lumpy plastic soccer ball on the ground at his feet.

"What's this surprise you have for me?" she called out as she crossed the courtyard, the grass tickling her feet in her flip-flops.

"Well, it's half for you, half for Bing. I thought he would love it, and it would give you entertainment—and a way to run off some of his energy when he's driving you nuts with his puppyness. If he likes it."

George bent down, pressing a button on the top of the plastic orb. A tiny motor inside immediately began to hum—and a moment later bubbles began spurting from the top in a steady stream.

Bingley barked—his high-pitched puppy yip—and immediately leapt toward the bubbles, trying to catch them in his mouth.

A laugh slipped out of Charlotte's mouth. "You got my puppy a bubble machine?"

"I thought he might like it." But George wasn't watching Bingley make an absolute fool of himself over the bubbles. He was watching her, his gaze soft and a little nervous.

The warm feeling in Charlotte's chest shifted. "You know, don't you? What today is?"

He nodded. "Elinor told me. And I know you want to be alone. I'm not trying to crowd you. I just wanted you to know you didn't have to be, if you don't want to. And I thought this might make you smile."

Her heart melted. She swallowed thickly. "Thank you."

His cheekbones grew rosy—she loved when George blushed. "There's one other thing." He reached into his back pocket, pulling out an old paperback that looked like it had been through several wars. The weathered book curved between his hands, and Charlotte barely stopped herself from telling him to stop abusing the cover—which was already cracked in so many places she couldn't make out the title.

"I know you already have copies of most of them, but you said your mom wasn't as into *Emma*, so I thought you might have missed this one and I always liked it, so…" He stopped awkwardly wringing the book and extended it toward her.

She accepted the battered book, the pages soft beneath her fingers from so much use. "How many times have you read this?"

"A few," he admitted, blushing again—and suddenly Charlotte's throat was tight and thick with emotion.

"I always liked this one too."

He'd done this for her. He hadn't wanted her to be alone when she was feeling all her messy, ugly feelings…and maybe she didn't have to be.

"Do you want to come back to my place and watch *Clueless*?"

His smile was quick and warm and so perfectly George. "How about my place instead?" he suggested. "I got a fresh box of wine and bunch of junk food, in case you wanted company today."

Her heart thudded hard again. "You're one of the good ones, you know that, Mr. Leneghan?"

"That's what my sisters tell me, but they're very unreliable."

Charlotte smiled as he bent down to turn off the bubble machine. Boxed wine, junk food, and rom-coms. None of the Darcys would have lowered themselves to serve her boxed wine—but they also wouldn't have cared that she was sad about a day on the calendar. They wouldn't have tried to cheer her up with a bubble machine. They wouldn't have even known her well enough to know what *would* cheer her up—always with the tennis bracelets and pearl earrings.

George was a different breed. And he'd been right there all along. Mr. Knightley, smiling and friendly and calling her Charles...though she realized these last couple weeks, he hadn't done that.

"Why did you stop calling me Charles?" she asked him as he picked up the bubble machine and they headed back toward his place with the dogs.

"Did I?" he asked, not quite meeting her eyes. "I don't know. Once we started sleeping together, I guess I thought I should try out your real name."

Something about his evasiveness tickled at her instincts. There was more there, but she wasn't quite sure what it was. All she knew was that she missed the way he said it. The way it made her feel. That connection between them of the long-running inside joke.

"That's too bad. I kind of liked it."

"So you want to be called Charles in bed?"

"I mean, I wouldn't *hate* it."

He smiled—and she had the distinct feeling he would have kissed her if they hadn't both had their arms full of dog leashes, books, and bubble machines. "As you wish," he said. "Charles."

She smiled, feeling inexplicably bubbly herself. She never expected to feel this light today. To feel like she could float away into the sky on a happy breeze. Her mom's birthday was always hard. But then there was George. And George changed everything.

"Does watching Jane Austen stuff bring up memories of your mom?" George asked, making his tone casual as he mixed a sriracha slaw for the fish taco recipe Mac had given him.

They'd finished *Clueless*—with much admiration of the never-aging Paul Rudd—and then watched the Keira Knightley *Pride and Prejudice*, before they'd decided they couldn't live off popcorn and M&Ms alone and he'd started making them dinner.

"Not really," Charlotte admitted, leaning against the counter and watching him work. He'd half-expected her to tense up at the question, but she seemed relaxed as she explained, "Sometimes when I read the books, there'll be a phrase that I hear in her voice—like she read it to me once and my subconscious has never forgotten—but I've read them so many times now that I'm not sure how much of it is actual memory and how much is me wanting to remember. Does that make sense?"

"Perfectly." He checked the fish in the oven, but it still needed a couple more minutes.

"Most of my memories of her are stories that get told over and over again—by Elinor, by my dad…He made us each these videos after she died. Compilations of home videos of her with each of us—and I must have watched mine a thousand times. But they were all videos from before she got sick, and I was so little I don't actually remember her like that. I'd try to tell myself I do, but it's like watching someone else's life because I don't remember those moments. Just this vague idea of how it *felt* to be with her before…"

When she trailed off, George looked up and she met his eyes with a sad little smile.

"There is one memory that I know is mine. She was so sick. It was only a few weeks before she died, and we were watching the Colin Firth *Pride and Prejudice*. When it ended—or maybe it was in the middle, I don't know—she hugged me so tight and said, 'You're going to have such a big love story someday, baby.'" She huffed out a breath, shaking her head.

"She was probably sad she was going to miss seeing you grow up and get married," George murmured.

"I know. She was so young. Only eight years older than I am now. It was so unfair."

George reached out, catching her hand and twining their fingers together. Charlotte looked down at their linked fingers and then up at him, her smile wistful.

"Sometimes I think I hold on to feeling sad I lost her because I'm afraid if I let that go, I'll be letting her go. So I create these rituals. Watching Austen. Because that's how I know her. I think of her as a romantic. I try to be what she would want me to be. Chasing this idea. Trying to make her proud. As if that would help."

He tightened his hand around hers. "She would be so proud of you."

"I hope so," she whispered, then seemed to shake herself. "Enough. We never did open that box of wine you promised me."

She pulled away, and he didn't hold on, taking his cue from her and moving back to check the fish. 'Charlotte opened the cupboard to get the wineglasses and he jerked his chin toward the dishwasher.

"They're in the dishwasher. It's clean. I just didn't get around to unloading it."

"The ones with the long stems?" Charlotte frowned, already opening the dishwasher to investigate. She straightened a moment later with one of the large goblet-shaped wineglasses in each hand. "You can't put these in the dishwasher, George. You have to do them by hand."

"I always put them in there," he told her as he pulled the fish from the oven. "Can you get the plates?"

"You're going to break them," Charlotte said, getting out the plates, while still griping about the wineglasses. "This is why you only have three, isn't it? One of them broke in the dishwasher."

"I plead the fifth," he said—and then couldn't stop his smile.

"What are you smiling at? I'm serious."

"I know. I just like arguing about the dishwasher with you." He leaned over to steal a kiss, and Charlotte shook her head when he pulled away.

"You're a strange human, George Leneghan. Luckily, you're also an amazing cook."

George just smiled and plated the tacos. He knew he was being ridiculous, that arguing about how to load the dishwasher wasn't really a necessary ingredient in a healthy relationship, but it felt good to be here with her like this. Like something he'd always wanted was finally clicking into place.

Chapter Thirty-Two

I must learn to brook being happier than
I deserve.

—*Persuasion*, Jane Austen

A week later, Charlotte stood in the world's longest food
truck line, wondering whether it was possible to be *too*
happy.

She'd taken flying trapeze classes during undergrad—the
best elective she'd ever crammed into her overloaded over-
achiever schedule. It had been impossible to be stressed
about her next organic chemistry test when she was throwing her body through the air a few dozen feet off the ground.
She'd loved the challenge to her muscles and her mind,
but also the incredible, buzzy, adrenaline-filled freedom of
releasing from the trapeze and flinging herself toward the
catcher.

This felt like that. Like she was flying through the air,
and all it would take was a single slip of timing for her to
miss the catch and go plummeting down to the net below.
George always seemed to catch her, but there was still that

fear whispering in the back of her mind—irrational as it might be—wondering if he always would.

But at the moment, she was *really* enjoying the flight.

The Old Fourth Festival was in full swing around her, and after-parade crowds densely packed the town square. Pine Hollow had been chartered in 1761, and they took the Fourth of July *seriously*. Since the holiday was on a Tuesday this year, the initial festivities had been scheduled for Saturday to kick off the long weekend. Little kids in Revolutionary War uniforms ducked and wove through the groups, playing some elaborate game of tag after having finished the annual recitation of the Declaration of Independence.

Food trucks had been set up around the edges of the green, and the lines wrapped around the square as locals vied for space with tourists who had come to town for the holiday celebration. Charlotte stood in the line for the barbecue truck—since it was the only line where she could wait for food and still have a view of the bandstand.

Her boyfriend's band was performing.

And they were *incredible*.

Not that Charlotte had doubted they would be, but she'd sort of thought they would sound like a group who played together in a rec room sometimes. Not like *this*. They could have been professionals.

George had such a tendency to downplay his achievements, and he always clammed up when she asked him to play for her, claiming that no one ever serenaded someone with a bass guitar, but he was *good*. Bob sat at the drum kit, still wearing the Revolutionary War uniform he'd put on to light the ceremonial cannon to start the parade this morning. He had to be melting in the heat, but his focus never wavered.

Mac sounded amazing on the vocals—which surprised no one who had ever heard him at karaoke—but it was Howard who stole the show. The guitar *sang*, and Howard seemed to almost be in a trance as he milked each note for maximum impact.

Charlotte glanced around, hoping to spot Vivian Weisman—she *had* to see this. The older couple had been flirting since *Casablanca*, but Vivian was still insisting that she wasn't looking for romance. When Charlotte searched the crowd, instead of Vivian, she saw Kendall moving toward her with a pair of pastries in her hands.

"Don't say I never did anything for you," Kendall said by way of greeting. "I had to fight a soccer mom for the last lemon bars. Mags looks like she'll be entirely sold out in under five minutes." She handed Charlotte a lemon bar. "Is it just me or are the crowds worse this year?"

"It isn't you. We were included in a BuzzFeed listicle of best places to spend the Fourth. The tourists love a best-of list."

"That they do." Kendall bit into her lemon bar and moaned appreciatively.

Charlotte took her own bite and closed her eyes in bliss. "Did you really fight someone for these? Because it was worth it."

"Sadly, only in my imagination. The soccer mom in question was in front of me in line, and I had a series of vivid fantasies about knocking her out of the way so she didn't buy these babies before I could snag them." Kendall jerked her chin toward the bandstand. "I'm not sure if you've noticed, but your boyfriend's band is freaking amazing."

Charlotte smiled—more than a little smugly. "I did notice, but thank you for the confirmation that I'm not biased and my boyfriend really is a rock god."

"I think technically Howard is a rock god, and George is getting proximity deification," Kendall corrected. "When they get signed to tour with Prince's hologram, promise me you'll take me with you. I could use an escape hatch."

There was such a layer of exhaustion beneath the words that Charlotte tore her gaze off George on the stage and focused on Kendall—and the dark circles under her eyes.

"Are you okay? You look exhausted."

Kendall's mouth twisted wryly. "Gee, thanks."

"You know what I mean. What's going on?"

"Just more of the same." Kendall stalled as the barbecue line shuffled forward, but Charlotte waited her out until she finally admitted, "It's these conferences at the resort. I hate them—it's one headache after the next, troubleshooting and smiling and making sure the staff remember all the special requests. But we need something to keep the lights on through the summer."

Her worry sharpened as Charlotte heard what Kendall wasn't saying. "The resort isn't in trouble, is it?"

Kendall shrugged, her mouth twisting downward. "It isn't great. I keep trying to convince my parents to open up the mountain to bikers and run the lifts through the summers, bring in revenue that way—we could even put in a skate park or a ninja course—but my dad's worried having a bunch of adrenaline junkie athletes hanging around will 'tarnish our brand' and scare away the suits-and-PowerPoints crowd. It's like he doesn't even remember that he used to be one of those athletes."

"Or that you were."

Kendall made the same face she always made when Charlotte or Magda referred to her aborted athletic career. "Let's talk about something else. Me complaining isn't going to change anything. Or better yet, let's just listen to your boyfriend being awesome. That whole swearing off men thing really stuck, huh?"

"You're the one who said I didn't need to swear off men, just assholes."

"That I did. I'm brilliant like that. And how are things with Mr. Not-an-Asshole these days?"

Charlotte flushed. "They're good."

"Good? That's all I get? You usually can't stop talking about your relationships."

Because usually she was trying to convince herself how wonderful they were, that she was doing the right thing by sticking it out. This time she was scared if she talked about it, she would jinx it.

George was singing harmony now, leaning into the microphone—and he seemed to be looking right at Charlotte. He winked at her, and she couldn't fight her smile.

"Ugh." Kendall made a face. "Please tell me he has flaws."

"You could have dated him," Charlotte reminded her. "I set you up." *And thank goodness you didn't hit it off.*

"He's too nice for me," Kendall said dismissively.

Charlotte kept watching George. "He is nice." The man was perfect. Considerate to a fault. "Do you think I'm taking advantage of him?"

Kendall groaned. "Uh-oh."

"What?"

"You're self-sabotaging."

"No, I'm not," Charlotte insisted. "I'm just wondering if he's too nice to me."

Kendall snorted. "Replay that last sentence in your head and see if it sounds as messed up to you as it does to me."

"You said he was too nice!"

"For *me*. When have we ever had the same taste in men?"

Charlotte struggled to put into words this unsettled feeling. "It's just that he never says no to me."

"How terrible for you," Kendall drawled, dry as chalk.

"I'm serious. He gives me everything I want before I even know to ask for it. It's like he's still trying to win me," Charlotte said—realizing as she said it what had been bothering her for the last few weeks, finally identifying the source of her underlying fear.

He was Mr. Knightley...but no one ever talked about what happened after THE END. What if Mr. Knightley decided Emma was really more trouble than she was worth?

"What if he gets sick of me? What if he realizes the reality of being with someone like me for the long haul is just too much?"

"What if you're freaking out and self-sabotaging when what you need to be doing is enjoying the fact that someone nice is crazy about you?" Kendall countered. "Are you really finding it this hard to just be happy?"

"No. I just..."

"Are used to dating jerks so you don't know how to behave when you have someone decent?" Kendall offered.

Her face heated. "Maybe."

"Do me a favor. Try to enjoy the fact that your life is awesome right now."

"I am," Charlotte insisted.

"If you say so." Kendall's phone binged and she glowered at it. "I should get back to work."

"You aren't staying for the carnival?"

She shook her head. "We have a dental conference this weekend. I just needed to get away for a minute. It's not like I have a perfect boyfriend to play carnival games with anyway."

Charlotte frowned. She hadn't been aware that Kendall *wanted* a boyfriend to play carnival games with. She'd been relationship-shy for years. "You could always play with us."

"The dental conference is preferable to playing third wheel, but thanks." Kendall gave her a quick hug. "Happy Fourth."

"Will you be at the fireworks?"

"Barring unforeseen dental disasters."

Charlotte watched Kendall go, worry pinching her brow. Kendall hated it when she meddled, but Charlotte would have happily jumped in and tried to fix Kendall's life—if she only knew what to do. Because she wasn't sure a puppy would really solve Kendall's problems.

The line shuffled forward, the angle temporarily blocking Charlotte's view of the stage. George would be playing for another twenty minutes. She'd been hoping to have lunch for both of them in hand when he got offstage so they could refuel before they hit the carnival, but the line was taking forever.

She went up on her tiptoes and craned her neck, trying to get a look at the front of the line to see what the hold-up was—but she was too far back and only managed to make awkward eye contact with a tall, dark-haired man a few people ahead of her in line. He smiled a little too warmly, and she looked away, turning her attention back toward the bandstand. She couldn't see George anymore, but she could hear him.

Another song ended and the line shuffled forward a few feet. She stretched to see how many people were in front of her.

The dark-haired guy was watching her.

Charlotte frowned, averting her eyes.

There was something familiar about his expression, even though she knew she hadn't met him. It was the appreciation in his eyes, the slight up-tilt of his mouth on one side. He looked like a man who knew he was handsome, who was absolutely confident he could have any woman he wanted, and who was currently considering whether she might be worthy of his attention.

He looked like every man she'd ever dated.

That look had once been her kryptonite. It had made her desperate for approval. Hungry for the reward of his attention. Tense and alert in a way she'd always mistaken for excitement.

Now she found it mildly annoying.

Who did he think he was anyway? Why should she care that some smug guy in line in front of her was looking at her like she was put on the earth for his enjoyment?

As Mac announced this would be their last song and the crowd groaned, God's Gift to Women got to the front of the line and had to stop watching her long enough to order—thank goodness—but as soon as he placed his order, he stepped to the side to wait for his food…and watched her some more.

She ignored him, but she should have known that was the

most surefire way to hold his attention. Guys like that always wanted what they couldn't have. It was only once they'd caught what they were chasing that they lost interest.

No wonder she was scared George was going to lose interest now that they were together. She'd been trained by all her past experiences to expect it—and the fear didn't care that George was nothing like those guys.

She was next in line now. God's Gift to Women was lurking closer, getting ready to make his move. He looked like he was itching to try to impress her with his knowledge of cryptocurrency.

She could write the script of the entire scene in her head, but she didn't want to play her usual part. She just wanted to get the food and see George—but then Lisa, who owned the barbecue truck with her husband, leaned out of the window and scratched a line through three of the items on the chalk menu hanging beside her.

Charlotte groaned as the tourist in front of her moved to the side and she saw what was left on the list.

"Sorry, hon. We're out of everything except French fries and coleslaw," Lisa said, confirming that she was too late.

They still needed sustenance, and Charlotte knew from painful experience that the wood-fired flatbreads on the other side of the square tasted like cardboard and were hard enough to chip a tooth.

"I guess I waited too long," she said, smiling for Lisa. "I'll take an order of each." She handed over a ten. She and George were scheduled to go to a cookout at her dad's before the fireworks anyway. They'd just be extra hungry when they arrived.

"It'll just be a minute," Lisa said, handing back her change.

Charlotte tucked it into the tip jar and stepped to the side.

"I'd be happy to share some of mine. I probably ordered too much anyway."

Oh, right. God's Gift to Women was still there.

Charlotte considered ignoring him, but that would probably make him even more determined. She gave him a bland smile. "No, thanks. I'm good."

"It's the least I can do. Since I stole it right out from under you."

She shrugged. "First come, first served."

He smiled, his teeth practically glinting in the sunlight. She'd bet her next paycheck he had them professionally whitened. "I can't let you go hungry. What kind of gentleman would I be then?"

The kind who listens to women when they say no, thank you? "I'm sure I won't waste away. Consider your gentlemanly duty satisfied."

"I'm coming on too strong, aren't I?" he said with a self-deprecating glimmer in his eyes, trying another tactic since playing Gentleman Savior wasn't working out. "See, I've been trying to think of a way to talk to you for the last half hour."

His gaze was warm, his smile charming. And she would have fallen for him hook, line, and sinker a few months ago. But right now, she couldn't have been less affected by the charm offensive.

"Sorry. I'm with someone." *And I shouldn't have to tell you that to get you to leave me alone if I'm not interested.* Just a few months ago, she would have found his persistence charming, thrilled that he'd chosen *her* to be the focus of his attention. Why had it taken her so long to learn her lesson about men like that?

His smile didn't even flicker. If anything, it grew. "He isn't here now, is he?"

The subtext screamed—*he can't possibly be as wonderful as me, can he? Don't you want to leave him for me?*

"It doesn't matter where he is," Charlotte said, with her best get-lost-buddy smile. "I'm not interested."

God's Gift laughed. "You're feisty. I like it." Their orders came up and he waved his pulled pork temptingly as Laura handed her the fries and slaw. "Last chance to share."

It smelled like heaven—and she'd never been less interested. "Nope. I'm good."

He smiled, his confidence undiminished. "Find me when you change your mind."

She watched him walk away—marveling that she'd ever found guys like that attractive.

"Someone you know?" George asked, appearing at her side.

Chapter Thirty-Three

No man is offended by another man's admiration of the woman he loves; it is the woman only who can make it a torment.
—*Northanger Abbey*, Jane Austen

George had told himself not to overreact when he looked down from the bandstand stage and saw Charlotte talking with some strange guy. He hadn't been able to see her face from his angle, but it had been pretty obvious from the guy's smile that he was trying to charm her.

He told himself he trusted her. That he wasn't worried she'd found her lightning guy and was about to trade him in for a better model, someone who made her heart race in a way George never had. He wasn't watching his girlfriend have a "meet cute" with another guy.

He told himself all that—but he still practically leapt off the stage as soon as their last song ended, making a beeline toward the barbecue truck.

"Hey! New guy!" Judith Larson called out. "Great job up there!"

George acknowledged the shout with a wave, not bothering to remind Judith that he had a name. When he finally fought his way through the crowds to Charlotte's side, she was watching the guy leave—which was probably totally normal. He'd probably asked her for directions and she was watching him to make sure he went the right way.

"Someone you know?" he asked, trying to keep the anxiety out of his voice.

"Hey!" Charlotte turned to him with a beaming smile that would have wiped away all of his anxieties if she hadn't also said, "Nope. Just someone who would have been exactly my type six months ago." He started to frown, but then she bounced, hooking a finger through his stars-and-stripes suspenders. "Why didn't you tell me I was dating a rock star?"

"You have a thing for musicians?"

"I have a thing for *this* musician. Though, sadly, I was so caught up in your awesomeness, I didn't get in line in time." She lifted her other hand, displaying two cardboard bowls. "There was a run on the barbecue, and this was all they had left," she explained. "French fries or coleslaw. Take your pick."

The fries smelled amazing, but she'd stolen fries off his plate enough times that he knew that was the one she would want, so he started to reach for the coleslaw. "I'll take the slaw."

"Oh." Charlotte's face fell—she had a terrible poker face—and he immediately backpedaled.

"Or, you know what, let me have the fries—"

"Ha! I knew it!" she crowed, holding both baskets away from him. "You only picked the coleslaw because you thought I wanted the fries!"

He frowned, confused. She was acting like she'd caught him at something nefarious. "So?"

"I don't want you to always give me what I want! I want to know what you really want."

"What if what I really want is for you to have what you want because I don't actually care?"

Her dark eyes narrowed. "Is that true?"

"Okay, in this circumstance I may have wanted the french fries," he admitted, "but I knew you wanted them too. Can't we just share?"

Charlotte pouted. "You're too nice to me."

And nice guys finish last. The words whispered in the back of his mind but were quickly drowned out by the Greek chorus of his sisters' voices telling him not to be an idiot.

"I like being nice to you," he said. "Is that a problem?"

From Charlotte's expression, apparently it was. "I just don't want you to feel like you have to be nice all the time."

"Okay." This felt like it was about more than the coleslaw, but he didn't know how to reassure her that he wasn't nice to her because he thought he had to be. He just *liked* doing things for her. "I promise to be meaner?"

She rolled her eyes. "Just take the fries."

He accepted the basket she shoved at him. "I'm serious about sharing." He wagged the fries temptingly, taking one and biting into it. "Mm, delicious."

"I suppose I can be persuaded to share." She snagged a fry, popping it into her mouth. "If you promise not to give me what I want all the time."

George grinned, bemused. He'd never had anyone complain about getting their way. "Deal. Are we still gonna play some of those carnival games? I heard a rumor the proceeds go to charity."

"Absolutely," Charlotte agreed, grabbing another fry. "But you better not let me win."

~

George absolutely destroyed her at the water pistols—and Charlotte had never been happier to lose. Though she was insanely competitive, so she tried to beat him every time.

After they polished off their snacks and she'd lost three games in a row, she chalked the french fry anxiety up to a low blood sugar moment and simply enjoyed being with George. She'd never had so much fun—or trash-talked quite so much—at the carnival. Some of the games were unconventional—like the stuffed animatronic pig races, which were completely random and ridiculous and she *adored* them, making him play three times in a row.

While the volunteer running the pig races reset the pigs for the third race, Charlotte announced, "Winner of the next one gets a creemee."

George met her eyes, his own warming as a small, wicked smile played around his lips. "I'm pretty sure you still owe me one from mini-golf."

Charlotte felt her face flushing as she remembered what he'd thought a creemee was back then—his eyes clearly telegraphing that he was remembering it too.

Then the race began and she pulled her gaze off George's, shouting encouragement at her little pig robot so loudly that they drew a crowd.

The faux-Darcys would have been appalled at the scene she

was making, but George leaned against the table, grinning at her like she was magical, rather than embarrassing.

It was heaven.

By the time they picked up the dogs and headed to her dad's for the cookout, she was buzzing on sugar from the creemee stand and the feeling of being herself—bright and brash and impulsive and loud. The cookout was even more wonderfulness.

George made her *happy*. In a way none of her exes ever had. It wasn't even that he got along with her family— George got along with everyone. It was how he made *her* so comfortable. Like she was capable of being even more herself when he was beside her. She'd never been with anyone like that before. Someone who gave her the confidence to be her entire self—a confidence she'd never felt like she lacked...but had always been missing in her relationships.

She had that with her family and with Magda and Kendall, but with the men in her life she'd always been insecure. She'd been chasing sweeping passion and dramatic love stories, but she'd never considered comfort. Friendship. *Ease.*

None of the Darcys were ever as kind as George. As *good* as George. And she was falling for him. Not in big, dramatic ways, but through every moment of everyday happiness.

Which scared the hell out of her. Happiness was tenuous. The second she took it for granted, something popped up out of nowhere to rip it away from her. Her childhood had taught her that lesson well. Perfect was always the calm before the storm.

She was scared to trust it.

It wasn't even George she didn't trust. It was the perfection. It was this feeling. The one that just kept building.

She was too happy.

Too happy when they dropped Duke and Bingley at the ski resort so they'd be on the opposite side of town from the fireworks, and George took a moment to cuddle both dogs and explain to Duke that he had to keep Bingley company and make sure he wasn't scared of the sky booms.

Too happy when they arrived at the field behind Pine Hollow Middle and High School, where the fireworks would be set off, and George took her hand as they searched for the perfect spot to lay their blanket—and he picked a space right next to Magda, because he knew Charlotte wouldn't be able to stand it if her friend was alone.

Too happy as she leaned against him, their hands tangled together as they waited for dusk and listened to the pre-fireworks music—which she thought was a recording until Magda pointed toward the platform off to one side where a gangly teen was strumming a guitar.

"That's my nephew Dylan," Magda said.

Charlotte's eyes widened. "Holy crap. He really is the next Ed Sheeran. No wonder he has a fan club."

"Right?" Magda grinned with pride.

Then Magda had seen one of her sisters and left to speak with her—leaving Charlotte alone with George—and her happiness swelled to unbearable levels.

The romantic music. The town she loved around her. The man she…well. She wasn't quite ready to think that yet. She wasn't ready to be quite that daring, but maybe she was falling for him. Maybe this feeling wasn't the music or the moment. Maybe it was him.

He lay down on the picnic blanket they'd spread out, and she stretched out alongside him, neither of them speaking, simply listening to the music and the sounds of the kids playing around them.

A few minutes later, the first fireworks burst in the sky, and a soft gasp pulled from her lips. She lay with her head resting on the muscle of George's arm, the warmth of him against her side, staring up at the sky as fireworks exploded above them, and each one seemed to also be exploding inside her chest. Tears pricked at the back of her eyes, and she tried to hold on to this feeling, this moment that seemed to stretch to infinity—but was still over far too soon.

The fireworks ended. Townspeople around them stirred, everyone gathering up their picnic blankets and folding up their chairs and trooping toward the parking lot. But Charlotte didn't move, and neither did George.

She turned her head on the pad of his arm and found him looking down at her. He wasn't wearing his glasses. Unlike Elinor and Charlotte before she had Lasik, his vision wasn't all that bad. He didn't need the specs to see her clearly.

He always saw her clearly. And somehow he still seemed to like what he saw. She couldn't get over the miracle of that.

She stared into his eyes, warm and soft and dark. "We should go," she murmured.

For a moment she thought he might say something. Something that would change everything and make more fireworks explode in her heart. But after a beat he just nodded. "Yeah," he murmured. "Time to go home."

She didn't know whether he meant her home or his, but as long as they were together, she didn't care.

The field was clearing out, and George volunteered to jog

ahead and bring the car around for her since they'd arrived late enough that they'd had to park down the road.

"You don't have to," Charlotte protested, folding up the blanket—and George leaned in to steal a quick kiss.

"Maybe I'm impatient to get you alone." His voice was husky, his lips brushing hers with the words—and sensation shot straight to her core.

"Run," she told him.

It was a sign of how hormone-addled she was that it didn't even occur to her until he was out of sight in the darkness that she could have run with him, both of them racing like impatient teenagers through the lingering crowds. But if she chased him now, they'd probably miss one another in the dark, so instead she headed toward the pick-up area in front of the school.

She was fidgeting impatiently, trying to distinguish his headlights from the dozens of other headlights moving slowly through the pick-up area, when a female voice spoke at her side. "Hey, Charlotte."

She turned to see one of the administrators from the Estates standing nearby with her three tiny daughters, waiting for her own ride. "Hey, Eileen. Happy Fourth."

"Happy Fourth. Always a zoo with these three." She glanced down at her daughters—one was fast asleep in the stroller, the other two waving glow sticks and spinning in circles. "You and George looked pretty cozy."

Charlotte felt her face freeze as she tried frantically to remember if they were supposed to have filed some kind of relationship form with HR. Eileen caught the look and laughed.

"Don't worry. You aren't breaking any rules—neither of

you reports to the other." Her smile was relaxed, friendly. "It's just good to see you both happy. And I'm glad someone else is trying to convince him to stay. With all the calls I got to check his references this week, I was sure we were going to lose him to one of those places in Colorado. Everyone seems to want him, and we can only offer him part-time, but maybe now he'll have a little extra incentive to stay."

All the calls to check his references.

Charlotte went still, her heart suddenly feeling like it was beating outside her chest, exposed and vulnerable.

He'd been applying for jobs. In Colorado. And they'd still been checking his references as recently as *this week*.

She'd known he might be going back. He'd told her weeks ago. But she'd been avoiding thinking about it. She'd hoped he wouldn't want to now. That he would be looking for jobs *here*.

She hadn't expected him to be actively applying for jobs in Colorado. And getting far enough in the process that they would be checking his references.

Eileen seemed to be waiting for a response, so Charlotte forced her frozen face to smile. "He is pretty great."

A car pulled to the curb in front of them and Eileen started toward it. "You two have a good night!" she called, herding her children toward the vehicle.

"You too," Charlotte echoed weakly.

Minutes later, the car pulled away, another one replacing it at the curb, and it wasn't until George rolled down the passenger window and called out "Charles?" that she realized it was his.

She quickly scrambled into the car.

"Everything okay?" George asked.

Her brain didn't seem to be working, and her instincts took over. The ones that told her to smile and pretend everything was great. To pretend her heart wasn't still beating strangely exposed outside her body.

"It's great! Let's go home."

She knew Kendall would want her to ask George about the job applications. Her friend would give her a hard time about how she was only scared to know the answer to questions when it came to her love life—but she *was* scared.

She might have kissed him in the middle of the town square and cuddled with him through the fireworks, but that didn't mean happily ever after and forever.

It might just mean he wanted a summer fling. Someone to date until he left.

And she didn't want him to leave. Even if they didn't stay together as a couple, even if it didn't work out—as painful as that would be—she couldn't imagine her life without George in it.

He had to stay.

She just needed to show him everything he'd be missing if he went back to Colorado.

Charlotte was always good when she had a mission. And her current mission was to show George Leneghan that everything he could ever possibly want was in Vermont.

So he never wanted to leave it. Or her.

Chapter Thirty-Four

Do not give way to useless alarm ... though it is right to be prepared for the worst, there is no occasion to look on it as certain.
—*Pride and Prejudice*, Jane Austen

George didn't know quite what had happened after the fireworks, but something changed.

Things had been good. Comfortable. And yes, part of him had been waiting for the other shoe to drop—but he hadn't expected Charlotte to kick into a frantically happy mode where she seemed determined to drag him to every corner of Vermont.

The rest of the Fourth of July weekend was a whirlwind.

He knew how fervently enthusiastic she could be about everything. He told himself this was just what she was like when she was happy, but he couldn't help feeling there was an edge of desperation behind her sudden need to *experience* Vermont, showing him all its glory. And that edge of desperation unsettled him.

On Sunday, she took him to Bingley Falls, leaping off the

top with him and splashing into the icy water side by side. Then they climbed a wilderness obstacle course and went zip-lining.

She took him to three different creemee stands—each of which claimed to have the best maple creemees in Vermont. And the soft-serve sweetness was delicious—but he was starting to worry he was going to go into a sugar coma if they kept up this pace.

Though he had to admit that kissing her with the soft, sweet ice cream on her lips was becoming one of his favorite pastimes.

On Monday, which they both had off, she took him floating down the river on an innertube, her fingers tangling lazily with his as they bumped closer together and drifted farther apart. She floated along in her giant sunglasses and oversized floppy hat, and the sun painted her skin, making her look like a goddess on the glittering water. It should have been heaven—but she never seemed to completely relax, always glancing at him, as if she couldn't stop checking to make sure he was happy.

That night they drove thirty miles on the curving country roads to the nearest drive-in, and Charlotte kept up a bubbly chatter the entire way about everything they passed—and how it could only be found in Vermont. The maple stands. The local cheddar. The moose crossing signs—though the only wildlife they saw were some wild turkeys that tried to run in front of his tires.

They looked like they were in the middle of nowhere, and he was starting to doubt there was actually a drive-in out here, but Charlotte seemed to know where she was going as she gave him directions.

"Take a right up ahead," she instructed—pointing to what looked like a thicket of trees.

"Where?" There was nothing remotely resembling a road.

"Right right right!" Charlotte yelped.

George slammed on the brakes and turned onto a slightly-wider-than-single-lane dirt track—with a half-hidden road sign reading ROYALTON TURNPIKE. "You've gotta be kidding me. In no world is this a turnpike."

"It is in Barnard. It's got history. You don't get history like this in Colorado."

George frowned—and focused on navigating the less-than-hospitable driving conditions of the pothole-filled road. After a few hundred yards, a hand-painted sign for the drive-in pointed them to the left, down an even narrower dirt road. Leaves brushed the side of the car—until the trees suddenly parted, and the dirt track spit them out at the back of a giant field.

There was a small building that looked like a glorified outhouse with a sign reading "$10 per car—cash only" and a bored teenager sitting on the steps. Farther down the field, George could see a few rows of cars already in position in front of a screen that didn't look much bigger than the one used for the movies in the square in Pine Hollow.

As soon as he rolled down his window to hand over his ten dollars, the pungent odor of livestock hit his nose.

"Is this a working farm?" he asked Charlotte, after the bored teen had taken their money, briefed them on the rules, and pointed them toward the front of the field.

"Yeah." She bounced a little in her seat. "They use one of the fallow fields, and it rotates, so the drive-in moves around some each year. Isn't it great?"

George threw his SUV into park and shut off the engine before twisting to face Charlotte. "Okay, what's going on?" he demanded, unable to wait any longer to ask the question that had been bugging him all day—all weekend, actually.

"What?"

"What's up?" he reiterated. "You've been in turbo mode all weekend. What happened?"

Charlotte knew she was staring at George like a deer in headlights, but she couldn't seem to stop. Yes, she might have been overdoing it with her "look how wonderful Vermont is, don't you want to stay?" campaign, but she hadn't really expected him to call her on it—though she probably should have.

It was almost a relief to talk about it. "Eileen told me you're still applying for jobs in Colorado."

She didn't realize, until she saw the vivid flash of guilt across his face, that she'd half-expected him to deny it. To say it was an oversight. Maybe a job he'd applied for months ago—back when she was still dating Jeff, even—and they hadn't gotten the message that he was no longer interested.

But from the way his face pulled into careful I-don't-want-to-upset-you lines, she knew her fears were about to be confirmed.

His voice was low. "I should have told you."

Her throat tightened. "You're leaving?"

He shook his head, his eyes holding hers. "I'm not sure. I'm applying for jobs in both places to see what my options are."

God, sometimes she hated how honest he was. But at least

she knew she could trust him to always tell her the truth, even when she wished he would tell her anything else.

"I guess you were always considering going," she reminded herself. "You told me weeks ago." *I just didn't think you still wanted to.*

George winced as if he'd heard the unspoken words. "It's not just the job," he explained. "It's my sister. She's going through something—might be getting divorced—and I want to be there for her. I should have talked to you about it—"

"No, it's okay. I mean. I knew you were considering moving. It makes sense."

"I should have talked to you," he repeated. "I just wanted to let things with work and Beks play out a bit so I'd have a better idea of the options. And I didn't want to presume anything. With...this." He waved a hand between them.

"Right." She mercilessly squashed the flash of hurt. Did he think their relationship would have run its course by the end of the summer? "That makes sense."

A question shifted in his eyes. "It does?"

"Yeah," she assured him—not even sure what she was agreeing to at this point.

She'd already completely abandoned all the rules she'd given herself during the Puppy Pact. No clinging. No desperate attempts to salvage the relationship.

She was supposed to be concentrating on Bingley. She was supposed to be strong and independent. How had she gotten right back where she always was? Chasing after a man. Except George wasn't a faux Darcy. So why did it feel the same?

All she'd ever wanted was to be the center of someone's world. To matter more than anything.

And she didn't. Maybe she never would.

But he had somehow become the center of hers. He mattered in a way she hadn't even realized until she thought she might lose him.

She was in love with George.

And he was leaving.

"Charlotte?" he said gently, probing.

She squirmed under his gaze. Why did he have to know her so well? "It's fine."

"Charles," he said gently—and she crumbled.

"I just didn't think about it. You leaving. I don't want this to end. I don't want *us* to end."

"We still have time to figure it out," he said. "I haven't gotten any offers yet. And I want to keep seeing you, too."

She almost said she could go to Colorado with him. The words nearly fell out without her permission. But they hadn't even said *I love you* yet. She was already clingy enough and now she was going to follow him across the country? Away from her family and her friends and a job she loved?

No. She couldn't do that.

"Right. We've got time," she said, but the words tasted like sawdust on her tongue. "September is almost two months away. We'll figure it out."

"Right," he murmured.

"Right," she echoed.

Maybe a great job would open up here. Maybe his sister would reconcile with her husband. Maybe George would decide he would miss Pine Hollow too much.

Maybe, when he left, he wouldn't take her whole heart.

Anything could happen in eight weeks.

Chapter Thirty-Five

It is not every man's fate to marry the
woman who loves him best.
                          —*Emma*, Jane Austen

George couldn't sleep.

This morning he'd gotten an invitation for an in-person interview. In Boulder.

He'd been putting off decisions. Telling himself he was living in the moment. Telling himself there was no point in rushing. But time hadn't stopped moving forward and he would have to decide soon.

Charlotte was sprawled on his bed on her stomach with one hand flung out over the edge. She was a restless sleeper, always twisting and thrashing, but for now she was still.

He should have told her about the interview, but he knew why he hadn't. He'd been afraid this would be a tipping point in their relationship—and he wasn't sure which way it would tip.

Though maybe this was why his exes had all left him. Because he wouldn't take the risk and put his heart out there first. Because he always waited to see what they wanted. Let them take the lead. Looked to his partners to define the future of every relationship—and then those relationships had ended.

Had he been playing it safe with his heart all along?

This was the first time it felt wrong. Like he might be screwing up—and about to lose something worth more than all those other relationships combined.

He needed advice.

He had a book club meeting this Saturday—but he also knew if he asked all his sisters for advice at the same time, it would be like chumming the water during Shark Week. The carnage would be spectacular. Instead, he texted Beks to see if she was free. His phone rang within seconds.

"You have good timing," she said in lieu of a greeting.

The words were dry, but her voice broke bitterly on the last word. George instantly shoved aside the question he'd been intending to ask. "Are you okay? What's wrong?"

Beks sniffled. "I talked to Scott tonight."

Oh shit. This did not sound like an it-was-all-in-my-head talk. "Beks..." he said softly, his voice thick with sympathy.

"He says he never slept with her." Another sniffle. "So that's great. He just texts her and talks on the phone. Apparently, they decided not to see each other in person because they know they would sleep together, and neither one of them wants to blow up their marriages. Isn't that sweet? He told me that, as if I'm supposed to be proud of him. To know that he wants to sleep with her so badly that he can't be in the same room with her, but he's choosing not to for my sake. Lucky me."

"Shit."

"Yep," she agreed bitterly. "And it's been going on for years. Since Logan was a baby. I guess he didn't feel like he could burden me with his problems because I was tired all the time—because I was taking care of *his children*—and she texted him one night and they got to chatting, and it was harmless, right? Just old friends catching up? Even if they were old friends who used to sleep together. It was casual and friendly—little inside jokes on her birthday. Funny memes and text messages whenever one of them had a dream about the other—no harm, no foul, right? Until he was talking to her about me. Confiding to her instead of me. The one who got away." She choked on a harsh sound that was halfway between an angry laugh and a sob.

"He doesn't even get that this is worse than an affair—or at least just as bad. It's an *emotional* affair. He *loves* her. He *admitted* that he wonders sometimes what his life would have been like if he'd married her instead of me. That the two of them almost ran away together before our wedding, but she wouldn't go through with it."

"What the hell?" George was suddenly very glad he wasn't in Colorado, because he probably would have driven over to Beks's house and killed Scott. "Why would he say that to you?"

"He was explaining to me that he never got closure. So that's why all this is justified, right? He *wonders* what would have happened if he'd run off with her and the *wondering* consumes him." Another bitter sob. "Poor baby. He has to live with his choices."

Shit. George's chest ached—his entire body radiating sympathetic pain for Beks. "What are you going to do?" he asked gently.

"Hell if I know." She sniffled. "He's sleeping at his brother's. Just don't tell the family, okay? I can't handle anyone else knowing until I know what happens next."

"Of course."

"He wants to stay. Work things out. He kept saying he would never do anything to hurt me or the kids—as if this doesn't hurt me. As if finding out our entire marriage has been a fallback plan—that she was the fantasy, she was the *One*, and I was just the one who said yes—as if that wouldn't hurt me. I actually thought we were the rom-com." She choked on more tears, and then pulled herself together with a broken, indrawn breath. "I loved our life. I thought we were the lucky ones. And yes, life gets hard when there are babies and mortgages and you're tired and you're stressed, but you get through it together, right? He never even told me he'd been struggling. Mr. Perfect Husband. And the entire time, he was talking to her and flirting with her—just so he could get through the days with me."

"Beks..."

She sniffed hard, making a deep humming noise in her throat as she fought to get herself under control. Beks hated crying. She hated showing weakness. And George wanted once again to dismember Scott for making her feel this way.

"Can I kill him? I'm coming to Colorado for an interview in a few days," he said, making the decision on the fly.

Beks laughed, jagged and cynical and half a sob. "If it comes to that, we should leave the murdering to Maggie. She's the one who reads all those serial-killer-among-us books."

At least she could still make jokes. He took some comfort in that.

But then she spoke again, her words low and soul-broken. "He broke the dream, George. How do we get back from that? He told me I was what he'd always wanted—and the entire time, that was a lie. He wanted her, and he still does, even if he'll never act on it. I'm the runner-up wife."

"You're the only wife," he reminded her gently.

"Yeah. But she's the fantasy."

Twenty minutes later, when George finally got off the phone, they'd barely talked about Charlotte. It seemed irrelevant now. He wouldn't have mentioned her at all if Beks hadn't brought up his relationship status at the end of the call, warning him to learn from her mistakes.

Duke whined softly, and George padded to the patio door, letting him out to pee. Bingley was still conked out in the crate they'd moved over here for him because Charlotte was spending all her nights here. Charlotte hadn't hesitated when he'd suggested moving the crate. She'd jumped in with both feet—but Charlotte never did anything by half measures. She was all enthusiasm and momentum.

But what would happen when she turned that enthusiasm in another direction?

George stood at the door, watching Duke, white patches on a dark blob in the night, and heard movement behind him.

"George?"

He turned, and there she was, standing in the doorway to the bedroom, her skin seeming to glow warmly in the light over the oven that he always left on at night since Duke didn't like the dark. She was wearing one of the tiny shorts and tank top combos she slept in—this one with I RUN ON COFFEE AND CHAOS printed on the front.

From her sleek, toned legs to her rumpled hair tumbling around her shoulders, she looked like a dream—his dream. But he couldn't get the sound of Beks's voice when she'd called herself the runner-up out of his head. Her low warning to learn from her mistakes.

He was the fallback position. Not her type. Not a Darcy. And yes, she deserved better than the guys she'd been with—but what if someday she met her lightning guy? Someone who made her heart race and who also treated her well? Could he live his entire life bracing himself for the moment when that would happen? When she would realize that she could have it all?

"Everything okay?" she asked, her voice groggy.

"Yeah. Duke just needed to go out."

A soft sound at the door had him looking down—and opening the door to let Duke in.

When he turned back to Charlotte, she was crossing the room to him.

"Come back to bed," she murmured, her voice husky, and she slipped her arms around his neck.

Her face tipped up to his—and he had to kiss her. He couldn't resist.

When he lifted his head, he confessed. "I talked to Beks. She's really struggling. I think I'm going to go out there for a few days. See if I can help." Worry whispered in her eyes, and he forced himself to admit, "I've been invited to interview for a job out there too."

Her gaze shuttered, but she nodded. "I understand."

He almost said he loved her then. But it felt like a promise, one he wasn't sure he was going to be able to keep. So he kissed her instead. And tried to pretend he was the kind of guy who lived in the moment. Tried to make this moment last.

Chapter Thirty-Six

I cannot fix on the hour, or the spot, or the look, or the words, which laid the foundation. It is too long ago. I was in the middle before I knew that I *had* begun.
—*Pride and Prejudice*, Jane Austen

I'm in love with George."

Charlotte expected some kind of fanfare, or at the very least a reaction, when she made her announcement as soon as Kendall and Magda were each settled with drinks—Kendall a beer and Magda a wine cooler—but neither of them so much as raised an eyebrow.

"I hate my job," Kendall said without missing a beat. "Are we just saying obvious things now?"

"I thought you loved the resort." Magda twisted to gawk at Kendall with all the shock Charlotte had mentally reserved for herself.

She might have overrehearsed this scene in her head.

They were at Charlotte's apartment, celebrating their first girls' night in far too long, and all day she'd been prepping for the moment she would tell her friends she was madly in love with George. Of course they would gasp with shock and squeal with delight, and then tell her what the hell she was supposed to do about the fact that he was getting on a plane tomorrow to go to Colorado to interview for a job.

Except none of that appeared to be happening.

"I do." Kendall bent down to accept the latest stuffed animal offering from Bingley—who viewed her as a god and brought her every toy from his toy bin in succession every time she visited.

"Thank you, baby," she told him, accepting his stuffed elephant, Sebastian, before continuing to Mags. "I love the resort. I love the mountain and the hotel—I just hate my job. I never wanted to manage people. Scheduling and hiring and payroll paperwork—I hate it. I just hate it. And now with all the event crap on top of everything, I don't have enough hours in the day to do it all. So I'm doing a crap job at something I hate, and it's destroying my family legacy." She lifted her beer in a mocking toast. "Fun times."

Bingley presented her with his squeaky ball, his tail wagging frantically, and her cynical smile softened as she took it from him. "Thank you, baby."

"Could you hire someone to take on the parts of the job you hate and focus on the things you like?" Magda suggested. "You're already doing the work of two people."

"If we could find the money in the budget, maybe. But it's already tight—and I'm not sure what would be left of my job once we took away all the parts that I hate. What I *want* to do is turn us into an adventurers' mecca, but my dad will never go for that. I guess I could keep the events—if I wasn't also having to manage the staff. But if we're going to be an event space, I'd rather we host something *fun*. Like the New Year's Eve galas. Or weddings."

Magda and Charlotte exchanged a look—but not quick enough that Kendall didn't catch it.

"What?" she demanded.

"Nothing!" Mags insisted, at the same time Charlotte said, "You're not exactly the hearts and flowers type. I didn't think weddings would be your thing."

"I know," Kendall agreed. "But it's not about the romance. It's about pulling it off. About everyone coming together for a good time. I loved arranging Ben's bachelor party for Connor. That was awesome. It was *fun*. And there were no grumpy suits bitching at my staff because the continental breakfast ran out of cheese Danish."

"You might need to talk to your parents," Magda pointed out gently.

Kendall groaned, sinking into the corner of the couch. "I know."

Bingley whined softly at Kendall's distress, and Charlotte crossed the living room to pick him up. He was starting to get too big—and too wiggly—for her to carry him around easily, but she was still able to lift him and dump him onto Kendall's lap. "Here. Hold the puppy. He's free therapy."

Bingley went into paroxysms of delight at his sudden proximity to his personal deity, wriggling wildly, and some of the stress on Kendall's face melted away as she smiled at his antics. "He is pretty great," Kendall acknowledged. "Maybe you're onto something with this whole Puppy Pact thing."

"Actually," Magda said, "speaking of the Puppy Pact, I have news too."

Charlotte had sunk onto her chair, but she instantly sat up straighter. "Is this about the *Cake-Off*? Did you get an audition?"

"No. Not yet." Magda smiled shyly. "I'm getting a dog."

"What? Mags! When? Who?"

She smiled, quietly pleased. "Her name is Cupcake."

"Oh my God, that's *perfect*," Kendall groaned.

"She's a pit bull mix, and she's the *sweetest*—which is how she got her name. Apparently she was found on the road and brought to the shelter after the Fourth of July. They think she must have gotten scared of the fireworks and run away, but she wasn't microchipped and didn't have a collar, and so far no one has claimed her. Astrid started calling her Cupcake because she's such a doll, and I guess it made Ally think of me because she called and asked if I might be interested in fostering her until her owners come forward or they can find her another home. But I just looked at her and knew she was meant to be mine. She doesn't bark, and she's already house-trained—they think she's about two."

Charlotte loved the idea of Magda getting a dog, but protective worry rose up. "But what if you get attached and her owners come back from a long vacation and want her back?"

"Then I'll be heartbroken, and I'll deal with it. I'm tough. I can take a little disappointment. And being afraid it might not work out in the end sounds like the worst reason not to try."

And there they were right back at George again.

Well, Magda and Kendall weren't back at George. They were still discussing Cupcake—who did sound incredibly perfect for Magda. If she got to keep her.

Only Charlotte was suddenly fixated on the terrifying fragility of her happiness with George.

She was so lost in her thoughts it took her a moment to realize her friends had fallen silent and were watching her, as if waiting for her to answer a question she hadn't heard. "What? What'd I miss?"

Bingley had settled down and now curled adoringly in Kendall's arms. Kendall idly scratched the puppy's head and eyed Charlotte. "So . . . George."

"Yeah. I'm in love with him. And he might be leaving. In fact, he *is* leaving tomorrow. But he might be leaving for good in September." She didn't say *and I'm going to lose it if he leaves*, but she was pretty sure Kendall and Mags both heard the subtext from the concern on their faces.

"Why is he leaving?" Magda asked.

"His family is all in Colorado, and his contract was only for two years—"

"I thought they loved him at the Estates?"

"They do," she confirmed to Kendall. "But Claudia's coming back, and they can only offer him part-time—"

"And you haven't told him you love him," Kendall guessed, the words more statement than question.

"I told him I want him to stay. He knows."

"He knows you want him to stay because he's a great fuck buddy? Or he knows you want him to stay because you're head over heels for him and have never felt this way about another human?"

Charlotte glared at Kendall—why had she thought it would be a good idea to talk to her? She always had such an unfortunate tendency to tell Charlotte exactly what she needed to do—and didn't want to do—to sort out her life.

"You don't want to tell him?" Magda asked, more gently.

"It's not that I don't want to tell him." She fidgeted, searching for the words. "I just want him to say it first."

Except that didn't feel entirely true.

Her best friends were watching her. Waiting. Giving her the space to think it through.

"I think he loves me," she said finally. "Or at least he thinks he does. But he's been chasing me for a while— even if I didn't know it—and I've seen what happens when people get what they want. They don't always want it anymore."

"He isn't like the Darcys," Kendall reminded her softly.

"But I'm still me. I still want too much. I'm still...*this*." She waved at herself, trying to encompass all her greedy, messy, ugly emotions. "I thought a relationship with him would be easier, but it matters more. It's real. And it's slipping through my fingers. It's like the universe is showing me everything I ever wanted—but I don't get to keep it. Because of course I don't."

"He might stay if he knew how you felt," Magda put in gently.

"So I beg him to stay—and what? He stays because he's a nice guy, because he always gives me what I want—except I already told him that I want him to stay, and he still doesn't know what he wants. He isn't sure. And I'm right back where I always am."

"What if the only reason he isn't sure is because he doesn't know how you feel? What if he's waiting for some sign that you're really in this?" Kendall asked, sounding so reasonable, so rational—and so terrifying.

Charlotte had thrown around the word *love* before,

waving it like a magic wand, as if she said it often enough it would make itself real—but this time she couldn't say it.

Kendall got up first, then Magda followed suit, the two of them coming up on either side of the oversized chair she sat in and cramming themselves in next to her, wrapping her up in their arms because right now words wouldn't help, but knowing they would always love her, no matter what, did.

But Kendall had to add words too—because Kendall had tough love down to an art.

"You don't want too much," Kendall told her, her chin resting on Charlotte's hair. "You deserve to be happy. You deserve to be loved. And I'm not going to tell you to do anything you don't want to do—but if you don't tell him how you feel, he might leave. Are you gonna be okay with that? Wouldn't you rather know? Wouldn't you rather blow up your relationship in a blaze of Charlotte glory than play it safe?"

"I'm just scared," Charlotte admitted.

"I know." Kendall gave her a squeeze. "Luckily, you're also brave. And tough as hell."

Chapter Thirty-Seven

I come here with no expectations, only
to profess, now that I am at liberty to
do so, that my heart is and always will
be...yours.
　　　—*Sense and Sensibility*, Jane Austen

The book sat on her kitchen island. Taunting her.

It was the book George had given her on her
mother's birthday. The much-read copy of *Emma*. She
hadn't opened it—she'd already read the story a dozen
times—but it had been tucked into her bedside drawer
in a place of honor for the last several weeks, where she
could take it out and trace her fingers over the cracks in
the spine.

Last night, after Kendall and Magda had headed home,
she'd gotten it out and put it on the island as a reminder
so she wouldn't chicken out.

She needed to talk to him today. Before he went to
Colorado. She'd volunteered to watch Duke for him. She'd
also offered to drive him to the airport, but he'd known she

already had plans to meet up with her sisters this afternoon, so he'd turned her down.

But he still had to drop off Duke. Which meant she would see him. And tell him how she felt.

"No big deal. Just my entire heart on the line," she said to Bingley, who sat attentively at her feet, wondering why she was standing in the kitchen without getting him a second breakfast.

Getting Bingley had been one of the best decisions of her life. She'd needed the Puppy Pact. Needed it to wake her up to the fact that she *could* be on her own, she *could* lavish all her love and affection on a puppy for the rest of her life... but she didn't have to.

Because there was George. Wonderful and frustrating and kind—*too* kind. *Too* considerate. And what would happen when he got sick of her? He was everything she'd never known she always wanted. He always made her feel like she mattered—and she was terrified she didn't deserve it. Terrified he was going to wake up one morning and realize that she was more trouble than she was worth. Too needy. Too much. It felt like flying without a net.

But she would regret it forever if she didn't tell him she loved him before he slipped away.

So today was the day.

She took a long time making herself cute. George had said they were squeezing in a band rehearsal this morning before he left, so there was no point in her going over to his place early anyway.

So she primped. Charlotte knew she cleaned up well, and she wasn't above using every weapon in her arsenal. She picked out a sundress that was casual enough it wouldn't be out of place on a Saturday morning, but also showcased her legs—which she knew he loved—and the bright yellow print made her feel confident.

Another hour with her hair and makeup made her look "natural" and like she woke up this way—though George had seen her bed head often enough to know better than that.

She was dithering over shoes when Bingley begged to be let out, so she shoved her feet into a pair of old sneakers to take him out to pee. She was planning to return to her apartment right after and continue the shoe debate, but when she stepped into the courtyard, she saw George, and her best-laid plans went right out the window.

Duke was wandering the grass beyond George's patio, with his owner pacing beside the sliding door. She didn't know whether he was already back from his rehearsal or hadn't gone yet, but her heart kicked into high gear and she could practically see the neon sign from the universe flashing above his head: TELL HIM, DUMMY! DO IT NOW!

Charlotte took a deep breath and started across the grass. She was nearly there when she realized he was on the phone. He still hadn't looked up. She forced herself not to turn back. She would tell him as soon as he finished his call.

Then she heard the words.

$\sim$

"Thank you. It's an incredible opportunity. A lot to think about." George paced on his patio, barely aware of his surroundings, focused on the call routed through his earbud. "When do you need an answer?"

He hadn't expected a job offer on a Saturday morning.

He'd just finished packing and was getting ready to head to the band rehearsal when his phone had rung while he was letting Duke out to pee.

It was a good offer. A freaking *great* offer. Undeniably better than part-time here. The rehab center in Colorado was a massive specialized facility that could afford to employ him full-time and give him a better benefits package than he currently had.

He should want it. It should be an easy call.

Dave was still considering moving back to Colorado. Beks needed him, and he wanted to be there for her—but there was so much more holding him in Pine Hollow than there had been a few months ago. He didn't know what to do.

"We can give you a week to think about it," the voice on the other end of the phone said. "If you can let us know by Friday, that would be ideal."

"Friday. Absolutely. I'll have an answer for you by then," he said, more on autopilot than aware of what he was saying. "Thank you. It's a very tempting offer."

The hiring manager said something else, but George barely processed the well wishes and goodbyes. His thoughts were already thousands of miles from Colorado.

He needed to talk to Charlotte—

He turned, and there she was, standing right on the edge of the patio, her expression strangely blank. Strange until he realized she must have overheard his half of the conversation.

"You heard?"

"They called on a Saturday morning. They must really want you," she said, her voice oddly flat.

"They're open seven days a week." *Why are you talking about hours? Tell her you aren't going!*

"It's a tempting offer?"

She sounded like she was quoting. Had he said that? He couldn't remember. "It's a big rehab center near Denver. They can afford a lot."

"More than little old Pine Hollow."

This wasn't going well. "I'm not—"

"You should take it," she interrupted, before he could finish telling her he wasn't sure he wanted to go.

"What?"

"You're never going to get an offer like that here. You must be considering it. You didn't say no."

He met her eyes, trying to see past the guard that was up in them. A barrier that had never been there before in bright, honest, open Charlotte. Who didn't know how to hide her true self if she tried.

"I wanted to talk to you first," he tried.

She was shaking her head before he finished speaking. "I don't want to be a part of the decision. You shouldn't be influenced by what I want. This is a lot more important than french fries."

"French fries." He shook his head. "Is that a joke? I'm sorry I got a great job offer in Colorado—but I haven't accepted it. I still want to be with you."

"Of course you say that, because you think it's what I want."

"Charlotte." He frowned. "Don't mistake me wanting to make you happy with not knowing what I want. Because I have *always* known what I want. Even when I was too scared to admit it to myself. I am in love with you. I have been since freaking mini-golf."

She kept shaking her head, not meeting his eyes—not

exactly the response he'd hoped for with his romantic declaration. "You're going to get tired of me. I'm great in small doses, but no one wants this all the time. And then you'll be stuck here, and it'll be my fault."

"Charlotte, I *know* what I'm getting into with you. I want this. I want you to be the person I argue with about the freaking dishwasher and get mad at when you watch something from our Netflix queue without me." The memory of Beks's voice on the phone came back vivid in his ears. "But I don't want to be anyone's runner-up. I know I'm not Mr. Darcy. I may not be the romantic lead—but I deserve lightning. I deserve someone who doesn't think of me as the fallback guy she's settling for because I'll put up with her—and that isn't an unreasonable ask."

"I never thought of you that way! I love you! But…"

He'd thought all he needed was to hear Charlotte say she loved him. Turned out one little *but* changed everything.

"But?"

"But I don't want someone who's only with me because he's too nice to walk away."

"Seriously? This again?" He heard his voice rising, but he couldn't seem to control it. "Or are you just running away? Because I don't think this is about me being too nice. I don't think it's ever been about that. I think you're just looking for a way out."

"I'm not the one with one foot in Colorado!"

"Yes! I want to be closer to my family and have a reliable job. I worry about Beks and not having a future here, and I want to be able to talk to you about that without having you decide I really want to leave and I'm only with you out of *niceness*. I want to be both places, Charlotte. Yes, maybe I've been holding back. Maybe I should have told you that from the start." He raked a hand through his hair in frustration. "I'm not good at relying on people. I'm always the guy who's there for everyone else, and that's comfortable for me. But I want someone who wants to be there for me, too. I can't ask you to leave your family and your job and your entire life, but I don't know what the answer is. I love you, but I want a relationship where we can make these decisions together. Where you don't always assume I'm going to give in to you, so you refuse to even tell me what you want. *What do you want?*"

An alarm went off on his phone before she could answer.

"Shit," he swore. "I'm late for rehearsal." He looked away from her, taking a breath. After a moment, he sighed. "Maybe we should just take some time to think about things. Cool off a little. Let it all settle."

When she didn't respond, he looked back at her. She nodded, swallowing.

"I'll be back on Wednesday. We can talk then."

"Right," she whispered.

"I love you, Charlotte."

"I love you, too." She didn't move.

George forced himself to turn away. He'd never realized how much those words could sound like *goodbye*.

Chapter Thirty-Eight

Friendship is certainly the finest balm for
the pangs of disappointed love.
—*Northanger Abbey*, Jane Austen

What's this I hear about you taking a job in Colorado?"
George froze in the act of unpacking his bass, his
head snapping up at Mac's question. Luckily Howard and
Bob were on the other side of the rehearsal space and didn't
appear to have heard. "Where did you hear that?"

"From Howard."

"Howard knows?"

"It's the hot rumor around the Estates."

George swore under his breath. He was in no mood for
this conversation.

Mac lifted his eyebrows. "So it's true? I thought you were
staying for good. No more Mr. New Guy and all that."

"It's complicated. Family stuff."

"Right." Mac nodded.

"You talking some sense into him?" Howard called across
the room—and George realized Howard and Bob weren't
nearly as oblivious as he'd hoped.

He'd been putting off this conversation, trying to avoid talking to the band until he was sure, but it looked like it was time. "I'm sorry I didn't tell you. Things are still up in the air, but either way, I'll be here for the talent show. My contract isn't up until September."

"I don't actually care about the talent show," Howard said, his hands stacked on his cane as he eyed George. "Don't get me wrong, I want to blow the roof off that place, but really all I wanted was to be in a band again."

"You'll find another bass player. I think if we're being honest, I'm not at the level of the rest of you anyway."

"It's not about levels. It's about chemistry." Howard sank down onto a chair, groaning slightly as he reached for his guitar. "I've been in a lot of bands, and I can guarantee you the best bass player isn't always the best bass player. You'll be missed, young man."

Something caught in George's throat. He would miss this. Miss them. If he left. After that blowup with Charlotte he wasn't sure what was going to happen. Everything he hadn't let himself say over the last few weeks had all come out at once, and he had no idea what would be left of their relationship once the dust settled.

"I'm not a hundred percent sure I'm going," he admitted.

They loved each other. That was great. But he wasn't sure in this case that love was going to conquer all.

It was tempting to go back to Colorado. Easy. It had always been easier to do what his family needed. To do the "right" thing for someone else and feel like it was out of his control.

"So why are you leaving?" Howard asked. He looked to Mac. "Did you get that out of him?"

"We didn't get that far."

"The rumors have been inventive," Howard said dryly. "I try not to listen to that stuff. Though there does seem to be one common theme. This have anything to do with Dr. Rodriguez?"

George winced at the thought of the rumors. "I'm not leaving because of Charlotte."

"But you aren't staying because of her, either, are you? I thought you were crazy about that girl."

He was, but... "It has to go both ways."

Howard laughed. "You trying to tell me she wants you to leave?"

"No. She wants me to stay."

"But?"

George gave up on avoiding the conversation. "She thinks I'd only be staying because she wants me to. But we both know I'm not her type and she's only biding her time with me until some perfect guy comes along."

Howard looked to Bob. "Were we that stupid?"

Bob arched his bushy white eyebrows. "Of course not. We were worse."

Howard snorted. "You're not wrong." He turned to George, his guitar cradled in his lap. "You need to start paying more attention when I talk. Didn't I just tell you that the best bass player isn't always the best bass player? It's all about chemistry, kid. It's not about being perfect— it's about finding that perfect fit." Howard eyed him. "You really that scared she's gonna decide she wants someone else that you'll move halfway across the country?"

"That wasn't why I was moving. My job. My family...I didn't have what I wanted here."

"Do you have it now?" Howard demanded.

He did. But... "It's a big decision to hinge on something that might not last." They hadn't even been able to talk about the possibility of him moving without it erupting into a fight.

Howard nodded slowly. "Sit down. I'm gonna tell you a story."

"We aren't going to rehearse?" George asked.

Howard stabbed a finger toward a chair. "The blues'll wait. I'm about to change your life."

"Well, in that case," George drawled, sitting down. Howard smiled.

"You ready? Everybody comfortable?"

Bob snorted. "Just talk, old man."

Howard had his guitar in his lap, and he casually flipped Bob off as he began to speak. "When I was young and stupid, all I thought I wanted in this world was to be one of the great guitarists. Jimi Hendrix. Stevie Ray Vaughn. B.B. King. I was going to write my name on history. I had this hunger, this ambition that drove everything I did. All that mattered was the dream. If I got it, I'd be happy. If I *made it*. And then the craziest thing happened..."

George arched a brow. "Let me guess, you realized there was more to life than fame and fortune."

"Nah, worse. I got the dream."

George blinked, surprised. "What?"

"I made it. The recording contracts. The fans. The critics calling me the Next Big Thing. You should google me sometime. Though I performed under a stage name then. Bo Raines."

"Holy shit," Mac whispered.

"You've heard of me." Howard grinned. "I was only big for a couple years. One band that struck gold before we fell apart. A few hits."

"And then you realized there was more to life than fame and fortune?" George prompted.

"You really want that to be the moral, don't you? Stop trying to tell my story." He glowered over the guitar, absently tracing the strings. "It was tough. It wasn't always perfect. Getting everything you ever wanted doesn't mean someone waves a magic wand and it's all easy. It didn't always feel like I thought it would—and that's when you have to decide whether that life is what you really want, or if it was the idea of it you loved. Did you want to be a great guitarist? Or did you just want the fantasy of it you'd built up in your head when you were dreaming and striving all those years? It's an adjustment. And it can be hard to reconcile the reality and the dream. But if you wanna walk away, you've gotta stick in it long enough to figure out whether it wasn't your dream after all, or if you're just scared someone's going to take it away from you, so you run first. Because if you run from something you really love, you're always gonna regret it."

Howard gave him a pointed look. "You following my story?"

George felt his face heat. Howard wasn't exactly subtle. "I think I got the point."

"You sure? Because it sure seems like you chased after that girl for two years and the second you got her, you started packing your bags."

"That's not exactly how I'd put it."

Howard nodded. "Because you think you're the fill-in

guy. Just someone she's with because you were handy, and she wanted to be with somebody."

"No, she didn't want to date at all—"

"You don't say? In fact, Vivian was saying she'd sworn off men entirely, and then she fell so hard for you she gave up on her big pact, so she could be with you—not with some other perfect guy."

George flushed harder. "That isn't exactly what happened." But it wasn't far off. Why had he never thought of it that way?

"Yeah, no, I bet you're right," Howard agreed too readily. "You go ahead and run back to Colorado. I'm sure you won't regret that at all." He strummed a chord. "We gonna play or what?"

"I was just waiting on you." George picked up his bass, but his thoughts didn't transition as quickly to the music.

Howard might not be entirely wrong, but that didn't make the decision suddenly simple. Beks was still in Colorado. His job was still only part-time here. And he still needed to get on a plane today.

He would have to see where he stood with Charlotte when he got back.

Maybe it would last. Maybe it would all work out. But if it didn't, he couldn't stay here and watch her fall in love with someone else. People could say that Charlotte seemed crazy about him, but people had said that about his past relationships, and they'd all gone up in flames too.

People were romantics. They wanted to believe in true love. They saw it everywhere. But he needed to be sure.

Chapter Thirty-Nine

She was one of those, who, having once begun, would be always in love.

—*Emma*, Jane Austen

He hadn't called her Charles.

Of everything that had happened during that disastrous argument, that was the piece that Charlotte couldn't stop fixating on. The rest of it felt like too much.

Over the last few weeks, she'd started to hear something else behind the name when he called her Charles—like it was his *as you wish*. As if he was telling her he loved her every time he used the nickname. And today, he'd called her Charlotte. The distance in that, the formality in it, had killed her.

Of course, she'd already been hanging by a thread.

He hadn't turned down the job.

She'd thought she was okay with him interviewing in Colorado—anxious, but okay. Until she heard him get the offer. Deep down she'd believed he would decline it, like his heart would instantly reject the idea of being away from her and everything would become clear and she would run into his arms like something out of a Disney movie, complete with spinning and rainbows and birds bursting into song.

Except life wasn't a Disney movie.

And he'd asked for time to think. He'd needed time to consider—and her heart had broken a little bit.

For a heartbeat, she'd thought *I could go with him*—but what if he wasn't ready for that? She was already a clinger, and she refused to be the clinger who chased a man halfway across the country. She always wanted too much, pushed for too much.

She wanted him to choose what *he* wanted, not be influenced by the tidal wave of her wants. When he'd told her he loved her, she couldn't make herself believe he meant it. Wasn't he always telling her what she wanted to hear?

She badly needed to schedule a therapy session.

After he left, she'd returned home with Bingley and Duke, for once not charmed by the way Bingley bounded around the condo in his enthusiasm to be home, checking on all his toys.

She shot a quick text to her sisters to say she wasn't going to make it today—telling them something had come up with Magda and Kendall so they wouldn't ask questions. Then she texted Mags and Kendall so they could corroborate her story.

That done, she pulled an oversized gray hoodie on over her sunshiny dress and flopped down on her couch, pretty certain she'd just massively screwed up the best thing that had ever happened to her. She'd known this was going to happen.

Bingley and Duke came over to her, Bingley with his little puppy tongue licking her face and Duke climbing up beside her to curl on top of her legs. It was the dogs who finally broke her—and the tears started.

"I should have stuck to the Puppy Pact," she whispered against Bingley's silky soft head.

She would always be the most important person in the world to Bingley. The idea that she could matter that much to anyone else was ridiculous. George *should* choose his family and a great new job over her. She was a mess.

She didn't know how long she wallowed, cuddling the dogs, before a knock came at the door. Bingley had fallen asleep, but he bounded off the couch, racing toward the door to see who had arrived—and Charlotte moved almost as quickly. What if it was George? Maybe he'd left his rehearsal to see her.

But when she opened the door, it was Kendall.

"Oh. Hi."

"Hi." Kendall's eyebrows arched up high as she crouched to say hello to the dogs—and took in what must be a somewhat rumpled and tear-stained appearance. "Magda's stuck at the bakery, but she thought I should come check on you after that weird text, and now I'm thinking she was right. What happened?"

Charlotte sniffled, trying to keep it together. "It's George. He got a job in Colorado, we had this huge fight, and now he's on his way there."

"Oh shit." Kendall straightened. "I'm sorry, hon. I'll tell Mags it's bonfire night."

"What? No. We aren't broken up." *Yet.* "At least I don't think so."

Kendall frowned. "Okay, you're going to have to explain. Because this definitely looks like breakup mode."

Charlotte retreated back to the couch, groaning and flopping down again. The dogs joined her as Kendall shut the door and followed. "Well?"

"I went over there this morning to tell him I was in love with him—just like we talked about—but when I got there, he was on the phone with someone in Colorado who was offering him this great job."

"And he accepted it?" Kendall prompted.

"No, but he didn't say no. He said he needed to think about it—and then he hung up and saw me standing there and was all, 'It's a great job.'"

"So you told him you were in love with him and asked him to stay," Kendall prompted.

"I couldn't! It would be just like the french fries! He would give me what I want, but I would never know if it was really what he wanted or if he was just being too nice."

"Okay, I have no idea what the french fries mean, but I'm going to pretend that made sense. So you what? Asked him to stay without telling him how you feel?"

"I told him I didn't want to be part of his decision."

Kendall groaned, her head falling back so her next question was directed at the ceiling. "Are you *trying* to sabotage yourself? You are the most direct person I know—how can you continue to be so indirect when it comes to men?" She leaned against the kitchen island, her eyes narrowed at Charlotte. "You keep inventing these tests for him, to see if he really loves you, when anyone with eyes can see he's been in love with you since the day he met you."

"That isn't love!" Charlotte insisted, her own voice rising.

"That's infatuation. And what happens when he gets sick of me—"

"Charlotte, the man knows what he's getting into. He knows you don't have an off switch. He knows you're a sucker for Jane Austen and rom-coms and that the way to your heart is through ridiculously long hikes and buying presents for your dog. He is the *only* guy you have ever dated who knows you, so why are you so scared he's going to wake up one day and stop loving you?"

"*Because* he knows me!" Charlotte shouted—startling herself with the words. "Because he's not an asshole. He's amazing. And if he rejects me, I can't tell myself that deep down I always knew that he wasn't right for me and I deserve someone better. Because there isn't anyone better, and if he rejects me, it will be *real*."

The starch immediately went out of Kendall's spine. "Honey."

She crossed the living room, dropping down beside Charlotte on the couch and taking her hands. "I know those idiots you dated before messed you up. I know there has been a parade of people walking through your life telling you that you're too demanding and you want too much, but you deserve everything you want. You want the big love story because it will prove you're worthy of it? Honey, you were always worthy. It was those assholes who weren't worthy of *you*." She squeezed Charlotte's hands. "But George is different. He is crazy about you. And you are going to have to be honest with him about how much you love him—or you won't be worthy of him. Doesn't he deserve the big love story, too?"

"He does," Charlotte whispered.

That wasn't the problem. That had never been the problem. She had always known he deserved the big love story. She was the one who hadn't.

She saw the weathered copy of *Emma* on the kitchen counter. George's copy of the book her mother had always hated.

Her mother, who had told her she would get the big love story. Her mother, whom she'd been trying to make proud for her entire life. As if that would bring her back.

"Charlotte?"

She met Kendall's eyes. "I think there's something I need to do."

Chapter Forty

Seldom, very seldom, does complete truth
belong to any human disclosure; seldom
can it happen that something is not a little
disguised, or a little mistaken.

—*Emma*, Jane Austen

Emergency session of the Leneghan Family Book Club
will come to order." Maggie smacked her gavel on an
end table, the sound echoing even louder in person.
"George, you have the floor."

He'd only been in Colorado a few hours before Beks
had taken one look at him and called an emergency book
club meeting. They'd driven over to Maggie's, where Lori
was already waiting, and Evie had joined via Facetime on a
tablet Maggie had set up on an armchair in her living room,
where they all sat with glasses of wine.

"Is this about the Hot Doctor?" Evie asked before he
could begin.

"Sort of," he admitted, a little reluctant to talk about it
with all of them.

His sisters had surprisingly mixed feelings about his relationship with Charlotte—though he supposed he shouldn't be surprised. Beks was down on love in general, and the others loved the idea of him moving closer to home, which was less likely to happen if he was madly in love in Vermont. Only Lori seemed to be firmly on Team Charlotte. But then she'd always been a hopeless romantic. Ninety percent of the romance novels they ended up reading in the book club were Lori's picks.

"I got a job offer in Colorado," he began. "A good one."

He expected a chorus of congratulations. Cheering and toasting. *Something*. What he got was silence.

He frowned at the carefully blank faces around the room. "No reactions? I thought you'd be jumping for joy."

"We would be," Maggie said, speaking for all of them. "If you hadn't said it like condolences are in order. What happened with the Hot Doctor?"

He grimaced. "She heard about the job offer and we, uh, argued."

Maggie and Evie cringed. It was Lori who asked, "Are you guys still together?"

"I think so. For now. I kept thinking about it on the flight. She said she didn't want to be part of the decision because she didn't want me to only stay because *she* wanted me to, but that sounds like something you say when you're not invested, right?"

"Or maybe she didn't want you to stay because of her and then resent it later," Evie offered.

He shook his head. "I don't know."

"Why are we here?" Beks asked.

"You called a meeting—"

"I know. That's not what I mean. Why are you conflicted? What's with the face? You know what you want. You wouldn't be this upset about getting a job offer here if you really wanted to come back."

He didn't want to come back. He'd been thinking about it on the entire flight, feeling like he was flying farther and farther away from home, rather than returning to it. He wasn't ready to leave Pine Hollow. It wasn't just Charlotte. It was Howard and Mac and Bob and the way this summer Pine Hollow had begun to feel like home. It was the way he could see himself there now.

He'd somehow stopped being the new guy. The town knew him—but what's more, he knew the town. The people meant something to him.

And Charlotte…he loved her. Yes, it had started as a crush, but what he felt now was a far cry from that initial infatuation. It was more real—and more dangerous. He was in love with the messy, tempestuous, loving, erratic reality of her. And he was freaking scared…

"I'm not upset about the job offer. It's…"

"Charlotte," Beks filled in for him, when he trailed off.

"You were the one who said—" He broke off before he outed Beks's marital troubles to the whole group.

"Who said what?" Beks waved at the others. "Go ahead. I was going to tell them soon anyway."

"Tell us what?" Evie's tablet asked, but George was focused on Beks. On the hard challenge on her face.

"I'm not her fantasy—isn't that what you were warning against? Falling in love with someone who will always be wondering what life would have been like with someone else?"

Maggie turned to Beks with a frown. "Why would you warn him about that?"

Beks held up a finger. "Okay, first of all, you got the absolute wrong message from my situation." She turned and met their sisters' gazes head-on, not flinching. "Scott is in love with someone else—his dream girl from before we got married—but they haven't slept together and he doesn't want a divorce and he says he still loves me too, so I'm trying to figure out what to do with that." Her gaze moved back to George. "But I wasn't warning you not to be *me*, you idiot. I was warning you not to be *Scott*."

George frowned. "How would I be Scott? That doesn't make any sense."

"I don't want you to run back home and spend the rest of your life wondering what if. Wondering what could have happened with the One if you'd only had the balls to go after her—*really* go after her and not hold anything back."

The words shifted around inside him. "How do you know she's the One? I thought you didn't even like Charlotte."

"I don't know Charlotte!" Beks threw her hands up. "I know you. And you spent the last two years reading Jane Austen for her. Are you saying she *isn't* the One?"

"I..." He shook his head. "I don't know."

"Well, we can't help you with that," Beks said, quick, like ripping off a Band-Aid. "And I don't think we can tell you whether to take this job you got offered, either. And don't use me as an excuse to run away from what you want. You're a great guy, George. You always want to make everyone happy. But this is your life. And only you can decide what's going to make you happy."

He grimaced, and Beks read the nerves on his face, her

expression turning sympathetic. "It's better to know the truth of where you stand now. Trust me."

He did. He knew she was right. But even knowing she was right, it still felt like leaping out of an airplane and hoping he had a parachute after he was already falling— because he'd been too nervous the answer wouldn't be one he liked to ask if it was there before he jumped.

Maybe not a perfect metaphor, but the fact remained. He was going to have to talk to Charlotte. To tell her what he really wanted. And hope she wanted it too.

Chapter Forty-One

I wish, as well as every body else, to be
perfectly happy; but, like every body else,
it must be in my own way.
—*Sense and Sensibility*, Jane Austen

Charlotte wasn't in the habit of visiting her mother's
grave.

It was beautiful—the gravestone was ornately carved
white marble, and the grass on the little plot was meticu-
lously tended. A bouquet of fresh white roses sat in a place
of honor. Someone had been tending to Emily Laughlin
Rodriguez's grave. Her father, or one of her sisters.

Charlotte sat down on the grass, crisscrossing her legs. It
hadn't rained today, but damp still seeped through her jeans
as she faced her mother's monument.

"I don't know why you hate *Emma*," she said to the
slab of rock, releasing a soft, almost bitter laugh. "I don't
know a lot of things about you. Maybe you wouldn't like
who I've become. Too much Emma Woodhouse and not
enough Charlotte Lucas. I'm not sure I'll ever understand

why you named me after her. I mean, Lizzie, I would get. She's awesome—if at times slightly judgy. But Charlotte is the walking embodiment of settling for less in life, so why would you want that for me?"

A white rose petal had fallen on the grass, slightly browned around the edges, and Charlotte picked it up, running the soft petal between her fingers.

"I know you didn't choose to leave us, but I was still so mad at you," she told her mother's headstone. "For getting sick. For leaving before I really got to know you. And I thought I was bad for being angry. You told me to be good for Daddy, and I wanted to be, so I never told anyone I was mad at you. I didn't even let myself think it. Had to make you proud. Had to be perfect. Had to be good enough that everyone would forget I'd ever felt the ugly awful thing and been mad at you when you died." Her voice cracked on the last word and she stopped.

The petal was so soft, falling to pieces in her hand.

"I've spent so much of my life trying to be something for you, I'm not sure I ever figured out how to just be happy." She swallowed thickly, trying to squish down the unflattering emotion as she always did. "George is good for that," she whispered to her mother. "You'd like him. Everyone likes him. I don't know if you'd think he qualifies as my big love story. But he's the best person I've ever met." She chewed on her lower lip. "I've been screwing it up. I kept trying not to hold on too tight. Like if I wanted it too badly it would all go away."

She inhaled, releasing her breath on a soft, humorless laugh. "That's probably about you too. Being scared people will leave. Feeling like if I were just good enough they would stay."

A rustle nearby made her look up.

Anne stood a dozen feet away, looking uncertain. "Hey. Kendall told me you might be here. I can leave if you want to be alone."

"No, it's okay." Charlotte had been holding it together, but suddenly her eyes were filled with tears as she waved her sister closer. "I'd like the company."

Anne didn't comment on the tears, coming to sit beside her, setting a box of Magda's pastries between them on the grass. "I started coming here when I first got diagnosed," she said. "Talking to Mom. Sometimes yelling at her for giving me her shitty cancer genes."

Charlotte looked at Anne in surprise. She didn't think she'd ever heard her sister swear before—let alone admit to the ugly emotions that seemed to be more Charlotte's forte.

"I don't come as often anymore," Anne went on, as if it was the most natural thing in the world to yell at a gravestone. "But I still try to make it every year on her birthday, and mine. And Jane Austen's, of course."

Charlotte studied the etching on the marble stone. "Do you think she was really as obsessed with Jane Austen as we remember? What if it was only a passing thing, but we all fixate on it because we want to have some way to know her?"

"I don't know. But I'm glad there's something that always makes me think of her."

"Me too," Charlotte agreed softly. But maybe that was all it needed to be. A reason to think of her. A fond memory—or an echo of someone else's fond memory. Maybe it was time to stop trying to live out some role she'd had in her head that her mother wanted for her. The person her mother had wanted her to be. "Do you think...do you think she would have liked me?"

"Charlotte," Anne said gently, putting her arm around Charlotte's shoulder. "She *loved* you. She would have been so proud of who you've become."

It felt so good to hear those words, that she figured Anne might need to hear them too. "She would have been proud of you too." Charlotte leaned into Anne, wrapping her arm around her sister's waist.

"I know," Anne said simply. "Because I'm happy. That's all she wanted for us. You know that, right?"

"Yeah." Except she hadn't known. She hadn't been chasing happiness. She'd been chasing worth. This idea that if she was just good enough then she would *earn* the happiness. If she was just good enough, then no one would ever leave. A mental rut that had been carved into her brain when she was nine years old. But life didn't work that way. Being *good* wasn't going to make George stay. But being herself, warts and all, being vulnerable and accepting that she might love him and he might still choose to leave…that was so much scarier. That was out of her control.

But as Anne had said, you didn't get what you wanted without the courage to go after it. And Charlotte finally knew what she wanted.

Now she just had to figure out how to show him.

∼

"Okay. Operation Grand Gesture." Kendall clapped her hands, rocking back and forth on the balls of her feet like a quarterback about to call a play. "Time to make George feel like a Darcy."

"Not *a* Darcy," Charlotte corrected. "*The* Darcy. Or any

leading man. I want him to feel like it's ridiculous for him to even think that he would be the fallback guy. We need *lightning*, folks."

"Right." Kendall rocked some more, channeling energy into her brainstorming. "Lightning."

"I'm assuming not actual lightning?" Elinor asked. "Because it's supposed to be clear for the next week."

"Metaphorical lightning," Charlotte confirmed.

Anne and Elinor were in charge of the DVD collection—calling up the most romantic declarations of love—while Magda sat at the kitchen counter with a pile of romance novels in front of her, including every Jane Austen edition Charlotte owned.

Magda frowned as she set down a copy of *Sense and Sensibility*. "Have you noticed how all of the romantic declarations are by men in these books?"

"That's because saying yes or no to a marriage proposal was pretty much the only agency over their own lives women were allowed in Regency times," Anne explained. "It would have been wildly improper to make a declaration first. Austen's frustration with the limitations placed on women by her society is especially evident in the way she talks about inheritance."

"But I am a strong, powerful woman who does not live in Austen's time, so I'm declaring myself first. Or maybe technically second, because we already said we love each other, but I messed that up, so we're starting from scratch."

Magda was no longer listening; her attention was rapt on the copy of *Emma* she was holding. George's dog-eared copy. "Charlotte, have you looked at this?"

"Of course. I could probably quote it from memory."

Magda's gaze was still riveted on the text. "This is seriously romantic."

"Yep. Jane was a genius."

That brought Magda's eyes off the page. "Not *Emma*. The notes."

For a second she didn't get it—then Charlotte felt the blood rush away from her face—and straight to her heart. "What?"

Magda turned the book toward her.

She was barely aware of accepting it. Everything in her had sharpened and muted at the same time.

George had written her notes in the margins.

He'd underlined parts of the text.

Charlotte's knees wobbled. She flipped through the pages, her eyes racing as fast as her heart.

Where Emma had explained how much of her happiness depended on being *first* in Mr. Knightley's interest and affection, George had written *You will always be first in my heart*.

It was a love letter.

The entire book was a love letter.

"Oh my God," she whispered.

And suddenly she knew exactly what to do.

Chapter Forty-Two

In vain have I struggled. It will not do.
My feelings will not be repressed. You
must allow me to tell you how ardently I
admire and love you.

—*Pride and Prejudice*, Jane Austen

George spent all day Sunday talking to Beks—or, more
accurately, letting Beks talk. She unloaded all her
fears, and by the end of the day he wasn't sure she'd decided
what she wanted to do, but she at least knew she didn't have
to do it alone. Regardless of where he ended up, George
would be coming back to visit often.

He stayed for his interview on Monday, and it went
great. He was probably going to have multiple options in
Colorado to choose from—but he also had a lead on a job
in Albany, which would be a lousy commute from Pine
Hollow, but he might only have to do it a few times a week
if he could keep some part-time work at the Estates.

It felt good to have choices.

He moved up his flight by a day and texted Charlotte that

he was coming home early. She texted back that she couldn't wait—which he hoped was a good sign. They'd texted a few times since he left—little notes to let her know he'd arrived safely, updates on how Duke was doing—but he couldn't wait to get home, even if he was nervous about what would happen when he did.

As if the fates knew how impatient he was, his flight had a tailwind and he got in over an hour early.

When he got back to the NetZero Village complex, Charlotte's car wasn't in the parking lot, even though she should have finished work hours ago. He tried calling her, but the phone rang endlessly, not even going to voice mail. He'd already sent a text letting her know he'd landed, with no reply.

Where was she? Off on some hike in the middle of nowhere?

He was still staring at Charlotte's name on the screen, trying to decide what to text, when a voice called out, "George! You're back early!" Kendall leaned out the window of her Jeep at the side of the road, where she'd paused when she saw him.

George jogged toward the Jeep. "Kendall! Have you seen Charlotte?"

"Yeah, you're supposed to meet her at the inn." She lifted her hand in a wave, pulling back onto the road. "Good luck!"

"Wait!" George shouted, but Kendall was already driving away. *"Which inn?"*

George groaned as he watched the dust rise up in a trail behind her tires. Of course it came down to this. This town and its freaking insider knowledge, expecting you to magically know which cute little inn they meant when the town was practically infested with them.

Except he did know.

George went still. Charlotte only ever went to the Bluebell. It was where Anne worked. It was also her favorite. Of all the inns, it was the only one that looked like it could have been plucked right out of a Jane Austen novel. The others felt more like hotels, but the Bluebell felt like you'd walked into a nineteenth-century home, complete with a parlor.

Exactly the kind of place a hero in an Austen novel would profess his love to the heroine.

He took the road between the ski resort and the town too fast, hoping he didn't run into Levi or one of his deputies, but willing to risk the ticket. Pine Hollow on a gorgeous summer evening was packed with tourists and locals alike, enjoying the sunshine—and the traffic in the square slowed to an agonizing crawl as he made his way toward Maple Street and the inn. Several locals waved as he inched past, some calling out, "Welcome back, George!" as if he'd been gone for weeks.

He spotted Charlotte's car in the tiny gravel parking lot beside the Bluebell—but the lot was full, and he had to park two blocks away on a side street. He jogged back toward the inn, too impatient to walk, and was covered in sweat by the time he got to the Bluebell grounds—not exactly Darcy appropriate.

The mayor walked past with his wife while George was bent over, trying to catch his breath—and Ally smiled at him as if she knew something. Everyone seemed to be looking at him that way.

He took a moment on the front step to smooth

his plane-wrinkled clothes, suddenly wondering why she'd asked him to meet her here—and why she'd sent Kendall with the message instead of just calling or texting him. Her phone had to be working in the middle of town, didn't it?

He'd never find out if he didn't go in.

George stepped into the blessedly cool air of the formal entry, grateful the inn had added the modern luxury of air conditioning. To his left was a sitting room and straight ahead a staircase with polished, hand-carved banisters leading up to the guest rooms. There was a tiny check-in desk, tucked into a nook in the curve of that staircase, but no one appeared to be manning it.

He heard voices from deeper in the mansion, laughter and the clink of glass, which reminded him the Bluebell hosted happy hours for its guests—but he didn't follow the sound of those voices, turning instead to the right and the room Charlotte had gushed about the last time they were here.

It felt a little off—like he should have a butler announcing him—but George pushed open the door to the parlor.

And there she was.

She didn't notice him at first, her back to him as she arranged something on the piano. She wore a pink cocktail dress that looked like a modernization of the one she'd worn to the Jane Austen Tea, with her hair pinned up in a style he recognized from every BBC Jane Austen adaptation they'd watched together.

She held a laminated card in her hand, and there were half a dozen others already strewn around the room, as well as a stack sitting on the settee. There was one on the fancy end table right in front of him, pointed straight at him, and George glanced down, reading the words.

If I loved you less, I might be able to talk about it more. —*Emma*

He glanced down at the pile on the settee, reading the top card.

There could have been no two hearts so open, no tastes so similar, no feelings so in unison. —*Persuasion*

It was all the quotes from the Jane Austen tea. She was filling the room with quotes about love.

Charlotte finished arranging the card in her hands and turned toward the couch for another, catching sight of him in the doorway. She gasped, her hand flying to her throat. "George."

"Hello, Charles."

⁓

He was too early.

How had he even known she was here? Had he seen her car in the parking lot? She wasn't ready—

"What's all this?" he asked, picking up one of the quotes that littered the room.

She'd had a whole plan. Each quote would be perfectly arranged, the sequence of them from the door to where she waited would have been a literary journey. And then she'd give her speech—which she would have had time to perfect.

She'd wanted it to be sweeping and romantic, and now she was standing there in bare feet because she'd taken off her shoes to spare the old carpets and there was no more time.

She just had to say it.

Her gaze locked on the quote in his hands. *You must allow me to tell you…*

But she didn't want to use Jane's words.

"I used to think there was nothing more romantic in the world than Jane Austen," she said, one hand braced on the piano for support. "My whole life, this has been what love meant." She waved to the room. To the quotes. "This was what I was looking for. And then I met you."

He watched her, his dark eyes intent behind his glasses. "Charles…"

He took a step toward her and she held out both hands, instinctively stopping him. "Let me say this. Please."

He nodded, and she wet her lips, going on. "I kept looking for this. I thought I'd been in love before. I thought I'd had my heart broken, but I didn't miss those relationships when they were gone, because I hadn't really been happy. I'd missed the potential for future happiness—the happiness that I'd always been so sure was coming if I could just get through this one last rough patch—but I hadn't actually been happy. Not like I have been with you."

She wet her lips nervously, her heart in her throat as she continued. "With you it was only happiness, right from the start. And if you got sick of me or you left—" Her voice cracked, but she got it under control. "I was scared to let myself love you, because I already loved you so much."

His brow pulled together.

"I know. That doesn't make sense," she said before he could protest. "But you have to understand—I thought I was in love before, but I had no idea. I certainly didn't know how to *be* loved. I didn't know how to be myself and let someone see that and make me feel like being just me was enough—and not too much, because I was always too much, always too clingy and too needy, and I didn't want to be that with you. I didn't want to drive you away, so I tried not to hold on too tight. I tried not to let you see how badly I wanted you to stay. Or to go with you—which you haven't asked me to, but I would go, if you asked, but now I'm inviting myself—"

"Charles."

"Sorry." She caught herself, reeling back in the verbal flailing. "I was scared I was the fantasy, and as soon as the first blush wore off, you wouldn't want the reality anymore, so I kept trying to be perfect for you—"

"I was scared too."

Her heart leapt up into her throat, cracking her voice. "You were?"

"I'm not Darcy. I'm not the one who sweeps the girl off her feet. And I can't settle for being settled for. Not with you. I was afraid of spending my life looking over my shoulder for the guy who was going to make you realize you wanted more than me. Running back to Colorado was safe."

"I am not settling." She picked up the copy of *Emma* resting on top of the piano, gripping it tight. "Did you mean what you said in here?"

He nodded, his eyes never leaving hers. "I wondered if you'd seen what was inside."

"I hadn't. Until you were gone." She clenched the book. "George... You aren't a Darcy or a Wentworth or a Knightley. You aren't some fictional ideal. You're real, and you're *better*. And I am madly, wildly, completely in love with you. *You* are my lightning."

His eyes widened.

"Are you really surprised? It's not about all this." She waved a hand at the quotes. "And it's not about what you do for me—though I have never met anyone as kind and as giving as you are. You don't have to earn my love by always doing what you think I want. I don't just love you because you love me. Not that I'm presuming that you still do—"

"Charles—"

She spoke over him, scared to let him get a word in. "I've begged people to stay before. I've cried and pleaded. But it was always about not wanting to be alone. About clinging to this idea of love. But you..." Realization shuddered through her. "You matter more than anything to me, George. I always wanted to be the most important thing in someone's world. And it turns out, you're the most important thing in mine."

He crossed the distance between them, gently framing her face in his hands. "Can I talk now?"

She nodded, all her words used up.

"Charlotte Jane Rodriguez. I have been crazy about you since the day I met you. And it's not because I built up some fantasy idea in my head of who you are. It's because I *see* who you are."

His deep brown eyes gazed into hers, intent, but also crinkling with affection. "I have always thought that the sexiest thing a person can be is at home in their own skin—and you, *Charles*, are the sexiest person I've ever met. I know you. I know you're impulsive. And brilliant. And moody—especially when you're hangry. I know you think you're too much—but I love it when you're the most. I've seen you when you say you're jealous and selfish—and I've seen you go out of your way to do something kind for someone else—over and over again— because you never want them to feel left out or alone. And you do it without thinking, as if doing nothing hadn't even occurred to you. Because it's part of who you are. And I love every bit of you."

"You do?"

"Especially the messy parts. I didn't know how to tell you, so I put everything I was feeling into that book. Because it was safer than saying out loud how much I love you." His thumb gently stroked her cheek. "I don't want to go to Colorado."

She gripped his shirt. "I don't want you to. Unless I can come too."

He shook his head slightly. "You'd miss Pine Hollow too much. And so would I. This is home. I have a band here. And I even know which inn is which now. Besides, I have to see if Howard and Vivian ever actually get together. It's painful to watch those two drag their feet when anyone can see they're perfect for each other."

"Give 'em a break. It took me a while to figure out what perfect looked like, too."

His eyes crinkled as he smiled. "And to think it all began over puppy poop."

She slipped her arms around his neck. "That's not where it started."

She didn't know the exact moment she'd started falling for George. Looking back, she couldn't seem to pinpoint a single time in the past when she hadn't adored him.

But maybe when she looked back on this one day and told their grandchildren the much-embellished story of how she had fallen madly in love with the ultimate Austen hero, she would say it was the moment he'd given her a dog-eared copy of *Emma* with notes in the margins and then kissed her in the parlor of the Bluebell, surrounded by Jane Austen quotes.

It made a good story. And if the reality was even better, if it was takeout and twisted ankles and her trying to set him up with all of her friends? That was just for her and George to know. Sometimes truth was better than fiction.

"I love you, George Leneghan," she said, just because she could.

He smiled, his dark eyes twinkling. "I love you, Charles."

"Are we late?"

At the question, they both looked to the doorway, where Mac stood, grinning broadly, with Howard and Bingley and Duke and what looked like half the town crowded behind him. "I heard this new guy was gonna be coming, and we were supposed to point him toward the parlor at the inn, but it looks like he's already here."

George looked back at Charlotte, his eyebrows arched high in a question. "Did you invite the whole town?"

She shrugged. "They wanted to help. You're one of us now. Whether you want to be or not."

He smiled, emotion shining in his eyes. "It's good to be home."

Epilogue

It's such a happiness when good people
get together—and they always do.
                              —*Emma*, Jane Austen

K endall is trying to back out of *Hamilton*," Charlotte
    complained, glaring at the message on her phone.
"She says she has to work."

"Tell her we'll kidnap her and drag her with us," George
said without looking up from his putt. "Then put your
phone away. Mini-golf is serious business."

Charlotte smiled at the admonishment and pocketed her
phone as soon as she'd sent her reply. George had surprised
her with *Hamilton* tickets for her birthday and arranged for
a big group of their friends to go with them. She'd been
looking forward to it for weeks.

"I still can't believe Kendall gave away the tickets when
Duke was sick," Charlotte grumbled, as soon as George had
taken his next shot—a magnificent standing-on-one-foot
miss. "I mean I *can* believe it, since she gave them to some
VIP at the resort who wanted to impress his new trophy

wife by flying her to freaking Burlington in his helicopter for the show, but *still*." She took her place at the tee, frowning at her cheerful yellow ball as she lifted one leg. "She needs a life outside the resort."

"Uh-oh."

She looked over at George, still standing on one foot. "Uh-oh?"

"You have that look. Like you're about to start meddling in someone's life."

"Of course I'm going to meddle," she said with a sweet smile. "Sometimes a person just needs an intervention. Or a Puppy Pact." She lowered her foot as an idea began to take form. "Didn't Ally say one of the puppies from Bingley's litter needed to be rehomed?"

"Kendall might want a say in whether she's ready to adopt a dog."

"She'll have a say," Charlotte assured him. But something needed to happen to shake up Kendall's status quo.

Charlotte wasn't meddling to avoid her own problems anymore—but that didn't mean she stopped butting her nose in other peoples' lives. She just had different motivations now.

She smiled brightly at George. "I just think everyone needs to be as happy as I am."

She stood on one leg—and sank her putt. That lovely little clink and George's groan were equally satisfying as she crowed her victory.

"Kiss," she demanded, pointing to her lips to claim her reward for winning the hole.

George dropped a kiss on her lips, smiling the entire time—and then moved to sink his ball.

It was two years to the day since George had started working at the Estates—and therefore two years to the day since the day they met and he first called her Charles. He'd suggested mini-golf as a fitting way to celebrate, and so far Charlotte was soundly trouncing him. Though his full attention didn't seem to be on the game.

She wasn't surprised he was distracted. He had a lot going on these days.

He'd decided to take the part-time job at the Estates, but they hadn't ended up cutting his hours after all. Two weeks before she was supposed to return, Claudia had been offered a research fellowship and decided to take that instead. Which meant George was just as busy as ever, being the residents' favorite PT.

After his band—which now called themselves the Diamond Dogs, in honor of *Ted Lasso*—had resoundingly won the talent show, which, yes, wasn't technically a competition, but they had *absolutely* won, they'd started playing once a week at the pub, and at various other events around town. Charlotte went to every gig—as did Vivian Weisman, though she and Howard were still being very secretive about whatever they had going on.

George also had plans to begin taking regular trips back to Colorado—his sister Beks had recently started going to counseling with her husband, and George still worried about her. Charlotte was scheduled to go with him on his next trip, which she was incredibly nervous about. She only hoped his sisters liked her when they all met in person. She was secretly hoping to score an invitation to the Leneghan Family Book Club someday.

She and George completed another hole with their eyes

closed and went through the windmill putting backward between their legs before arriving at the last hole. Charlotte's ball ricocheted out of the hole and she glared at it menacingly.

"I would just like it stated, for the record, that this hole is clearly rigged. There's something in there that spits my ball back out."

"You think so?" George asked. "Why don't you take a look?"

"I bet it's a secret switch or something," Charlotte insisted, as she approached the cup on the eighteenth hole. "It looks totally normal, and then they push a secret button under the counter and *bam*, spits your ball right out."

"It's a reasonable theory," George acknowledged. "I bet if you felt around inside you could feel the mechanism that knocks your ball out."

Charlotte frowned at him suspiciously. "Is it going to bite me? Did you tell them to make it grab my hand?"

George laughed. "What? Don't you trust me?"

"There better not be spiders in here," she muttered, approaching the Cup of Doom and slowly reaching her hand into the dark black hole.

She didn't feel spiders. She felt a small velvet-covered box.

"What…" She pulled it out, frowning at what looked for all the world like a ring box, and turned to find George on one knee in the middle of the eighteenth fairway.

Her breath whooshed out. *It's happening.*

He nodded toward the ring box in her hands. "You gonna open that?"

Her heart had never beaten so hard in her life. She opened

the box. Nestled inside was the most gorgeous vintage ring she'd ever seen.

"Magda and Kendall and your sisters all helped pick it out," he said, when she couldn't take her eyes off the ring. "And my sisters. It was kind of an odyssey."

There was humor in his voice. And love.

She looked up, meeting the eyes that had become the most important in her world. At the man who had made her feel safer and more special and more *herself* than she'd ever felt before.

"Do you have a question for me?" she said, already smiling so hard he must know her answer.

He took her hand—the one that wasn't still clutching the ring box like she was never going to let it go. "Charlotte Jane Rodriguez. Charles." She giggled, and his lopsided dimple flashed. "Will you be the one to tell me when I'm loading the dishwasher wrong? Who will never watch a new episode of *Cake-Off* before we can watch it together? Who will meddle in my life when I'm stuck in a rut? And who will let me love her for the rest of my life? I realize this is fast, but you're my lightning. Do you think you might want to marry me?"

Charlotte smiled until she felt like her face might split, her throat tightening and tears threatening. How was it possible to be this happy? "Abso-freaking-lutely."

George flashed her his devastating dimple—and slid the perfect ring onto her finger, surrounded by fake grass and chipped plastic windmills.

She'd wanted the fairy tale. The big love story. She'd wanted to be the center of someone's world.

He hadn't been what she'd thought she wanted.

He was more.

Her Darcy. Her Wentworth. Her Bingley and Knightley and Edward. Her best friend. Her everything.

Her George.

Don't miss Lizzie's next book,
FOUR WEDDINGS AND A PUPPY,
coming Fall 2023.

Acknowledgments

From the moment Charlotte and George appeared on the page in *To All the Dogs I've Loved Before,* I knew they were meant for each other, and I couldn't wait to write their story. So the romance should practically write itself, right? Yeah. Not so much. This book was a beast, and I'm so incredibly grateful to everyone who helped me make it better, one painstaking step at a time.

Huge thanks to my editor, Leah Hultenschmidt, and her assistant, Sabrina Flemming, for their incredible patience as they helped me wrangle this book into shape. I'm also so fortunate to have an amazing cohort at Hachette working on the Pine Hollow Series. Thank you so much Joelle, Francesca, Stacey, Lori, Estelle, Dana, and the rest of Team Hachette.

To my agent, Michelle Grajkowski, thank you for quite a bit more hand-holding on this one than I normally require. Sometimes it really does have to get worse before it gets better, but I'm so glad you were in my corner as I dismantled the Franken-book and put it back together again.

And, you guys, Kim Law is a miracle worker. She might argue that she just talked me down a few times, read twenty-seven versions of The Chapter That Shall Live in Infamy, and convinced me to listen to my instincts when I was doubting myself, but trust me when I say *Kim Law saved this book*. Or at least my sanity. Kim, you're a rock-star goddess.

Speaking of rock-star goddesses, huge thanks to my two very-best-friends-in-the-whole-wide-world, Kali and Leigh, who are, in fact, the best friends in the history of friends and make me feel so incredibly lucky that you are in my life (and let me spoil your children).

Many thanks to Kris and my mom, who still read every single book when they're rough and awful and love them anyway. Also, special thanks to my wildly supportive and extremely analytical dad, and the rest of my sprawling family—I'm so lucky when I get to be with you guys. I love you tons.

I've been fortunate to have many wonderful canine inspirations for the dogs in these books, and I'm grateful to all the shelter workers and volunteers who have shared their stories with me, and who do such important work in animal rescue. I also sincerely appreciate everyone who answered my many questions on my various research trips to Vermont. Thank you for sharing your state with me.

And finally, thanks to Jane Austen. Not unlike Charlotte, I fell in love with Jane's characters early and have reread her books over and over again, always finding something new in them. (*Persuasion* is my personal favorite.) I wanted this book to be a love letter to Jane. Fiction can get us through some of the hardest moments and give us hope when we most need it. I only hope this book can be that to someone else.

So *finally*, finally, thank you to the readers, booksellers, and librarians. Whether you are just discovering me or have been with me on the entire Pine Hollow journey, or started way back with Reality Romance, or even in the Vivi Andrews years, thank you for reading and sharing your enjoyment of these stories. You're the best.

About the Author

Lizzie Shane was born in Alaska to a pair of Hawaii transplants and grew up in the extremes of the 49th and 50th states. After graduating from Northwestern University (Go Cats!), she began writing happily-ever-afters while also exploring the world. She has now written her way through all fifty states and over fifty countries. Lizzie is a three-time finalist for RWA's RITA® Award and also writes for Hallmark Publishing, but her favorite claim to fame is that she lost on *Jeopardy!*

She is currently based in Alaska and can occasionally be found on Facebook, Twitter, or Instagram gushing about her favorite books...and her favorite dogs.

Learn more at:
LizzieShane.com
Twitter @LizzieShaneAK
Facebook.com/LizzieShaneAuthor
Instagram @LizzieShaneAK